IN PURSUIT OF SHADOWS

"He didn't show?" Little's voice sounded tight.

"No. I waited, but nobody approached me."

"Did you wear the white handkerchief like I told you?"

"Yes."

"And he didn't show?"

Palmer could sense the tension at the other end of the line. "What is it?" he asked.

"Lookit, Palmer. Get out of there. Fast. I don't like it."

"What's wrong?"

"The meeting was set up. I double-checked with the guy just two hours ago. He should have been there. Get out of there, Palmer."

Palmer started to ask a question, but the line went dead. Harvey Little had hung up, and he had been scared. . . .

ZEBRA BRINGS YOU EXCITING BESTSELLERS
by Lewis Orde

MUNICH 10   (1300, $3.95)

They've killed her lover, and they've kidnapped her son. Now the world-famous actress is swept into a maelstrom of international intrigue and bone-chilling suspense—and the only man who can help her pursue her enemies is a complete stranger . . .

HERITAGE   (1100, $3.75)

Beautiful innocent Leah and her two brothers were forced by the holocaust to flee their parents' home. A courageous immigrant family, each battled for love, power and their very lifeline—their HERITAGE.

THE LION'S WAY   (900, $3.75)

An all-consuming saga that spans four generations in the life of troubled and talented David, who struggles to rise above his immigrant heritage and rise to a world of glamour, fame and success!

DEADFALL   (1400, $3.95)

by Lewis Orde and Bill Michaels

The two men Linda cares about most, her father and her lover, entangle her in a plot to hold Manhattan Island hostage for a billion dollars ransom. When the bridges and tunnels to Manhattan are blown, Linda is suddenly a terrorist—except *she's* the one who's terrified!

Available wherever paperbacks are sold, or order direct from the Publisher. Send cover price plus 50¢ per copy for mailing and handling to Zebra Books, 475 Park Avenue South, New York, N.Y. 10016. DO NOT SEND CASH.

THE ZUKOVKA EXPERIMENT

NATHAN GOTTLIEB

ZEBRA BOOKS
KENSINGTON PUBLISHING CORP.

ZEBRA BOOKS

are published by

Kensington Publishing Corp.
475 Park Avenue South
New York, N.Y. 10016

First printing: September 1984

Printed in the United States of America

For Thea and George

*I do not think we need fear too much about the Communists drop-
ping atomic bombs on Washington. They would kill too many of
their friends that way. . . .*

— Joseph McCarthy
June 14, 1951

PROLOGUE

Bethesda Naval Hospital — April 30, 1957

It was the same face, and yet it was not. The photographers at the foot of his bed had been snapping his picture for years, yet today he seemed a ghastly stranger.
His face had turned a sickly yellow, the once bright eyes
now grey and watery. He could barely raise himself up
on his elbows, dry lips trembling from the effort.
Squinting through their lenses, the cameramen tried to
reconcile this wasted creature with the driven man they
had shadowed for so long through the halls of the Senate, the most photographed man in America. It was a
hopeless task.

"Lean this way a little, Joe. Try not to look directly at
the camera."

"You guys want me to smile?"

"Whatever you think, Joe."

"Might as well. Wouldn't want all those bastards in the Senate to think Joe McCarthy was dying, right?"

The cameramen laughed uneasily. This was not an assignment any of them relished. Most preferred shooting their stiffs after they got to the morgue.

"Give 'em hell, Joe," one of them said.

"You bet."

McCarthy raised a clenched fist. The room exploded with flashes. It was a familiar picture: the scourge of the Senate shaking a fist at the Red Demon. There must have been two dozen of the same shots on file. The only difference was that now McCarthy's battlefield had shifted to a hospital room. The senator from Wisconsin was dying.

"Raise the chin a little Joe."

"Sure."

The chart hanging at the foot of McCarthy's bed listed the Senator's ailment as hepatitis. It was being referred to in the early Fifties as a new disease, although it wasn't really very new at all. Doctors had been diagnosing the same symptoms for years as catarrhal jaundice. Rest, a strict diet, and keeping the cap on the booze usually cured it.

The only problem was in McCarthy's case, he did not know how to abstain. When he did something, it was all the way or nothing. It was like that when the first list of names came his way. People told him to check the information out first, but Joe turned a deaf ear and plunged in headfirst, waving the list for the TV cameras. A trusted friend in the White House had taken him aside in the halls of the Senate one day and whispered: "You're on the right track, Joe, but you've got to go at it more delicately. A lot of these people have important friends, if you know what I mean." McCarthy knew all right. That's why he went after them. McCarthy sent the Red bastards scurrying like rats to their hiding places in the walls of government. He might have purged them all, had the lords of the Senate let him finish the job. . . .

So it wasn't much of a surprise to anyone who knew Joe McCarthy that when his liver started acting up in the fall of 1957 and his doctor told him to slow down, McCarthy just plowed straight ahead. And when the pressure got a bit too much, why any good Irishman knew the best medicine was a nip on the bottle. In McCarthy's eyes, the stakes were just too high for him to slow down. The Ruskies had stepped up their space program, and who knew what they'd drop on us once they got control of things up there. Even three years after he had been censored in the Senate—and McCarthy was sure the Reds had had a hand in that—the senator continued to tour the country, naming names and driving home the message to loyal Americans. It was an exhausting task, and it took its toll. McCarthy lost a lot of weight. He drank hard and went long stretches without sleep. The senator cut a gruesome figure in early April of 1957 when he showed up at a Milwaukee Press Club gridiron dinner. Newsman there were shocked at what they saw. McCarthy had dropped forty or fifty pounds, his skin was yellow, the fire gone from his eyes. "The guy's dying," they whispered, and weren't wrong.

McCarthy's wife Jeannie had made a last-ditch attempt to stop him from self-destruction. "If not for yourself, then do it for the baby," she had pleaded, holding up tiny Tierney Elizabeth for the senator to hug. In January of that year, with the help of their friend, Francis

9

Cardinal Spellman, the McCarthys had adopted a five-week-old girl from the New York Foundling Home. In less than three months, the baby had become the joy of McCarthy's life. He fussed over her constantly, stocking the nursery with enough toys for quintuplets. She was going to be first lady president of the United States. Providing, of course the Commies didn't take over things by then.

So Jeannie McCarthy's plea had had the opposite effect, serving to intensify her husband's crusade. Two weeks after his ghastly appearance at the Milwaukee Press Club dinner, the senator became violently ill. He was taken to Bethesda Naval Hospital where a team of doctors gave it to him straight. His liver was badly inflamed, barely able to carry on normal functions. They placed him immediately in an oxygen tent, and it was touch and go for several hours. Now, having shown some improvement, McCarthy had talked the doctors into allowing the photographers in. Also at his insistence, the oxygen tent was removed. McCarthy wanted to let the Commies know he was still alive and kicking.

"Just a couple more pictures, Joe, okay?"

"Take as many as you want, fellows. I'm not going anywhere."

There was nervous laughter.

"Anybody got a flask?" McCarthy said, knowing damn well Wally Jenkins of the *Star* always had one on his hip. Jenkins avoided McCarthy's eyes. "Don't get pale, fellas. I'm not going to drink it. I just thought it'd make a helluva picture, me with the flask tilted. I bet some of those bright boys you got on the copy desk could cook up a dandy caption. Something like: 'HIGH LIVER— Joe McCarthy, hospitalized for an inflamed liver, shows he's lost none of the zest for life that put him where he is today.' "

McCarthy let out a bellow of laughter and the photographers caught it with their flashes.

" 'STILL FIGHTING — Ailing Senator Joseph McCarthy puts up a brave front despite being confined at Bethesda Naval Hospital for acute hepatitis.' "

The *Star* would carry the photo and a short story buried inside beneath a wire service report on a drought in southeast Texas.

Twenty minutes after the photographers had left, an exhausted Joe McCarthy was just nodding off inside his oxygen tent when a nurse came in.

"Are you awake, senator?"

"I am now."

"Sorry," the nurse said, blushing. She was a registered Democrat, but sympathized with McCarthy. Her brother had been killed by the Communists in Korea. "You have a visitor, but I'll tell him you're not feeling up to it."

The nurse turned to go.

"Who is it?" McCarthy said, struggling to raise himself up on his elbows.

"His name is Henry Smith. He says he's an associate of Jim Bell. I'll tell him you had a tiring session with the photographers and—"

"You'll tell him no such thing, young lady. I don't suppose you know who Jim Bell is, do you?"

"Of course I do, senator. I followed the hearings on the TV. I thought you were very impressive."

"Thank you. So did the Communists. That's why they had their friends try to silence me. But that's neither here nor there. Jim Bell is one of the best lawyers in

11

this great country of ours and a loyal and trusted friend. I can't keep an associate of his waiting. Send him in."

The nurse headed for the door.

"Before you go, could you remove this?" McCarthy pointed at the oxygen tent. "It wouldn't look right."

"I understand perfectly, senator."

When the nurse returned she had with her a tall man in a grey suit. His black tie was thin, the knot crooked. He looked more like a bureaucrat than an attorney, except for the eyes, which were deep-set and intense. The nurse left and McCarthy gestured toward a bedside chair. The man moved the chair several feet away and sat down, never taking his strange, dark eyes off the senator. McCarthy spoke first.

"So how's Jim? How come he didn't come himself? Old Joe McCarthy not important enough anymore?"

The man stared a moment at the senator. McCarthy had the uneasy feeling he was being soaked in.

"Senator McCarthy," the man began in a voice that was both soft and yet powerful. "My name is not Henry Smith. I am also not an associate of Mr. Bell. I do have a rather important message for you, however."

McCarthy sat up in bed, thrown off balance.

"Say, what is this?" Tired, badly in need of a drink, McCarthy's Irish temper started to flare. "Who the hell are you, pal?"

"My name is not important."

"Oh no? Then neither are you."

McCarthy reached for the buzzer.

"Please, senator. I don't think you want to do that. What I have to say will mean a lot to you."

Slowly, McCarthy lowered his hand, eyes riveted on the stranger's. Something told him to listen.

"Okay pal. Spit it out."

The man cracked a smile. "You are very direct, aren't you."

"Is that what you came to tell me?"

"No. Of course not." The man smiled again. "I have watched you for a long time, you know. It seems strange to be meeting you after all these years."

"That so? Well you've got five minutes to say what you have to say and then I ring for the nurse."

"Okay, senator. I came to talk to you about your crusade. You did an excellent job. Better than we could ever have expected."

There was something about the way the man said "we" which unnerved McCarthy.

The stranger took out a pack of Lucky Strikes. "Mind?"

"Suit yourself."

He lit up, inhaled deeply, then blew a stream away from the bed.

"You were set up, Joe," the man said flatly. He studied McCarthy for a reaction. The senator gave none. "We fed you all the wrong names."

"Names?"

"The list, Joe. All those card-carrying Communists."

McCarthy bolted up in bed, about to argue, when the stranger interrupted.

"I know what you're thinking, Joe. The man who gave you the list was a trusted friend, he wouldn't steer you wrong. Not knowingly, anyway."

"What are you saying?"

"The list was planted on him by someone with authority. It was suggested that he give it to you, a senator with the guts to use it."

13

"Why?"

"We wanted you to stir things up."

McCarthy wiped perspiration off his forehead.

"And who is this 'we'?"

The stranger paused and then lowered his voice: "The Red Menace. The Commie bastards, as you call us."

"You're crazy."

"Think so, Joe? You mean all these years you never had any doubts about the names, even when one by one the cases you tried to build crumbled beneath you?"

McCarthy said nothing. Sure he had had his doubts. More than he cared to admit. But he had always blamed himself and his staff. If they had done a better job, the cases would have stood up. He believed in the names . . . he had to. . . .

"What you're saying doesn't make any sense," McCarthy said weakly, trying to take the offensive. "Why would the Commies want attention drawn to them?"

"Let me read something to you, Joe."

The stranger took a folded piece of paper from his jacket.

"This is an excerpt from a survey taken by the American Political Services Foundation in 1954. It says in part: '. . . After the censure of Joe McCarthy in the Senate, the number of people in the United States worried about the threat of communism was less than one per cent. Nearly one-third of the population could not name a senator who had taken a leading part in the investigation of communism, not even Joe McCarthy . . .'"

"So?"

"Don't you find it ironic, Joe, that less than four years after you began your witch hunt few, if any people, gave a damn about the Red Demon? Can you imagine how little anyone cares now?"

McCarthy shrugged uneasily. "People are like that," the senator said.

"Yes, they are, Joe. We counted on that. They reach a saturation point and then don't want to hear anymore. It's elementary psychology. And that's what you did for us, Joe. You made the American public sick of Red-baiting."

"Think so, pal?" McCarthy said, the words coming thickly.

"We know so. That's what we counted on all along. That's why we put you up to the witch hunt. The atmosphere is right now, Joe, thanks to you."

"Right for what?"

The stranger smiled and slowly got to his feet. He turned his back on McCarthy and started for the door.

"STOP! DAMN YOU! Tell me what you're saying! The atmosphere is right for what?"

The stranger turned around.

"We're moving in now, Joe. In every branch of government. And nobody will bat an eye. You made it all possible."

"Nobody, huh? Nobody?" McCarthy forced himself up in bed. "You made a mistake coming here, pal. Joe McCarthy's still alive and kicking. I'll tell everybody what you've said. I'll let them know the Communists are moving in."

"But Joe," the stranger said, smiling. "You already tried that, remember?"

Part One

ONE

In a black mood, Alex Palmer stormed across the lobby of the Washington Plaza and headed for the elevators. He had been snubbed and nothing short of a scalding shower and several jolts of whiskey was going to take the bad taste away. It would have been better if he had simply punched out the guy, but you just didn't go around throwing fists in the office of the secretary of state. Palmer's jaw muscles twitched as he recalled what the secretary's aide had said: "I'm sorry, Mr. Palmer, but the secretary refuses to see you."

"Refuses to see me? You mean he's too busy?" Palmer had said.

"No. Refuses to see you. As in turns down your request for an interview."

The underling, a cocky young Ivy League type whom Palmer had grown to hate at Yale, barely suppressed a smile.

"Didn't you tell him who I am?"

"Yes. That's why he refuses to see you. He said he's read both of your books and can think of no single printed sentence in either of them that would serve as a recommendation for you. Those are the secretary's exact words, Mr. Palmer."

Palmer had thought about scaling the desk that separated him from the underling but had decided the risk to his typing hand was not worth it and left, slamming the door ferociously behind him. Now, passing the lobby newsstand, Palmer's eye was caught by a picture of President Demic on *Life*'s cover. It was still a shock to think of Demic as President. Palmer bought *Life*, the *Washington Post* and the *New York Times*, slipped them into his briefcase and entered the elevator.

Upstairs in his room on the twenty-first floor, Palmer poured a couple of fingers of Wild Turkey over ice and sat on the bed, sipping quickly as he flipped through the *Life* article on the new president, titled: "A STANDBY STEPS FORWARD." Demic had stepped forward all right. Stepped in it was more like it. Ten months ago Joe Demic was just a bookend at the White House. His presence on the Democratic ticket had stunned a lot of people, especially after the bitter campaign he had waged against John Pierson. It had been pure political expediency, of course, an attempt by Pierson to bind the party. But not since Kennedy and Johnson had hooked up had there been such an unlikely pair of political newlyweds.

Palmer had met Joe Demic just once. It had been

while Palmer was still with the *Washington Post* and had been assigned a piece on the possible effects a congressional clampdown would have on the CIA. Demic, a former deputy director of the CIA, was California's junior senator at the time, and Palmer had hoped he could milk him for a little deep background on the agency. Palmer had come away oddly disturbed by Demic. The man had been friendly, but had given away nothing about himself or the agency that wasn't already a matter of record. Not a drop. In his career, Palmer had interviewed hundreds of people, and they had all revealed at least a scrap or two they hadn't intended to. All except Demic. He was the most airtight man Palmer had ever met. And now he was president of the United States.

Palmer had been in Santa Barbara trying to track down one of Joe McCarthy's victims when the news about John Pierson had come over the radio in his rented car. Just ten months after he had taken office, five days shy of his fifty-sixth birthday, President John Pierson had dropped dead of a heart attack while attending a Baltimore Orioles-New York Yankees' game at Municipal Stadium. Stunned by the news, Palmer had pulled off the road at a tavern and watched the spectacle unfold on TV. The bar was jammed with a ball-and-beer crowd, and though they had all probably cursed out Pierson while he was alive, they now sat transfixed by the procession of footage the networks were dumping on the screen. Palmer was reminded of the day Kennedy was shot. He had been in a high school gym class when news of the assassination was announced. Palmer was shaken the way kids are when the world tilts without asking them. Pierson's death, however, had affected him differently, but Palmer wasn't able to put a finger on it until he had drained a dozen beers and then it hit him with such clarity that he laughed out loud. The boys in the tavern didn't take too kindly to some college-type asshole chuckling while one of their presidents was being buried, so Palmer had decided it was wise to leave. It would have been impossible to explain his reaction to the president's death. John Pierson was dead and Alex Palmer didn't give a shit. It was that simple. It could have been a D.C. sanitation man for all he cared. Palmer's father had been a suicide. That meant something. John Kennedy, a man whom Palmer had idolized without really knowing why, had been cut down by a sniper. That one had hurt, too. But John Pierson: What had he ever done while alive to make you care that he was dead? The newsman in Palmer wondered if the jaded D.C. sportswriters were taking Pierson's fatal heart attack at an Oriole's game as seriously as the boys in the tavern. He thought not. No less than ten jokes linking Pierson's death to the fate of the Orioles came to mind as Palmer drove back to Los Angeles that day.

In the two weeks that had passed, Demic had been sworn in and had chosen popular southern congressman Gary Thornburg as his vice president. Demic had left Pierson's cabinet more or less intact, retaining David Schuyler—a boyhood friend of Palmer's—as president's counsel. Palmer had at least one thing to like about Demic's presidency.

Just who Joseph Demic was and what he was going to do, now that he had taken over the most powerful elected office in the world, was a question on a lot of people's minds. *Life* had tried to answer it, but the story was shallow and conformed to a formula: Scratch a president and you discover the American Dream. *Life* had approached him with the outline for an Horatio Alger story, and the secretive Demic had been only too happy to fill in the standard blanks. Born on a farm in Long River, California, Joseph Demic had had the kind of childhood that builds character. He had milked cows, fed chickens, and studied long hours in a hayloft. He had graduated first in his high school class, gone off to Harvard and . . .

Palmer tossed the magazine away. It was not his kind of story. When Alex Palmer wrote something, he always milked the dirty angle. Palmer's editor at the *Post* had always known that even if he sent him out to cover a meeting of the Baltimore Garden Society, he'd come back with some story about how club funds were being funneled to back a former horticulturist with Communist leanings who was running for county freeholder. The same formula had worked later when Palmer had written two best-selling books. The *Life* writer had glossed over the fire on the Demic farm that had killed both of the president's parents, probably because Demic had not wanted to talk about it. Now that was ground Palmer would have dug into. Maybe Demic hated his parents and set the fire himself. What a story that would make. . . .

Life wasn't the only one wondering what the new president was made of, Palmer thought. Apparently the Russians were eager to test him, and the fighting that had flared up again between Iran and Iraq had provided a convenient excuse. Palmer picked up the *Times* and read the lead story. According to government sources, two weeks before Pierson had died, the CIA had convinced him that fighting was about to erupt between Iran and Iraq. Pierson, according to the sources, had been afraid one of the warring nations would close the Strait of Hurmuz—the Persian Gulf passage through which sixty per cent of the world's oil imports are shipped—and had sent four AWAC command planes to Saudi Arabia, the United States's chief ally in the region. It was a minor gesture, but as soon as Demic took over, the Soviets had pounced on it eagerly, dramatically beefing up their troop levels in Afghanistan. The possibility of the war escalating was very real. It was some mess to dump on a novice president's lap.

Palmer was about to pour another drink when the phone rang.

"Is this Alex Palmer, the famous investigative author?" a muffled voice said.

Palmer paused, debating whether to hang up on the crank.

"Yes this is, more or less," Palmer finally said wearily.

"I just called to find out if there was any truth to the rumor that you're in Washington investigating the possibility that Richard Nixon may have had a sex change operation and was really born Rachel Nixon."

Palmer recognized the voice before it cracked up in laughter.

"Hello David, how are things at the White House?" Palmer said.

"Fine, Alex. If you discount the fact that we've changed presidents in the last two weeks and that the Russians are trying to goad us into World War III."

"How'd you know I was in town?"

"Not because you called me, that's for sure."

"I was going to do that later."

"How thoughtful."

"Was it those assholes over at the State Department?"

Palmer asked.

"Could be. Can't reveal my sources, though. You ought to understand that, being in the trade."

"Right."

"What brings you to town?" the president's counsel asked.

"I'm doing a book on Joe McCarthy, the one who didn't manage the Yankees. I've got some interviews I want to run through down here. Haven't gotten off to a good start today, though, as I'm sure you've heard. Anyway, I'm having lunch with Charlene Lowenstein over at the *Post,* but I'm free for dinner."

"Charlene? I thought that was long buried?"

"It is. I just wanted to say hello. We're still friends."

"Whatever you say, Alex."

"We on for dinner?" Palmer asked quickly.

"Drinks."

"Too busy to eat?"

"Don't you read the papers?"

"Okay. Where do you want to meet?"

"Brant's? The room in the back is nice and quiet. Nine okay?"

"Fine."

"See you then."

"Say, David. What's Demic going to do about this mess in the Middle East?"

"The Iranians have petitioned the UN for a meeting. If it comes off, the Soviet president is going to be in New York and Demic's going to grab him for a summit at Camp David. That's all off the record, of course. Especially for Charlie Lowenstein's ears."

"Gotchya."

Schuyler lowered his voice.

"Alex . . . what do you think of Demic?"

"I don't trust him," Palmer said flatly.

"Me neither. And I'm the president's counsel."

The line went dead.

TWO

The sound was all wrong. Charlene Lowenstein closed her eyes and listened. From isolated pockets of the office came a rhythmic, muted tapping. Voices dominated over machines. Charlene wondered what her father—a *Times* correspondent for forty years—would have thought about an editorial room without typewriters. He probably wouldn't have liked it very much, Charlene thought, opening her eyes. She turned her attention to the keyboard of her own computer terminal. Function. Control. Scroll up. Scroll down. Christ, some day they'd invent a computer which would gather the news. The thought made her cringe. She had grown up in her daddy's office at the *Times* and was at home in an atmosphere thick with smoke and the heavy staccato beat of typewriters banging out the news. Charlene wished she had her old Remington manual back.

After finishing her story, Charlene edited it and coded it into the city desk file. She wanted to ask city editor Bernie Harrison what kind of play the story would get, but was too professional to play the superstar. Instead, she started work on a Sunday magazine piece. She wondered how many of her fellow workers were as truly professional as she. Most were just on an ego trip. Writing the news was a way for them to get ahead and be visible. A lot left the business the minute a better job came along. Some of them—because of ties cultivated with senators and other politicians on the beat—would become press agents. Other would go corporate, churning out public relations dribble. Charlene could never see herself as anything but a reporter. Life began and ended for her with the three words: by Charlene Lowenstein. The fact that she wrote for a prestigious paper was just icing on the cake. She'd have worked for the *Nutley Sun* if need be. Her byline was her anchor in the world, especially on mornings after a night of hard drinking and bad conversation when she'd wake in a fog, intimidated by shower handles, electric coffee pots, and clocks that ticked much too loudly. Sometimes, when mornings were particularly bleak, she would wonder if she would be better off in the warmth of a comfortable marriage with kids tugging on her skirt, but then she would pick up the *Post* from the front porch and life would fall right back in place. Reading her story over breakfast, she would wonder how many thousands of people held her in their hands at this very moment, and she would feel the beat of life in a way she had never been able to describe to anyone.

There had been a lot of bad nights ever since Alex Palmer had tossed her a kiss and walked out. It had been two years, and yet she was still affected. She knew it by her reaction to his call earlier. The sound of his voice had made her heart seem to float up in her chest. He had wanted to take her out to one of their old haunts, and although she desperately wanted to go, she was afraid in a vague sort of way and said no. Instead, she had asked him to stop at a McDonald's on the way over, suggesting they chat over burgers in the office.

After he had hung up, she had thrown herself into her story. More than once she had been tempted to rush to the women's room to fix her face, brush her hair. But she had refused to give in. She was a working lady and he would find her like that: hair messy, sleeves rolled up, fingers smudged with ink.

"Lunch," a voice said behind her, and a McDonald's bag plopped onto her desk.

"Hello, Alex," she said turning. She blushed, not knowing why.

"I hope I'm not disturbing a potential Pulitzer."

"Hardly."

Palmer sat on the edge of Charlene's desk, studying her. "You look good, Charlie."

"Not really. I'm a mess today." Charlene ran one hand quickly through her long, brown hair. She was sorry she hadn't brushed it.

"Dig in to your haute cuisine," Palmer said.

"Aren't you eating?"

"Not my style."

"To each his own."

Charlene lifted the top bun off the hamburger. "Oh Palmer, dammit! I told you to hold the pickles. You know I hate pickles."

"Sorry. Let me fix it."

29

Palmer slid the pickles off with one finger. "Voilá." He handed it back to Charlene.

"I don't suppose you've washed your hands in the last day or two, have you?" Charlene asked.

Palmer shrugged. Charlene bit into the hamburger, avoiding his eyes.

"Why are you in Washington, anyway, Palmer?"

"I'm doing a book."

"More dirt?"

Palmer laughed. "I'm writing a book on Joe Mc-Carthy."

"What have you dug up? Let me guess. Joe Mc-Carthy was a fag, and his right-wing lover was black-mailing him into carrying on an anti-Communist crusade. That sounds right up your alley."

Palmer smiled. "You have a low opinion of my books."

"That seems to be the common denominator among semi-literate people. Actually, I haven't really read either of them. Just the reviews and advertising blurbs."

"That's not exactly fair."

"No. You're right. I'll remember to be more fair the next time you look me up in two years."

Charlene wanted to say more. She wanted to explain that she hadn't read the books because she was afraid she couldn't handle having anything in her apartment with his name on it. What would be the use, though. He wouldn't understand.

Palmer was suddenly sorry he had come. "What do you think of Demic?" he asked, shifting subjects.

"Well, it's a little early to tell, isn't it? He's only been in office two weeks."

"Charlie, you're a reporter. All reporters have opin-ions. You probably had Demic sized up while he was taking the oath of office."

"Okay," Charlene said smiling, "he's not my cup of tea."

"Profound, very profound. Have you thought about working up an op-ed piece on that theme?"

"Very funny. Actually, it's hard to explain my feelings about him. I covered the Pierson-Demic campaign — whistle stops and everything. Never saw the man once he let his hair down. Even when he drank. He was always on guard. I never met a man who was put together that way, and frankly I suspect there's a lot more to Joseph Demic than meets the eye. And that's what bothers me. What about you?"

"I guess I feel the same way. The odd thing is he's not really unapproachable in the way Nixon was. You can get near him, but you might just as well be light years away for all it matters."

"Maybe he's just a very private man."

"In a very public job. Bad mix."

"I guess." Charlene reached across her desk for *LIFE*. "Want to see something fascinating?"

"I saw the story. Hardly what I'd call fascinating."

"Not the story. The pictures."

Charlene flipped through the magazine. "Here. Look at this," she said. It was a photo of a teenage Demic with his arm around a boyhood buddy. The two kids were standing in front of a tractor. The caption identified the friend as Jeffrey Hanlik. The future president looked like something out of an O'Dell's hair tonic ad: dimpled smile, hair parted sharply to one side, a pompadour in front.

"Yeh? So?"

"Now look at this."

Charlene opened a manila envelope and took out a yellowed snapshot. She handed it to Palmer. There was a boy standing in front of a patch of trees, squinting in sunlight. It was also Demic.

"So?"

"My sister took that."

"How did she know Demic?"

"She didn't."

"I don't understand."

"That's not Demic."

Palmer put the photo next to the picture in *LIFE*.

"Looks like Demic to me. Right down to the pompadour," Palmer said.

"I know. As I said, fascinating."

A copy boy walked over and dumped a wad of wire printouts on Charlene's desk.

"Well, if it isn't Demic, then who is it?" Palmer said, intrigued.

"Remember me telling you about my older sister, Elizabeth?"

"Yes. The one who was killed in Russia."

"Right. Well, when she was over there with Mom and Dad she met this boy. Dad was covering Moscow at the time and they had taken a vacation at one of the resorts—I forget the name. Elizabeth was out hiking one day when she came across the boy. He was very nice and spoke excellent English. They arranged to go into Moscow and some very strange things happened to them there. The boy got beaten up at a workers' meeting and—"

"How do you know all this? You weren't even born then."

"It's in Elizabeth's diary. I have it at home. The boy

was studying in some kind of accelerated program which included gobs of English. He studied tapes of American radio programs and read several of our newspapers daily. Elizabeth was fascinated with him . . . This was right before she was killed . . . 1953.

"It must be strange having had a sister and never met her," Palmer said.

"Yes. But from reading her diary and talking to my parents, I really feel I know her."

"You ought to show this picture to Demic. He'd get a kick out of it. Tell him you've got proof he's really a Communist spy, then dump this on his desk.

"That's something Alex Palmer would do."

"Darn right."

Charlene took a bite out of her hamburger. She made a face and put it down.

"I offered to take you out," Palmer said.

"Couldn't handle it."

Palmer waited for an explanation, but none came. It was just as well.

"You really think I should show this to the president?" Charlene said.

"Of course."

"Maybe I will. They've called a press conference for today. I'll try and finagle an audience with Demic afterwards. Something big must be up."

"I know."

"You know?"

"I spoke to David Schuyler at the White House earlier today."

Charlene leaned toward Palmer. "Yes? And . . .?"

Palmer glanced at his watch. "Getting late. I don't want to hold up your work." He got up to leave.

"Alex, don't leave me hanging like this. You've already ruined my lunch. Don't kill my whole day."

Palmer started across the office. A few heads turned to see what the commotion was. As he reached the elevator, Charlene came running up behind him.

Palmer pressed the down button.

"You're really not going to tell me what Schuyler said?"

"Can't. My lips are sealed. By order of the White House. You don't fuck with the White House, right?"

"Palmer, you're a bastard. You haven't changed one bit."

"Thanks."

The elevator door opened and he stepped in.

"Do me a favor, Palmer. Don't come back to visit me for another two years, huh? I don't want to see you."

"I know you don't mean that, deep down in your heart."

"I do, Palmer. I truly do."

The doors closed.

Charlene stood there a moment staring, her chest heaving.

"Dammit," she muttered to herself. Love sucks. She turned and stormed away.

THREE

Gen. James Worthington stared at the little Mickey Mouse map the people at the National Security Council had sent over. It always amazed him how the NSC prepared reports as if they were for third graders. The map was the perfect example. There was a large land mass in the center shaped like the United States, and just in case the presidential counselor had trouble figuring it out, the words UNITED STATES were printed in capital letters across it. There were two black dots about an inch apart along the East Coast and they were labeled New York and Washington — upper and lower case — presumably to distinguish them in significance from the UNITED STATES. Jamie Worthington liked that touch. A lot of people in those two cities thought it should be the other way around. Off the East Coast there were three shadows shaped like airplanes, and although they were not labelled,

Worthington took the liberty to presume they were just that. The planes were about three inches apart and connected by dots to form an arch over the Atlantic Ocean (appropriately labeled). The dots ended at a little land mass shaped like an arthritic finger. Cuba. Upper and lower case. It was a dandy route the Russians were flying, and Worthington wondered how long the Soviet Bears had been penetrating gaps in the U.S. radar defense. It was chilling to think about it.

The general heaved a sigh and sank back in his chair. From the top drawer in his desk he took out his favorite pipe, stuffed imaginary tobacco in the bowl, tamped it with his finger and then struck a wooden match, holding the flame over the empty bowl as he puffed. Five years of this routine had all but wiped out the last smell of tobacco. Damn doctors. In order to keep you from dying, they sanitized you to the point where you were all but dead anyway. No smoking. No drinking. Easy on the exercise. Christ, doctors did a helluva better job monitoring his defenses than the air force was doing.

Worthington picked up the inter-office phone and dialed the president's counsel down the hall. David Schuyler's secretary told the general that her boss was on the phone.

"Have him call me when he gets free."

"Will do."

Worthington sucked nervously on his pipe. The Russians were up to something and he didn't like it. Demic just didn't seem to grasp the ramifications. The Russians wouldn't have tried to pull this crap if Jack Pierson were still around. Pierson was a former marine, and had maintained a military sensibility when it came to international politics. He was a hard-nosed man who took a no-nonsense approach to global affairs. Under Pierson, there were no billion dollar bribes to banana republics in the guise of financial aide. If the bastards wanted to align themselves with the Cubans, let them. If our navy needed more nuclear subs to keep pace with the Russians, he gave it to them. The way Pierson reasoned, it made no sense to steal money from the military and funnel it to the inner cities if somewhere down the line we wouldn't have the defenses to guarantee there'd be any cities. Jack Pierson had understood all this, and that was one of the reasons General Worthington had let himself be lured away from UCLA and brought back to Washington.

Jamie Worthington had thought he had seen the last of the city when he had retired three years ago as army chief of staff. The professorship at UCLA was something he had dreamed about for a long time. In addition to being a crack soldier, Worthington had long been recognized as a distinguished historian — albeit an amateur one. Several of his publications had drawn praise from respected circles. The job at UCLA had made it all sort of official: Jamie Worthington was now a professor. It was to have been a new start for him. There would be no long days spent in a rocker flipping through an album of war memories. His life's work had been the military, but his passion had been historical research. It was the long march of history that had made him understand and accept how little his own jaunt through time mattered. No one man meant all that much in the scheme of things. It was a working concept with which he could deal with the world in the autumn of his life.

When Jack Pierson had won the presidency and invited him to his Texas ranch, the general had a strong feeling something was about to threaten the balance of the neat world he'd built. Pierson had made it all sound so logical. The problems of previous administrations had been caused by ambitious young men lording it over the White House, the Haldermans, the Powells. Pierson wanted someone who had had enough power in his lifetime, an older man more intent on serving his country than owning it. It was a shrewd argument. Pierson knew it would touch a cord with Worthington. The two had met eight years earlier at a fund-raising party for the senator from Texas. They had struck it off right away. Pierson had admired the general's rugged individuality, his dedication to country, and his honesty. Worthington had liked Pierson because he was a man with power who understood he was only as good as his advisors, and he had always chosen the best.

Pierson had known how deep Worthington's passion for history ran, so he had played on it. "This will be a chance for you to write a chapter in history, Jamie, not just study it. We're going to do great things. It will be an important era for the nation, and you, as my top aide, will be a part of it. You'll have your finger on the pulse of the most vital White House in the last thirty years . . ."

Worthington was to be given the title of presidential counselor. It would be his job to link the White House staff to the cabinet. He would have cabinet status and authority over the two major White House policy organs — the National Security Council staff and the domestic policy staff. The White House chief of staff would serve under Worthington and would supervise day-to-day business, including relations with the press and Congress.

And so, history beckoning, Gen. James Worthington had returned to Washington. Now, ten months later, it was like a bad dream. President Pierson was dead. Demic was in the Oval Office, and although Worthington had been retained, his authority had been substantially reduced. Where Pierson had given the general considerable leeway in daily operation, Demic monitored everything. Nothing escaped the man's eye. Nothing. He was the most demanding, un-trusting man Worthington had ever encountered, and that included Patton and the rest of them.

So when the NSC had passed on the intelligence about the secret Soviet flights down the coast of Cuba, Worthington had been stunned at how lightly Demic had treated the information. "Get me all the intelligence you have on it and I'll study it and get back to you," Pierson had said.

That was three days ago, and the president still had not said anything about it. Worthington half suspected that Demic had filed the information away somewhere and forgotten about it. Yet that was inconceivable. Demic was a former deputy director of the CIA; he could not react so lightly to such an important penetration by the Soviets.

Worthington glanced back at the NSC man, then over at the dossier compiled on the Soviet flights. The Russians had detected enormous gaps in our radar defense system, and were able to fly nuclear bombers through without being detected. There was a lot of concern down at the Pentagon that small numbers of Soviet Bear bombers penetrating our radar in such a way could swiftly knock out missile installations and Strategic Air Command bases. They could easily penetrate our defenses by flying low enough to avoid radar detection—just as drug smugglers were doing daily in the Caribbean.

The NSC report outlined how the giant Soviet bombers were regularly testing our defenses electronically from two hundred miles off the coast, flying south along the Eastern Seaboard. The flights originated at Murmansk in north-west Russia, heading for Cuba, where they refueled and then turned back north to find gaps in our radar screen. How the Soviets had gotten the information about the gaps, God only knows, Worthington thought, but it was a nifty piece of intelligence. Maybe there was something to all that scuttlebutt down at the Pentagon about the Russians having a mole in the CIA.

In any case, Demic had hardly blinked an eye when Worthington had passed on another piece of intelligence disclosing that the Soviets had launched a nuclear-powered, missile-firing submarine of about forty thousand tons. Code named Tornado by our boys, it was the largest nuclear sub ever built. Coming on the heels of the *Omar, Typhoon,* and the *Delta*—new subs which use a titanium hull and can make fifty knots—this was bad news indeed. Demic had shrugged it off, however, promising again in that same noncommital way to "look into it." Worthington had checked with his CIA and air force sources, and if Demic had acted on it, they sure as hell didn't know about it.

Worthington was about to light up his pipe again, when the phone rang.

"Good afternoon, general. Private Schuyler returning your call."

"It's about time you called back. Listen, David, I've got problems. You're the Big Man's counsel and I need counseling."

"Legal?"

"No. Just general problems."

"I know a good psychologist."

"Don't get flip with me, private."

Schuyler laughed. He enjoyed his little sparring matches with the general.

"It's about Demic," Worthington said.

"What about him?"

"Can you come down here now?"

There was a long pause at the other end.

"I've got some people coming to see me in a few minutes, general." David Schuyler glanced at his watch. It was twelve-thirty.

"When will you be free?"

"Four o'clock."

"No sooner?"

"Can't. Big business. Hush hush."

"Okay. If that's the best you can do," Worthington said.

"It is. Sorry."

David Schuyler hung up. He tried to shrug off the uneasy feeling lying always gave him. Glancing again at his watch, he quickly slipped into his overcoat and went through to the outer office where his secretary was programing a computer.

"Sally, I've got to go out for a while. If anybody calls, tell them I'm in conference. Be back at four."

The president's counsel avoided his secretary's eyes and walked out.

FOUR

The black limousine was waiting for him in front of the White House. Schuyler got in the back. "Where to, sir?" the chauffeur said.

"Senate, Carl."

The black limousine made a right on Pennsylvania Avenue. Midday traffic was fairly light, and the chauffeur was able to move quickly. Schuyler glanced back through the rear window. A grey Ford LTD had come up behind them the minute they had emerged from the White House gates and was still there. Schuyler leaned forward.

"Make a left here, Carl."

"It's quicker if you go straight."

"I know. But there's something I want to see. I'm in no hurry."

The chauffeur made the turn. Schuyler looked behind him. The Ford did not follow. Schuyler released his breath, suddenly aware that he had been holding it for several moments.

"Traffic ahead, Mr. Schuyler. Told you we shouldn't have come this way."

"It's okay, Carl. I needed time to get my thoughts together anyway."

Schuyler tried to catch Carl's eyes in the rear-view mirror. Did he know? All these little midday trips. He must suspect something.

Reaching inside his suit jacket, Schuyler took out his wallet and began counting the bills. There were five crisp hundreds, two twenties, two tens, and a five. Schuyler took out one of the big boys and stared at it. New money always looked unreal to him. He somehow felt like a counterfeiter when he had to pass a crisp bill. Sometimes, if he had some new bills and wasn't particularly busy, the president's counsel would lay them out on his desk and then crumple them one by one. It was a silly thing to do, but it made him feel better, and wasn't this the age of feeling good? Some of his Washington friends were heavy drinkers, others snorted coke or smoked pot. So what was the big deal if crumpling new money made David Schuyler feel good? Once, after having gone to the bank, Schuyler had a bunch of new twenties, and after scrunching them in his fist, he laid them out on his desk. Just at that moment, his secretary had come in. It had been embarrassing. . . .

Money, the root of all evil. Schuyler laughed to himself. He put the hundred away and looked at his hands. His palms always seemed to get sweaty on these little trips, and he hated what that meant to him. Taking out a white handkerchief, Schuyler tried in vain to soak up the moisture on his hands.

Two blocks from the Senate, Schuyler had the chauffeur pull over and he got out, saying he needed some exercise. As always, Carl said nothing, glancing just once at the president's counsel in the rear-view mirror. When Schuyler was sure the limousine was out of sight, he hailed a cab, giving the driver the address of a high-rise on the outskirts of Georgetown. Once in the cab, away from Carl and what he stood for—the White House—Schuyler was able to relax a little. He lay back, opened his jacket and let himself breathe easy for a few moments. Then he slipped his tie off, stuffed it into his jacket pocket and undid two buttons on his yellow Pierre Cardin shirt. After hesitating, he undid a third. David Schuyler, blond and still boyish-looking at thirty-eight, had no Neanderthal mat of hair on his chest, so he wore an expensive gold chain to make him look more masculine. Three open buttons was the limit, though. Four made him seem too much on the make; two looked stuffy, something like you'd expect of a president's counsel.

A block from the high-rise, Schuyler felt his pulse quicken again. His palms grew slick. Quickly he took out his dark glasses and slipped them on. Almost reflexively, he drew his right bicep in toward his chest, feeling for the bulge of his wallet. It was there. He knew it was there because he had seen it a little while ago. Still, he wanted to make sure he hadn't lost it in the limousine.

Stepping out of the cab, Schuyler approached the canopied entrance. He didn't see the doorman, but knew he'd be there. Schuyler hated the condescending, stuffy look the man always gave him. Just once Schuyler would like to let the doorman know who he was really dealing with. President's counsel. The White House. Big-time stuff. But of course he couldn't do that.

"May I help you, sir?"

The long arm held the glass door open. David Schuyler stepped into the heated outer lobby. He stood there and said what at one time he had had to rehearse, but now came naturally: "Would you please tell Miss Jackson that Fred Mitchum is here."

FIVE

"Maybe I should put a cover on his food, Daniel."

"Leave it be."

"But it will get cold."

"That's all right. He knows what time we eat lunch."

Daniel Johnson avoided his wife's eyes and dug into more of her hearty Irish stew. The heat from the steaming mixture of beef and potatoes was drawing great drops of sweat from his forehead. From time to time he had to stop and wipe the moisture with his napkin. Eating Irish stew was a great way to chase away the chill of a Boston winter, but this was Santa Monica, California, and even in December, days were warm. Still, he would never dream of telling his lovely "bride" that what had kept her tummy warm as a kid growing up in Boston was out of place here. Jackie had never really felt at home in California, and he had always gone out of his way to do the little things that made her comfortable. If that meant fattening up on stew at lunch when he would have preferred a cool beer and a salad, so be it.

"Hi. Sorry I'm late. What are we eating?"

Twelve-year-old John Fitzhuh Johnson quickly slipped into the seat beside his father, dropped his school books on the table and dove into his stew.

"Books off the table, young man," Jackie Johnson said.

"Aw, Mom."

Johnny glanced at his father, who was staring at him, a spoonful of stew suspended in front of his mouth. The look said he was skating on thin ice, so Johnny picked up the books and put them under the table.

"Why are you so late?" his mother said.

"Two black dudes stopped me on the way home and shoved me into their car. They robbed me at knife point and then left me tied up in an abandoned lot in Watts. I had all I could do to get free and back here in time to taste your delicious Irish stew before it got cold."

Jackie Johnson tried hard to hide her smile. Oh, that boy could spin 'em. Just like her dad, James Fitzhuh. The kid was a born liar, and though she always scolded him for it, she beamed with pride inside.

"That's a long tale to be telling, young man. You can't expect your parents to be believing the likes of that one, now do ya," Jackie said. She liked to put on a little of the Irish brogue at moments like this.

"Sure it be the truth I'm telling ya, so help me God," her son said, joining the game.

" 'Twas talk like that what put your poor grandaddy in his grave."

"That and the good stuff O'Hara and Grady served

47

down on State Street."

"None of that lip from ya, now."

It went on like that for a while. Daniel Johnson waited until the two of them had finished, then spoke to his son.

"You were also late for dinner last night, Johnny. Why?"

Johnny measured his words before speaking. His father did not have much of a sense of humor. What he liked to hear was the truth spoken in the fewest amount of words.

"I was doing my homework at Marty Pace's house."

"Why do you have to go there to do your homework?"

"Marty's dad is a mathematical genius. He helps us with our geometry. He's a physicist, you know."

"It's not right to have somebody do your work for you," Daniel Johnson said.

"I know. But Mr. Pace is so smart. It looks easy when he does it. There's nothing Mr. Pace doesn't know."

"Your father's smart, too," Jackie Johnson said quickly. "You could go to him if you want help."

"I know," Johnny said, eyes down on his stew. "It's just that Mr. Pace is a physicist and dad, well . . ."

". . . He's a truck driver. You're allowed to say it," Jackie said.

"I didn't mean anything bad by that. I know that Dad's smart. He's got the best collection of books around, more than our school library almost."

"But you still go to Mr. Pace with your homework, right?" Jackie said, angry.

"Leave him be. The boy doesn't mean any harm," Daniel Johnson said. "George Pace is a very smart man. I understand why he asks for his help. It's just that I

48

don't approve of it."

"Why don't you ever defend yourself?" Jackie said.

Daniel Johnson turned his attention back to his stew, and his wife knew that was the signal to drop the subject. She got up to clear the dishes from the table, cleaning around her silent husband and her son. In the kitchen, she went about loading the dishwasher, banging plates just loud enough so her husband would know she could not be dismissed so easily. Daniel Johnson was the most exasperating man she had ever known. They had been married fourteen years and in that time he had treated her the way a woman dreamed of. He was courteous, kind, attentive, and loving. He called her his bride, and she always felt their relationship was something special. There were times, though, when his stony silences infuriated her, and she had gradually come to recognize that there was a wall somewhere he hid behind, and their union would always be incomplete because of it.

She had been twenty-seven when they married, Daniel thirty-six. He was driving the truck for the brewery then, but she saw in him an intelligence that spoke of better things. Jackie had only gotten through high school herself, but knew from the books he read, his mind was special. Yet all this time, he had done nothing to further himself. It was almost as if he was afraid to get ahead. But if that was the case, Jackie thought, why did he keep devouring all those books, night after night. Sometimes he would be in his study and she would go up to bed and the next morning come down to find him asleep at his desk, head lying on an open book. There was a hunger there she did not understand. She had come from a family of ambitious men, and when they wanted something, they grabbed it. This man was different. He had no goals, no hopes, no desires she knew of. Just that unending hunger—for what she did not know. Driven, going nowhere. . . .

Daniel Johnson took a beer into his study and sat down at his desk. The room was not large, but every available inch of space had been utilized for books. He had put the shelving in himself, running the boards up to the ceiling. A beautiful old ladder he had bought in an antique store kept him in touch with the books furthest from reach: his Russian collection. He had a wonderful swivel chair he had found at a flea market, which when sanded and stained, made a handsome addition to his room. There was an architect's lamp on his mahogany desk and a worn leather couch at one end of the room where he could spread out when the night grew long and the book refused to let him go.

Today his interest was in the *Los Angeles Times*, which he had picked up on the way home and now, with the front page spread before him, he was reading it carefully. He had never been a newspaper reader, finding the stories much too thin and speculative. But when Demic had become president, well . . . that had made everything different. It had become a daily ritual. He would scour the *Times* looking for news about Demic, always feeling somewhat uncomfortable. It was almost as if he feared someone would guess his purpose. But of course that was silly. How could anyone possibly guess. It was too incredible for even him to grasp, let alone anybody else. Joseph Demic, president of the United States. . . .

Daniel Johnson did not have to look far to find news about Demic. He was on the front page, in the middle of

50

the Iran-Iraq crisis. There was a mug shot of him next to the story. Casually, Daniel Johnson picked up a pen and began to draw a beard on the president's face. He made it thick and dark, running from just below the eye down to the Adam's apple. It was the same beard Daniel Johnson had worn all these years, worn and hated. Johnson was suddenly uneasy. The beard changed everything. It was amazing. Johnson's fingers strayed to his own face. He sensed the fear rising in the pit of his stomach, the way it always did when he stared too long at the president. The dread . . . the fear . . . and the guilt.

Daniel Johnson's fingers began to tremble. Angry with himself, he hurled the pen across the room. "I must stop this," he said to himself. But he knew he could not. Fear and guilt spread like a band across his chest.

Daniel Johnson knew he had to do something, and it was this that scared the hell out of him. What could he do? And more importantly, what would they do to him if they discovered the truth?

Suddenly the study door opened and Johnny entered. Johnson reached for the picture of the president, tearing it from the page. He crumpled it and stuffed the scrap of paper in his shirt pocket. He tried to look casual, but the fear showed in his face.

"Dad . . . is there something wrong?"

Daniel Johnson took a long time before answering. "No, son. Everything's just fine."

SIX

"Another, sir?"

"Please."

Alex Palmer slid his glass across the bar. He knew he shouldn't be drinking this much, but the routine was so easy: You just pushed the glass across the counter, the man passed it back, brimming with golden bourbon and the good times rolled. Something was bothering Palmer and he couldn't get a handle on it. He thought maybe the booze would help him get in touch with it, but of course he knew it never worked that way. Drinking only closed more doors. Palmer had a rule which forbade him from getting excessively drunk during the writing of a book. It was a lovely little rule, and he always mentioned it at cocktail parties when he wanted to impress someone with how serious he was. Invariably his audience would be a woman and he would rattle on about how important it was for a writer to stay reasonably sober, pausing between breaths to put away more bourbon, so that by the end of the night he was quite drunk and more than a little embarrassed. The strange thing is that Palmer really meant what he said. He didn't think writers should drink during the writing of a book. The problem was Palmer had never followed anybody else's rules, so why the hell should he be bound by his own.

The best system, Palmer said to himself as he hoisted his fifth Wild Turkey on the rocks, is the French custom of piling up saucers on your table. When Palmer had been in Paris, it had always embarrassed him to have a tower of saucers. It was bad enough getting drunk in public, you didn't want to advertise it. Leave it to the French to provide a great city for a man to get drunk in and then make him feel guilty about it.

Palmer glanced at the entrance to Bray's Steak House. It was eight-fifty-nine and Schuyler was a minute away from being late. It was not like Schuyler to be late. He was punctual, trustworthy, dependable, and straight—had been for the twenty-eight years Palmer had known him. Straightest bastard in the world. David Schuyler was exactly the type of establishment man Alex Palmer hated, except that Schuyler was a sweetheart of a friend and they had been through so damn much together.

Palmer thought back to his meeting that afternoon with Charlene Lowenstein. It had gone poorly. He wondered why he had bothered to see her. He must have known she was still in love with him. Maybe that was the point. He needed an ego boost. Except that Charlene had ruined the day by implying that he was a muckraker. How dare she? What a thing to say, especially since she was more or less right.

Alex Palmer had made a small fortune riding the crest of the Watergate craze. He had quit the *Washington Post* to write a book on the dirty tricks presidents before Nixon had pulled off. It was an unusual move: leave a prestigious paper to do something on spec. People were always telling Palmer how much they admired his guts for doing it, and Palmer would nod modestly. Of course he didn't tell them he had quit simply because he couldn't take the routine anymore. All those obligatory parties and lunches, trying to pretend he was a nice guy, the sort of person you would trust your secrets to. And then there were the deadlines. The endless pressure. Produce, tell it right and do it quick. Who are your sources? Can we trust them? Maybe we should sit on this for a while. . . .

No, Palmer had gotten out because he couldn't take it anymore. He had saved up a few bucks and managed to stretch it out by living on peanut butter and jelly sandwiches and gallons of Gallo burgundy. He had rented an attic room from a middle-aged lady who owned a townhouse in Georgetown, and after a couple of weeks she had crawled into his bed and told him her life story and exhausted him with a sex drive that belied her forty-four years. It was a bit of a drag on his energies, but she had stopped asking for rent and always left sandwiches and beer on his desk when he came home from walks. At the end of a year, he had the book ready for market, was turned on to an agent by Carl Bernstein, and got a decent enough advance on *Dirty Tricks* to start another one. *Dirty Tricks* was a hit. The *Kent State Conspiracy* followed that one. Palmer had dug up some evidence that a group of wealthy, conservative businessmen had planted radicals among the student protesters. Palmer's theory was that several guardsmen were then paid off to fire shots, the idea being to frighten the students and discourage further demonstrations. The book was short on evidence, long on speculation, but it was written well and the subject touched a chord. It became a best seller and Palmer suddenly had lots of money. He spent a great deal of it and went through a lot of women until he let his guard down for Charlene Lowenstein and got in too deep. He had bailed out at the last moment, although it had been messy. He hated himself for what he had done—telling her he didn't love her anymore—which was a lie. Maybe it still was a lie. But life was much easier without all the doubts, jealousies, and pain, and Alex Palmer was always one for taking the easy road.

"Mind if I interrupt?"

It was Schuyler.

"Not interrupting a thing. I was just waiting for a friend, but he's late."

"You looked like you were pretty deep into it."

"I guess I was."

Schuyler grinned and pulled up a stool.

"My God, David. How can you smile at a time like this? Your best friend is in the process of ruining a great writing career by drinking himself to death, the president's body is only two weeks in the ground, Iran and Iraq are threatening to suck the rest of the world into war, and there you stand, grinning from ear to ear. Why is this man smiling, I ask you."

Recognizing the familiar signs, Schuyler said, "Let's take a booth."

"Why? I thought we weren't eating."

55

Schuyler ignored Palmer and started toward the rear of the restaurant. Palmer tossed a ten and a five on the counter and caught up with him.

When they had ordered drinks, Palmer said, "I know it looks like I'm getting drunk, but appearances can be deceiving. Actually, I'm doing some research into the effects of one hundred one-proof bourbon on a man's empty stomach. I'm morally opposed to the use of guinea pigs so I'm doing the testing on myself. The initial results are fascinating."

"Tell me about the new book, Alex," Schuyler said.

"It's about Joe McCarthy. I'm trying to prove that he was set up by a secret group of top Republican officials in order to pave the way for an Eisenhower presidency. Hardly new, but I've got some fresh evidence."

"More dirt-digging, huh?"

Palmer banged his fist on the table and stood up.

"Dammit! Why does everybody think that just because I bring out the tough facts that I'm a muckraker? Where do you come off moralizing about what I do?"

"I'm not moralizing, Alex, and would you please sit down."

Palmer had attracted a lot of attention. He fixed a glare on an elderly man, who looked away. Satisfied, Palmer sat down.

"I'm down. But I'm not on the canvas. I won't take this lightly."

"Take what lightly?"

"What you said."

"What did I say?"

"I don't remember. But it was bad. Oh yes I do. You said I was a dirt-digger. That's what you said. Mr. Clean called me a dirt-digger. Mr. Lawrenceville and Princeton implied that I wasn't playing the game by the good rules, what ever the fuck they are. David Schuyler, Dorothy in the *Wizard of Oz,* following the yellow brick road. Harvard Law School, Phi Beta Cumquat, married the right girl — Julie Baron, daughter of Mr. Robber Baron. Yeh, you've made all the right moves, but don't forget I know your humble origins in a garden apartment complex in Maplewood, New Jersey. I was the one who protected you when all the local hoodlums wanted to kick your ass. I was the one who'd argue until he was blue in the face that, yeh, Dave Schuyler acted like a yo-yo, but he was really a good guy."

"And I was the one who bailed you out of all your jams," Schuyler said, still smiling.

A waiter, hoping to quiet down Palmer, came over and asked if they wanted dinner.

"No. I don't want to spoil my experiment. More bourbon, please." The waiter disappeared.

After a few moments of uncomfortable silence, Schuyler said, "The new book giving you trouble, Alex?"

Palmer heaved a sigh. He had let it all out and now felt so damned empty.

"Yeh. Christ, how do you always seem to know what's troubling me, David?"

"We're blood brothers, right? Remember when we used your aunt's carving knife to seal our pact?"

"How could I forget? I got an infection from it."

Palmer smiled. The worst was over.

"I'm sorry, David."

"For what? Forget it. Tell me what's wrong with the book."

"I don't know. It started out so good. I wanted to do

57

something that would help me to come to grips with my dad's suicide. You know I've always thought he was framed to take the brunt of the heat in the *Amerasia* scandal. I wanted to do something about McCarthy's victims, something with social import. But then, like Pavlov's dog, the minute I started my research, I automatically went for the dirt angle. All sensitivity went out the window. I've got my hooks into a conspiracy angle now and I can't let go. I have an interview set up with Jim Bell in New York tomorrow. It could be the high point of my research, but I'm not the least bit excited. I don't even want to go. But will I go? You bet. Why? Because my nose smells big dirt just under the next rock . . . God, I wish I could be like you. Married to a wonderful girl, two beautiful kids, respect from everyone . . ."

"Alex, you're a best-selling author."

"Muckraker."

"Damn good writer."

Palmer pushed his drink away and smiled.

"You're right. I am a damned good writer. And you're a damned good friend."

"Thanks."

Palmer drew on his drink, sipping more slowly this time. Then he said, "So okay, we've established that you're a great guy and I'm a great guy. Now tell me one thing."

"What's that?" Schuyler said, smiling again.

"How did two great guys like us living in a great country like this wind up with Joseph Demic as president?"

David Schuyler stopped smiling.

SEVEN

People are staring at me, Palmer thought.

I cannot be imagining it. A drunk, a fornicator, a dirt-slinger, an emotional cripple, all these I may be. But paranoid? Not yet, at least. . . .

Still, Palmer could not figure out why so many people in New York's posh Four Seasons restaurant were obviously stealing glances at him. He had even gone to the men's room to check his appearance. He was not unduly funny looking, nor was he dressed out of place. He wore a brand-new, black pinstripe three-piece suit. His zipper was closed, his socks matched and he wasn't drooling. Sure he looked a little hung over, but that was no reason to stare at a guy. And since Palmer had never allowed photos of himself on the dust jackets of his books, or appeared on any talk shows, nobody could know he was a best-selling author, not that anybody'd give a shit anyway. Palmer had recognized Joe DiMaggio at a nearby table, and nobody was staring at *him*.

They had arranged to meet at Four Seasons—one of Bell's favorite haunts—and he had arrived forty-five minutes early, which was the second big surprise of the day. The first was that he had even made it to New York.

It had been a wild night, even by Palmer's standards. Schuyler had deposited him at the front entrance to the Washington Plaza shortly after midnight and left in a taxi. Palmer had the kind of drunk where if he lay down on his bed he knew he would have passed out fully clothed and barfed on himself sometime during the night. So instead of going to his room, he hit the hotel bar, and from that point on, it was all a blur. He remembered the outline of things—leaving the bar, talking with a bellboy about a woman, slipping the bellboy some money and then going to his room. Moments later there was a knock at the door and a girl appeared. Palmer did not remember if she was a big girl or a small girl or if she was thin, fat, pretty, or ugly. He just knew she was a girl because she had long hair and wore lipstick and a skirt. That much he could make out. Palmer wanted to go to bed with her but he was afraid he would be sick and somehow there was a part of him still dignified enough to feel there was no dignity in vomiting on a girl you paid to lay naked beneath you.

So he had given her a hundred dollar bill, patted her on the ass and sent her away. The rest he didn't remember. All he could recall was the seven o'clock wake-up call, the fuzzy cab ride to the airport, and the gradual responding of the senses to doses of caffeine aboard the nine o'clock Eastern shuttle to LaGuardia. He had taken a checkered cab to the Four Seasons, told the maitre d' he was meeting Jim Bell and had been shown swiftly to a table.

It was not the way Alex Palmer had wanted to take on Jim Bell, the infamous and evil Jim Bell. Palmer remembered hearing the man's name mentioned like a plague when he was a kid. Jim Bell, one of McCarthy's henchmen. Palmer's father had had a particular fear of Bell, although he had never mentioned what it was. All Palmer knew as a kid was that the word Bell was something terrifying. Palmer had wanted to review his research on Bell before meeting him in the flesh. Having facts at his disposal would help him avoid being emotional. Palmer wanted very much not to get emotional with Jim Bell. The risk, Palmer recognized, was that once he let his feelings out he might lose control. It would be an ugly scene and Palmer somehow felt that after the indignity of his father's suicide and what it had meant to his mother, Bell should not be allowed to drag another Palmer down. Getting drunk had not been in his plans. He had hoped to spend a good portion of the night and early morning poring over his file on Bell. Now he would have to wing it.

Palmer reviewed what facts he could remember. Bell had been recruited for McCarthy's campaign by Roy Cohn, the senator's righthand man. Bell had had a small private law practice in Virginia at the time and had run unsuccessively for the state legislature on a fierce and dirty anticommunist campaign. Once he had hooked up with McCarthy, his career skyrocketed. Linked with the senator throughout the hearings, Bell had found it easy afterwards to secure a position with a prestigious law firm in New York. Thirty years later, Bell was one of the most respected and feared lawyers in the city. In his late

61

sixties, Bell was semi-retired now, taking on only the most glamorous of cases. He had made a fortune backing several successful Broadway shows, and through a succession of affairs with beautiful stage actresses, was constantly mentioned in the social columns.

Palmer was interrupted in the middle of a thought by a tall, slim man in a light grey, double-breasted suit with steel-grey eyes and a thick head of silver hair combed straight back. "You must be Palmer. I'm Bell. You're early."

Jim Bell sat down, took out a cigar and bent his well-tanned face to meet a match offered by a waiter. Within seconds, a red phone was brought to his table and plugged in to an outlet on the floor. Bell waved to several people, then turned his attention on Palmer. His eyes were clear and piercing.

"Tell me, Mr. Bell," Palmer began. "Do I look out of the ordinary to you?"

"Out of the ordinary? Other than the fact that you show unmistakable signs of being hung over and your suit has never been worn before, I'd say no."

"How did you know this was a new suit?"

"You left a tag on your right sleeve."

Palmer blushed.

"Still, as I say, nothing out of the ordinary. Why do you ask?"

"Because either I'm becoming paranoid, or else I get the distinct impression that people have been staring at me ever since I sat down."

"Of course people have been staring at you, Mr. Palmer. You're sitting at Jim Bell's table," Bell said flatly.

Palmer nodded, impressed against his will. He tried to regain control by doing what he always did in situations where he felt overmatched: look for flaws. Palmer saw Bell's immediately. A handsome man with a hard, athletic face, Bell was losing the battle to old age. There were two thin red lines around his ears, undoubtedly the signs of cosmetic surgery. Lift the bags, soften the heavy lines. Vanity. The man was vain. But of course Jim Bell was vain. That would not qualify as a brilliant observation.

"You're probably wondering why I consented to this interview," Bell began. "Obviously our political persuasions are not even remotely similar. Your books, both of which I have read, are shrill and poorly researched. Muckraking, but very good muckraking." (My God, Palmer thought, there's that damned word again.) "What I find interesting about you is that you're a winner. I like winners. I'm one myself. And of course I've got guts. Even you would concede that."

Palmer nodded, mesmerized by the power of the man. A waiter came. He did not bring menus. Bell asked for a steak and recommended Palmer try the veal cordon bleu. He also ordered a bloody Mary for Palmer.

"So I agreed to this meeting because I find that interesting people, no matter how odious their convictions — and yours, what little of them I can discern, are quite odious — make life richer. I'm curious to see what makes a guy like you tick, and why you're scratching with your poison pen my way. What great theory about Jim Bell have you dreamed up?"

"Actually," Palmer said, "I'm more interested in your old buddy, Joe McCarthy." Palmer thought he detected a hint of disappointment in Bell. He decided to rub it in. "Although I find you interesting as a supporting actor, McCarthy was the star of the show."

"A very great man," Bell said sternly.

"So was Hitler."

"Really, Mr. Palmer, I expected more of you."

The phone rang and Bell picked it up.

"Yes? Hello Lawrence. What's up? . . . Nine? Your place? . . . Fine with me. See you then." Bell hung up. "One of my clients. A famous actor. So where were we?"

"We were talking about Joe McCarthy."

"Yes. And you were about to trot out all the tired, left-wing cliches."

"Not exactly."

"Then what?"

"I've got a theory."

"Ah yes, a theory." Bell let out a sigh. "And what is Alex Palmer's theory?"

"Joe McCarthy was set up by a secret group of influential Republicans to cause trouble for Truman and pave the way for an Eisenhower presidency. Then, when Ike took office, they went about cutting McCarthy loose, culminating in his censure in the Senate."

Palmer found he was sweating. He didn't know why.

"You know, Palmer," Bell said, relighting his cigar, "there is an assumption in your theory that a lot of people have made. Namely, that Joe McCarthy was wrong about the Communist infiltration. Since he was wrong, the thinking goes, then either he knew it and was a demagogue, or else he was sincere and was set up. All of the theories and such are, of course, beside the point."

"The point being . . . ?"

"Joe McCarthy was fighting a real evil. The fact that he did not succeed does not mean he was wrong."

"So says Jim Bell."

"Yes. So says Jim Bell. And what says Alex Palmer?"

"I think he was set up but didn't really care because he was a self-serving, unscrupulous red-baiter. The typical liberal line."

"A conviction born, no doubt, from the fact that your father killed himself over his own involvement in the Communist conspiracy."

Bell puffed deeply on his cigar, exhaling a large smoke ring which hung over the table a moment before drifting Palmer's way.

Palmer recognized Bell's bald statement for what it was: an attempt to ruffle him. Bell wanted to see if Palmer would make a scene. It would be sure to hit the society columns: best-selling, muckraking author had to be escorted out of posh New York restaurant after making a scene at attorney Jim Bell's table. The ruckus would serve two purposes: It would embarrass Palmer and get Bell's name in the news. Palmer didn't bite.

"Mr. Bell. I did not come here to debate Joe McCarthy's role in history. Nor do I care to discuss my family with you. I was hoping you could shed a little light on a period in American history which you personally helped shape."

Bell puffed again deeply, the hint of a smile coming to his face.

"You do not rattle easily, Mr. Palmer."

"Sorry if I disappoint you."

"Not at all. I don't like easy targets. They're unworthy of me."

The waiter brought Palmer's bloody Mary and he went for it quicker than he would have liked.

"I was wondering if McCarthy ever told you his source for the lists," Palmer said. He tried to sound casual.

"He did."

"Could you tell me?"

"No."

"I see."

Palmer drew on his drink again.

"It's nothing personal, Palmer. Actually, I find you sort of likeable. In a perverse sort of way, of course."

"Why won't you tell me?"

"Joe made me and Roy swear never to tell. If you know anything about Jim Bell, you know I never betray a trust."

"If I pursued a certain influential Republican senator as the chief source, would I be on the wrong track?"

Bell smiled.

"Really, Palmer. A question right out of journalism school."

The waiter arrived with food and a written message for Bell. Bell read it, then turned and waved at someone. Palmer absently cut into the veal and put a piece in his mouth. He couldn't taste it.

"Whom do *you* think gave Joe the list?" Bell asked.

"I can't tell you."

"So now we're at a standstill. But I'd bet the name you've got dripping from that poison pen of yours is a biggie. Why else would a best-selling author like you put aside his personal feelings to ask Jim Bell for help? Your dislike for me must run very deep, I would imagine."

"Not for you, Mr. Bell. Just what you represent."

Palmer felt Bell's eyes penetrating him. For a moment, neither of them said anything.

"You know, I had nothing to do with the *Amerasia* case, Palmer. It was before my time — and Joe and Roy's for that matter, too. But I did a lot of research into it at the senator's request. If it's any consolation to you, I have my doubts about your father's involvement in the case."

Bell let the statement hang in the air. Palmer recognized it for the gesture it was, but he could not acknowledge it.

"Understand this about me, Palmer. I am not a man without feelings. There were a certain number of people who were unjustly victimized by our efforts. Only an idiot would deny that. But the number was very small and the cause more than justified it. The lives of millions of Americans were at stake. It was a war, and in any war, innocent people are caught in the fallout. It has been that way throughout history. I look back on my role in the McCarthy hearings with nothing but pride. It was the high point of my life."

Bell had not touched his steak. He caught Palmer noting the fact.

"There is nothing wrong with my appetite, Palmer. Do not draw such a satisfying conclusion. Any waiter here will tell you that I have very little interest in food. Half the time what I have ordered is taken away uneaten."

Palmer nodded, feeling his respect for Bell growing. He fought against it.

"You know, I shouldn't be telling you this, Palmer, because I hate to see a grown man salivate, but Joe told me something when he was dying which should interest you."

Palmer put his knife and fork down. His dirt sensors shot up instantly.

"You're drooling, Palmer," Bell said with a smile.

Palmer smiled back.

"Sorry."

"It's all right. Just a hazard of your profession."

"Muckraking, right?"

Bell, a man not accustomed to being called names, just shrugged.

"Let 'em call us what they will. We do our job and we make good bucks."

Bell took out another cigar, slid it along his upper lip, sniffing.

"Do you smoke?"

"Cigarettes. Never cigars. I'm a womanizer. The smell drives them away."

"An honest man . . . but you don't want to hear about cigars, do you?" Palmer shook his head. "You want to know what little tidbit Joe McCarthy delivered on his death bed."

Bell lit the cigar, exhaled and leaned forward.

"It's really a crazy little story, actually. You know, of course, that Joe died of a liver disease. He was in Bethesda Naval Hospital. While he was there, he phoned me with this wild little story. Right up your alley. He said a Communist agent had visited him at the hospital and told him the Reds had set him up for the fall. It was the Reds, the visitor said, who had passed the first list to McCarthy through an unknowing influential friend."

"The Communists? But why? That's ridiculous."

"Of course it is. But the theory has its own perverse logic. The visitor told McCarthy that he was fed all the wrong names in order to create what would eventually turn out to be an unpopular witch hunt. Then, with the American public sick and tired of hearing about Reds, the atmosphere would be right for a real infiltration by the Communists. And nobody, the visitor said, would bat an eye. Intriguing. But of course ridiculous."

Palmer felt his mind racing.

"Joe McCarthy was a very sick man at the time. You have to understand that before you judge what he said. I prefer to remember him on his record, an outstanding, courageous American. He was obviously hallucinating."

Palmer was barely listening. A thousand doors had sprung open in his mind. His fork hung suspended with a piece of veal.

"Palmer, you're attracting flies. Either eat it or put the thing down."

Palmer shoved the fork in his mouth. He was suddenly ravenously hungry.

EIGHT

Palmer held his breath as the nose of the giant DC-10 lifted off the runway. He glanced out the window just once to see empty Shea Stadium pass below, then continued to stare straight ahead at the multi-colored wall rug in the front of the American Airlines jumbo jet. Ten minutes later, Palmer began to relax. The plane had leveled off and a pair of female attendants were heading down the aisle with a drinks cart. Not soon enough for Palmer, who noticed with disgust that his palms were glistening with sweat.

Alex Palmer, globe-trotting investigative author, veteran of hundreds of thousands of air miles, was desperately afraid of flying. He had calculated from a compendium of crash accounts that most accidents occurred "soon after takeoff," roughly within ten minutes, and he never felt at ease until that time span had passed.

Now, feeling relatively comfortable, Palmer opened his briefcase and took out a paperback copy of Harvey Little's book on the CIA which he had bought at La-Guardia. A bonafide graduate of a speed-reading course, Palmer hoped to finish *The Company Man* before he landed in Salt Lake City for his meeting with the former CIA agent.

Ever since Palmer had talked with Jim Bell earlier in the day, he had been speeding on his own juices. As tactfully as possible, Palmer had cut short his luncheon with Joe McCarthy's former henchman and rushed back to his room at the Grand Hyatt to call David Schuyler at the White House. Palmer recalled the conversation with a smile:

"David, I'm going to present you with a hypothetical question and I want you to be as objective as possible in your answer."

The hypothesis was an incredible one, hard even for Palmer to swallow. What if Joe McCarthy had actually been right, that the Communists were indeed trying to infiltrate the American government, but not when the senator thought? What if McCarthy had been set up to create an atmosphere conducive to a real infiltration. . .

"Alex, are you on dope?" Schuyler had said.

Palmer had laughed and then carefully recounted his conversation with Bell.

"That's ridiculous. Utterly insane."

"I know it is, David, but I'm asking you as a friend to just pretend for one crazy moment that it was true. What I want to know, is, if it were true, what branches of government would the Communists most likely have tried to infiltrate?"

"Oh hell, Alex. I don't know . . . the State Department, of course . . . Defense . . . CIA . . ."

Palmer sat up in bed.

"CIA?"

"Of course CIA. If you wanted to screw up the country, undermining the CIA would be a perfect place to begin."

"But wouldn't that be impossible? I mean don't they have extraordinary safeguards against such a possibility? I've never read once where it had been proven that a mole had penetrated the CIA."

"That doesn't mean it hasn't happened. People never knew Harry Truman did dirty tricks until crusading author Alex Palmer came along and dug them up."

"But the safeguards . . ."

"Tough. Very tough. Every applicant undergoes a rigid lie detector test administered by a highly skilled professional. And the test is repeated periodically during the agent's career."

"Then how . . . ?"

"Polygraph tests have been beaten. It is known to have been done. It's very difficult to do, but not impossible."

Palmer sucked in his breath.

"Surely, Alex, you're not going to take this thing seriously," Schuyler had said.

"I sure am. It's a better idea than I had for my book. You know I wasn't very pleased with the way it was going anyway."

"But this, this theory, it defies belief."

"Would you have believed twenty years ago that an American president could have been toppled from office because of a two-bit burglary that a couple of green reporters milked into the story of the century?"

There was a great sigh from the White House end of the line.

"Alex, you're going to fall flat on your face."

"That's what you used to tell me when we were kids." "And you usually did fall flat on your face."

"Okay, okay. So I'm just a fall guy. But humor me for a moment, will you? I need another favor."

There was silence from the White House.

"David, are you listening?"

"Unfortunately, yes."

"All I want you to do is come up with a list of the agents who joined the CIA in 1957."

"Is that all?" Schuyler said sarcastically.

"David, you're a sweetheart. I knew you'd do it."

Palmer had hung up before Schuyler could reply. He had to admit, though, that Schuyler was probably right. It was a pretty crazy notion. And the wildest thing of all was that here was Alex Palmer, whose father had killed himself because of a witch-hunting scandal, trying to prove Joe McCarthy had been right.

But as soon as Palmer had thought of the CIA angle, he had been hooked. It was right up his alley. A mole, or moles in the CIA. Who knows what damage they could do in there. Christ, what a notion. The CIA, of course, had been the first thing Palmer had thought of after talking to Bell. Being an addicted dirt-digger, Palmer had wanted a second, more objective opinion, so he had called Schuyler and waited to see if the CIA angle occurred to him.

Naturally, Palmer was already ten steps ahead of Schuyler. He had immediately thought of Harvey Little, the former agent who had had the balls to write a scathing book about the agency. With the list of names

Schuyler would supply him with, and whatever information he could milk from Little, Palmer would be off and running toward Best-sellerdom.

Little had not been an easy man to reach, however. Palmer had gotten the name of Little's agent from his publisher, but when he had called Benjamin Green, he found him reluctant to supply information about his author.

"I've got to verify you are who you say you are. Give me the phone number of your own agent," Green had asked, and Palmer had done so. Then, Green had carried the game a little further. "I also want you to tell me the name of the last restaurant you and your agent ate at."

"What?"

"I know it sounds bizarre, but my client is a very up-tight man. He has written some strong stuff, and he likes to keep his whereabouts unknown. When I can verify who you are, I'll call you back."

So Palmer had complied, naming the Chi Mer restaurant in New York's Chinatown, and a half hour later the phone rang in his room at the Grand Hyatt.

"Palmer?" the voice at the other end said softly.

"Yeh. Green?"

"Yeh. You are who you say you are."

"That's comforting. I've had my doubts lately."

"I understand. Anyway, your agent said he remembered the Chinese restaurant on account it was the first time in six months you'd picked up a tab."

"That's a lie. I treat a lot."

"He said you'd say that, too. You're definitely who you say you are."

Green had given Palmer a room number at the Salt

Lake City Hilton and Palmer had gotten in touch with Little. Although alerted by his agent, Little was still cold. He only grudgingly agreed to a meeting.

Palmer put his drink down on the tray in front of him. He felt a glow inside which was only partially due to the bourbon. He was in the hunt again, happy for the first time in ages. Yeh, maybe they were right. He was a muckraker. But he was a damned good one. And there was always something nice about being the best.

So Palmer picked up Little's book and began reading:

It started out as a desire to serve my country, but it turned into a living nightmare. . . .

NINE

Charlene Lowenstein made one last try at pleading her case.

"Lookit, Barry. This has nothing to do with politics. I'm not trying to beat any of the other papers. No one will even know I've been with the president. I just have something I want to give him, and I'm curious to see his reaction"

"I'll deliver it for you," Barry Abramson, the president's press secretary said, leaning back in his swivel chair.

"Oh Christ, can't you get it through that little head of yours that the whole point of me delivering the envelope is to see Demic's face."

"I understand, Charlie, understand perfectly. And you should understand my position as well. If I grant you this interview, I've got to take care of the *New York Times* and *Newsweek* and *Newsday* and the *L.A. Times* and—"

"Dammit, Barry, you aren't even listening to what I'm saying. This isn't a bloody fucking interview. I'm not going to print a God-damn word of it."

"Tsssk. Tsssk. Such language from a lady."

Charlene stood there trembling, trying to control her temper. It would not do for a *Post* reporter to make a scene at the White House.

"You know, Charlene," Abramson began, "I might be willing to make a concession to you in return for a favor or two on your part."

"The day I let you fuck me, Barry Abramson, is the day I start shoving horned toads up my twat."

"Well," the president's press secretary said with a smile, "I guess that about settles the compromise issue."

"It certainly does."

"And now, having been spurned by the *Washington Post* ice queen, would you be so kind as to leave me to my sorrow."

Charlene stood there with her hands on her hips.

"You're really not going to let me see the president, are you."

"No I'm not, my lovely."

"Barry, you're the pits. The absolute worst."

"Flattery will get you nowhere, my dear."

"Ron Ziegler was better than you."

"Aaaaaah . . ." Abramson put his hand over his heart. "Not that, please. You've really cut me to the quick."

Charlene gave him the finger.

"If it's not asking too much, could you at least deliver the envelope?"

"Of course. That's my job, isn't it, helping the press?"

Charlene dropped the sealed envelope on Abramson's desk.

"Don't bend it, will you. There's a photo inside."

"Of you, perhaps?"

"No."

"What a pity. I might have sneaked a peek in the john."

Charlene headed toward the door, then stopped and turned around.

"Say, Barry. Did you ever see the movie, *The Green Slime?*"

Abramson smiled. "I have the distinct feeling this is not going to be complimentary. But yes, Charlene, I did see *The Green Slime*. Why, pray tell?"

"Well, if it ever came down to it, I want you to know that I'd sleep with the Green Slime before I'd go to bed with you."

TEN

Down the hall from Abramson in the office of the presidential counselor, Gen. James Worthington sat in his easy chair with his feet up on a hassock, puffing on an empty pipe. On the table beside him were a dozen hardback books. The general eyed the stack the way a man who has to move a huge pile of furniture does.

General Worthington had never wanted to read any of the books written about Watergate. The historian in him did not trust first person accounts written by guilty participants, and the patriot in him was offended by the almost obscene way self-serving reporters had followed the scent of blood. They were all too much on the make, these so-called investigative reporters, building reputations at the country's expense. This is not to say that the general wasn't put off by the government's handling of the episode. He was. He had never been able to warm up to Nixon, and the men the president had surrounded himself with were a mirror of his own personality. It was inevitable they would lead him into some mess. What bothered General Worthington the most was the harm that had been done to his beloved country.

So it was not with pleasure that Jamie Worthington sat before the stack of Watergate books. It was after talking with David Schuyler and having his misgivings about the new president reinforced that the general had told an aide to "buy up every damned book about Watergate." Like Worthington, Schuyler did not trust Demic, yet could not articulate the source of his uneasiness.

Worthington knew he should not be wasting the afternoon skimming books. There was a lot to be done before the UN conference on the Iran-Iraq mess and the president's summit with Rublov. But Jamie Worthington found himself drawn to Watergate, and he had always followed his instincts. He would not admit that he was connecting Watergate and its abuse of presidential power to the new president. After all, Demic had done nothing wrong. Worthington would readily admit that. But why had the man cut himself off from his staff? Why had he not acted on information about the Soviet reconnaisance flights or the new atomic sub the Russians had launched?

There was more, but it was all instinctive. General Worthington had never trusted men who wouldn't look you in the eye, and the president never did. He would stare down at the floor or at a wall while you spoke, nodding his head, only occasionally glancing your way. Maybe that was just the man's style. Who knows? You certainly couldn't indict a man for that. But it went deeper than the eyes. It was the sudden change in the man after he had assumed the presidency. Demic had never been warm or outgoing as vice president, but he had been approachable. Now, he was like a man apart. Even Jamie Worthington—presumably his top aide—had trouble getting to see him. It was just too sharp of a change, and Worthington did not trust men who switched skins too quickly.

Maybe it all boiled down to the fact that Watergate had left an ugly scar on everyone in the White House, and the one thing Worthington desperately wanted to avoid was having a long and distinguished career ruined by someone else. That's why Jamie Worthington had to know what had happened in Watergate. Even if it was an imperfect account, it was better than nothing. If his career went up in flames, Worthington wouldn't be writing any breast-beating books afterward. He would not say he was just following orders.

So Worthington reluctantly approached the pile of books. He scanned the names. Haldeman? Erlichman? Woodward and Bernstein? Where to start?

Dean.

Worthington gave out a laugh.

Yeh, Dean. The number one breast-beater.

The general picked up *Blind Ambition* and dove in.

ELEVEN

"Let me say first off, Palmer, that I'm sorry you showed up. I was hoping that I was sufficiently rude to you on the phone to have discouraged your little trip. However, since you've come, I'll have to deal with you."

Palmer, his overnight bag at his side, stretched his legs on a coffee table in the lobby of the Salt Lake Hilton. There were real logs burning in the fireplace, and Palmer was close enough to feel the heat come in waves.

"Actually, one part of me is sort of glad you showed up," Harvey Little was saying. "I haven't wanted to admit it to myself, but I've been kind of guilty about the turn my writing career has taken."

Little paused and looked at Palmer, as if waiting for him to ask something. Palmer didn't know what to say.

"Christ, Palmer, you're supposed to ask the natural question."

"Which one is that?"

"What my new book is about."

"What is it about?"

"Forget it, Palmer. I'll tell you later."

Little sank in the deep-cushioned chair, pouting. He was a tall, thin man, balding and beginning to grey along the sideburns. Palmer stared, trying to get a beat on him.

"You're thinking, 'Gee, this Harvey Little character is flaky. How'd he ever get into the CIA?' Right? Well I'll tell you, Palmer, I wasn't always like this. I was a straight arrow. Neat little dark suits, accountant's manners, mathematical mind. But the CIA fucked me up. Ten years of that crazy crap and I changed. God, any sane man would. It's either that or turn into a machine. I mean, hell, I've got feelings, too."

Palmer nodded.

"You're troubled by me, aren't you Palmer? You didn't expect a former CIA agent to be like this. You're saying to yourself, 'If this guy's this buggy, maybe I shouldn't believe what he's got to tell me.' Well, I say fine, fuck you, too, Palmer. I wish to God you don't believe me. Because the stories I've got to tell are going to defy belief, and if you don't believe in Harvey Little, you certainly won't swallow what I say."

Little paused, mopping perspiration from his forehead with a Hilton Inn cocktail napkin.

"I've been hiding out, Palmer, trying to lose myself in a putrid, All-American novel I'm writing, and then you show up and remind me of who I am, or was. But I'm glad. Yeh, glad. Palmer, my man, I'm going to be a big help to you. But first, we're going to get drunk, stinking drunk, Salt Lake City style."

"What style is that?"

"You'll see."

Palmer found out fast. The bar was on the thirteenth floor. If you liked beer, you could drink on the thirteenth floor. If you preferred whiskey, wine, vodka, or whatever, you could not order a drink on the thirteenth floor. You had to ride the elevator down to the basement, where there was a state-licensed liquor store which sold miniature bottles. Upstairs, the bartender would set you up with a glass and ice, which would cost you a buck and a half.

"This is crazy, absolutely crazy," Palmer said, mixing his own bourbon on the rocks.

"This, Palmer, is Salt Lake City."

"Why don't they just sell you hard liquor in the bar?"

"Because, Palmer, the Mormons would not like that. The Mormons have begrudgingly allowed you to drink alcohol in their fair city, but they will not make it easy for you. In order for you to get drunk, you will have to ride up and down in the elevator all night, thinking about your sins between floors. Sometimes the elevator gets stuck and then if you are the least bit claustrophobic, you will suffer even more for your sins."

"God, and I thought the French had a great little system," Palmer said, staring down the bar at all the brown bags with little bottles of booze. "But this is better. Absolutely beautiful."

Palmer had bought five bottles of tequila for Little and five bourbons for himself. Little ordered a salt-rimmed glass with ice and a slice of lime, Palmer just ice in a glass.

"Okay, Palmer, let's get down to some serious talking and serious drinking. For openers, I want you to know I've read your stuff. It's good, good for a muckraker. You're not offended by that word, are you?"

"No. I'm getting rather used to it."

"That's good. You won't be worth a lick as a writer until you are free of guilt. Take it from one who knows. Did I mention what I'm writing now?"

"No."

"It's a great American saga about the pioneers. Actually, it's a big pile of shit but it will make me a lot of money and that's all I'm concerned about. I want to build a fortress somewhere where I can live in peace, safe from the CIA and from people like you. That's what I'm doing here in Salt Lake, tracing the path of some of the original Mormons."

"Sounds interesting."

"No it isn't, Palmer. Don't humor me."

Palmer twisted the cap off another bottle and ordered a setup. He was getting pleasantly high. The bar was circular and rimmed with big picture windows. There was a full moon and the snow-capped mountains surrounding the town looked like ice cones in the night. Palmer had the strange sensation that he had broken free from the grip of his life and was floating. It was a nice feeling, but then the former CIA agent broke the spell.

"Why exactly did you come to see me, Palmer?" Little said.

Palmer quickly went over his meeting with Jim Bell, explained his theory and where he was going with it.

"And where do I fit in?" Little asked.

"I want to know if it's possible that a mole could have

infiltrated the CIA."

"Not only possible, it's true."

"You have proof?" Palmer asked.

"Not the kind of proof that stands up in court, but enough to satisfy me. Certainly enough to tantalize a muckraker." Little smiled. Palmer thought he detected fear in Little's eyes.

"What does the name 'Trianon' mean to you?" Little asked.

"Trianon," Palmer repeated, thinking. "Spy. Soviet."

"Close. American. It was the code name of a mole we placed high up in the Soviet Foreign Ministry. His name was Anatoly N. Filatov."

"That's right. Now I remember. I read something about it a few years ago."

"Yes. He was tried and executed by the Soviets in 1978. He had been attached to the Soviet Embassy in Algeria in 1976. Our boys set him up in a sex trap, took pictures and convinced him to work for us. It was blackmail, but we didn't use words like that in the company. He was reassigned by Moscow to the Foreign Ministry. Less than a year later, he was caught, and a year after that tried and shot as a spy. It all happened remarkably fast. Fast enough to suggest that Trianon had been betrayed by someone within the CIA, a mole perhaps."

"An isolated incident, perhaps."

"Hardly. Why had the CIA failed to establish a single productive agent in the Soviet Union between the arrest of Col. Oleg Penkovsky in Moscow in 1962 and the enlistment of Filatov in 1976? I'll tell you why. It's hard to enlist foreign spies when the word is out that your agency has been compromised."

Palmer opened two more bottles.

"Ever hear of Victor Hamilton?" Little asked.

"No."

"He was a Syrian-born research analyst for the National Security Agency. Most people don't understand how important the NSA is to the intelligence game, even though it has more people working for it than other spy agencies, including CIA. The chief responsibility of NSA is to secure the channels through which the military, intelligence services, and leaders of government communicate. It's a very sensitive job, and it was compromised by Victor Hamilton. He defected to Russia, joining two other former NSA employees, Bernon Mitchell and William Martin, who had slipped away to the Soviet Union three years earlier. Do you think it's a coincidence that from 1958 to 1963, the period these men worked at NSA, that the Soviets were able to catch the CIA's two top moles in Moscow — Peter Popov and Oleg Penkovsky — both of whom were put to death?"

Palmer was transfixed. This was better than he had hoped for. He was barely able to contain his excitement. He noticed Little had finished the last of his bottles.

"More?"

"I'm ready. You?"

They took the elevator downstairs. The rug inside was soggy with puke.

"Happens all the time. It's the up and down motion. The Mormons planned it this way, of course," Little said.

Back upstairs, Palmer ordered setups. A working girl was making eyes at him. He ignored her and turned his attention to Little.

"What about lie detector tests? Don't they prevent infiltration?"

"Hardly. The CIA has never been known for quality control. Fluttering — as we call the tests — was used with the NSA employees, and they obviously beat it."

Little opened two bottles of tequila and dumped them both in his glass. He was getting very drunk. Lines of stress seemed to be drawing his face in tightly. His eyes were bloodshot but still alert, and they bore into Palmer now.

"I've got a theory, Palmer. I call it my Mole-ecular formula." Little took a big hit on his tequila. "Just about every major fuckup in this country in the last twenty years could be traced to a mole in the CIA. Bad information led to the Bay of Pigs fiasco. The CIA's involvement in JFK's assassination is well documented, I don't have to repeat that stuff for you. Then there's Vietnam. All those glowing reports coming back from the lines. Lies, preposterous lies. We had plenty of agents over there. Their reports were fed back through a couple of operatives in Saigon. Who's to say they weren't doctored before the president saw them? An unpopular war, damaging to the country, was perpetuated in part by optimistic reports coming out of 'Nam. And then there was Deep Throat."

"Deep Throat? What does Watergate have to do with it?" Palmer said, suddenly feeling like he was getting in over his head.

"A buddy of mine in the company told me he had absolute proof that somebody high up in CIA was Deep Throat."

"But why . . . ?"

"Christ, Palmer, isn't it obvious? Anything that creates turmoil in American society weakens the fabric of the nation. Wasn't it Watergate which made it possible for a weak little shit like Carter to win the presidency? And Carter and his spineless Baptist thinking is what made the Iranians bold enough to grab fifty-two American citizens and humiliate us in front of the world. It's what made the Soviets dare to march into Afghanistan. If this country is in trouble today, one reason is fucking Carter, and Watergate made Carter possible. I don't have to tell you where those two assholes from the *Post* would be without Deep Throat: covering Girl Scout picnics in Chevy Chase, is where. My buddy had all the goods, but he didn't want to burden me with it. Then he was transferred to Turkey and killed by a mugger, knifed in an alley. Coincidence, right?"

"Jesus, Little, why the hell don't you write all this?"

"Why? I'll tell you why. Do you have any idea what happens when you mess with CIA? I don't want to discourage you Palmer, but from the moment my book was published, my phone was tapped, my every movement was watched. I even caught them picking through the garbage I put out on the street. My brother, whom I loved more than anyone in the world, died with his wife in a car accident six months after my book came out. They swerved off the road and rammed a telephone pole. Coincidence, right? I'm paranoid, right? Then you're going to tell me, 'Why didn't they just bump you off instead?' Well I'll tell you why. They knew it was more painful for me to live with the knowledge of my brother's death, then to die myself. And besides, it's risky stuff going around killing former agents who squeal on the company."

Little opened up two more bottles and dumped them into his glass.

"And who gives a shit, anyway, Palmer? Why should

I write this stuff and risk my ass? Why? Tell me? What good really came of my book and Agee's?"

"Congress forced the CIA to clean up its act, for one."

"Temporary setback. Sure the company has to report to a shit-load of congressional committees and comply with Freedom of Information Act requests, but big fucking deal. Nothing substantially has changed. No, Palmer, I won't write what I know. If you want to know the truth, I'm scared. I'm forty-five and I've reached the point in life where I can no longer march to the beat of patriotic slogans. I love this country, but I'd cut her loose in a minute if it meant saving my ass. Oh yeh, when you're young, things look different. I was a government agent, strong, virile, vital. I had the world by the balls. I couldn't die, not me, I'm too important. CIA. But I'm not young now, Palmer, and my body is fucked up from too much drinking and too many nights lying awake in bed listening for footsteps in the hall which never came. I'm vulnerable now, a little turd in the toilet, and anybody can come along and flush me away. I'm not about to die for my country anymore. I'll leave the crusading and the dying to younger nuts like you, men who think the mountains will move if you just give 'em a shove in the right spot."

Palmer drained his drink. He was drunk now and had had his fill of Harvey Little. Even a muckraker can only stomach so much.

"I'm going to sleep, Harvey. I want to thank you for being candid with me."

"Palmer, if you had a brain in your head, you wouldn't be thanking me. You'd be forgetting every word I told you. You'd fly back to New York or wherever you came from, find a nice girl with big tits and no brains, marry her and live in peace in some neat little Long Island suburb writing novels about Nazis. But you know, Palmer, looking at you, I know you won't let it lie. There's something eating you up. I don't know what it is, and maybe neither do you. But whatever it is, it's got you by the balls and it's swinging you around. I wish you luck, pal."

Palmer got up and staggered out of the bar. Maybe Little was right, Palmer thought as he entered the foul-smelling elevator, maybe he had bitten off more than he could chew. Kicking around a few dead presidents was a lot different than messing with CIA. But Little had been right, there was something inside of him which wouldn't let go. Almost like a death wish. He couldn't back off. Not from anything or anybody. His father had been a quitter. He had copped out when things got rough. Palmer could never do that.

The red message light on Palmer's phone was blinking when he entered the room. He dialed the operator.

"This is Palmer, room seven twenty-one. My message light is blinking."

"Hold on, sir, I'll connect you with the front desk."

In a moment, another voice came on.

"Yes, may I help you?"

"This is Alex Palmer. Seven twenty-one. I've got a message."

"Yes sir, I'll check."

Palmer kicked off his shoes while he waited and lay back on the bed. There was a switch on the night table and he flipped it up. The TV came on. *Casablanca* was playing for the millionth time.

"Mr. Palmer?"

"Yes."

"A David Schuyler called. He said it was urgent. He left a number."

Palmer wrote the number down, hung up and dialed.

"Yes?" came the sleepy voice at the other end.

"Davis, it's Alex. What's wrong?"

"Oh God, Alex. I don't know how to tell you . . ."

Palmer sucked in his breath.

"Charlene . . . she's dead. It was a bad car accident. Oh Christ, Alex, I'm sorry. . . ."

TWELVE

From his vantage point in the American Airlines terminal at Los Angeles International Airport, Daniel Johnson had a clear view of where the president would be greeted by Mayor David Toth when he stepped down from Air Force One. Through the terminal building's huge windows, Johnson could see a crowd of newsmen and photographers pressing up against a police barricade some hundred yards down the tarmac. Johnson lifted his binoculars. He recognized one of the star reporters for Channel Two, Alan Swyer. It was Swyer who had reported the night before that the president would be coming to Los Angeles to attend a thousand-dollar-a-plate luncheon for Mayor Toth. Toth, who was running for reelection, had campaigned vigorously for the Pierson-Demic ticket and was apparently cashing in an I.O.U.

Johnson had been standing in the same spot for almost two hours now and felt weary. He needed to go to the bathroom, but knew the minute he moved, one of the fifty or more spectators behind him would scramble into his place and he would miss seeing the president. Daniel Johnson did not want to miss seeing the president.

He had knocked off work early, heading straight for his favorite gin mill, and there he had quickly pumped enough beer into his blood for the courage to come to the airport. He had made a scene at the bar, and recalling it was painful. Denny White was a good bartender and Johnson had no business taking things out on him. White always called him "professor" because of the books he talked about . . . Professor Bud, Anheiser-Busch's brightest truck driver.

Denny White had been in a talkative mood and when things got around to politics, the bartender took a couple of potshots at the new president. Johnson had tensed at the mention of Demic, and when White had parroted a few of the popular doubts, Johnson had exploded foolishly: "God dammit! It's not my fault he's president!" and then stormed out of the bar. What a stupid thing to have done. Nobody was blaming Daniel Johnson for Demic's presidency. Certainly not Denny White. Johnson recognized the outburst for what it was—guilt—and clenched his teeth.

"What time is he due in?" someone behind Johnson asked.

"Noon, I think," another voice said.

Johnson checked his watch. It was four minutes of. Anxiously, he spun the focus dial on his binoculars, fingers sweaty. What was he doing here? Why had he

94

come? If only the big glass window wasn't in front of him . . . if only he had a rifle . . . crazy, absolutely crazy . . . it was the guilt . . . an accident of birth . . .

"THERE!" someone shouted. "Isn't that his plane coming in?"

"Yup. That's Air Force One. I saw a picture of it in *LIFE*. The plane's specially equipped for the president. Cost a trillion bucks."

"Taxpayers' money."

"What do you want him to do, fly standby on Frontier Airlines?"

Johnson raised the binoculars. Yes, it was Air Force One. He watched it taxi toward the barricade. The crowd of newsmen parted as a trio of cops formed a wedge for Mayor Toth, who ducked under the barricade. Johnson watched as Toth adjusted his tie and fidgeted with his cufflings. He's nervous, too, Johnson thought. Johnson suddenly felt a painful pressure on his face and realized he was pushing the binoculars too hard against his eyes. He relaxed his grip.

"The door is opening!"

Through the binoculars, Johnson saw four secret servicemen step out and scan the crowd before descending. Then the tall, ruggedly built figure of Joseph Demic emerged from the dark hole of the cabin.

The president of the United States.

Seeing Joseph Demic in person for the first time in his life, Daniel Johnson felt his heart pounding.

The face . . . Johnson could see nothing else. Standing on the top of the metal stairs, the president looked beyond the crowd of newsmen toward the terminal building. Riveted to his binoculars, it seemed to Daniel Johnson as if Joseph Demic was staring straight into his

95

eyes. The blood pounded in Johnson's ears.

With a quick turn of his fingers, he twisted the president out of focus and melted back into the crowd.

THIRTEEN

Alex Palmer watched the suitcases float by on the United Airlines conveyer belt and wished he could be one of them.

"Now there's a good life," Palmer said.

"What is?" Schuyler said.

"Being a suitcase. You get to travel a lot and then they take you home and empty you of your burden. I wish somebody would do that to me. Pry me open and dump everything out."

Palmer spotted his bag and bulled his way through a crowd to grab it.

"How many drinks did you say you had on the plane?" Schuyler asked.

"All I can say is I was reasonably sober when we approached Washington. It was this damned snowstorm which forced me to dig out my private stash from my briefcase. Stacked up for an hour, going round and round. Not my fault. You could have done something about the weather. You're the president's counsel."

"There are some things even the White House can't control, Alex."

"Maybe. How many inches are they predicting?"

"Three."

"Terrific."

"There's the limo. Come on."

The chauffeur put Palmer's bag in the trunk of the black Continental.

"Home, James," Palmer said, sinking down in the back seat and stretching his legs. "You rich guys got it knocked."

"Are you going to sober up before the funeral?" Schuyler said.

"Why? Charlie would have come drunk to mine . . . just wish this was mine instead of hers."

Palmer felt tears coming to his eyes. He turned away, staring out the window as they left the airport. The snow was coming in big flakes now, a sure sign it would stop soon. That was good. He didn't want to get stuck in D.C. He had work to do. Life must go on and all that. Damn Charlie and her dying.

"How did it happen?" Palmer said.

"They haven't exactly figured it out yet. They think her brakes locked and she skidded."

"What the hell was she doing out at that hour anyway?"

"She was working late in the office. One of the other reporters said she got a phone call. Something about a story she had been working on. So she went to meet the caller."

"What time was it?"

"One in the morning."

"Why go out so damn late for a story?" Palmer asked.

"You of all people shouldn't have to ask that question."

"Yeh. I suppose not," Palmer said glumly. "Does this thing have a bar?" Palmer looked around.

"No. Taxpayers wouldn't stand for it."

Palmer slouched down in his seat.

"Who found her?"

"Cops. She probably died on impact, if that's any comfort to you, Alex. They estimate she hit the wall doing about fifty. She was dead . . . before the fire."

Fire. Christ. What a grisly way to go. Burned beyond recognition . . . Palmer stared out the window. The city looked dazzling in the snow. There was a clean, pure quality to it. Washington — the part Layette laid out — always seemed unreal to Palmer with its perfect pattern of broad streets, the clear, unobstructed views. What right did a city have to look so pretty, anyway? Cities were mean, dirty, and ugly. Cities were for piling garbage up in alleys, for nickle-and-dime hoods to stake out a corner. This city didn't make any sense . . . Charlene's death, that didn't make any sense, either.

"How long did you go with Charlie?" Schuyler asked, hoping to break Palmer's silence, which made him uncomfortable.

"Three years . . . three years, two months, six days and five hours. That's her accounting. She kept track of such things."

The chauffeur, who had been listening, cut a corner too sharply and the big car skidded sideways in the snow, narrowly missing a parked van.

"Sorry, sir," the driver said, glancing back in the mirror.

Schuyler noticed Palmer hadn't even tensed up in the skid.

"You okay, Alex?"

"No. Should I be?"

"No. I guess not."

Schuyler shifted to face Palmer.

"Want to talk about it?"

"About Charlie? Nothing to talk about. We loved each other, I couldn't handle it, I bailed out. No big deal. There's creeps like me walking around out there every day."

"You're being a bit hard on yourself, aren't you?"

"Sure. Why not? I made life hard on Charlie, didn't I?" Palmer turned to face Schuyler. "You know, I still loved her. I didn't quite realize it until . . . this. I tried to be so cool about her. I went down to the paper to see her, to convince myself she meant nothing. Bad thing about it was I think I convinced her."

They were heading out to Landover, Maryland. Charlene had died there, smashing into the wall of a freeway underpass. A local funeral home had her body . . . her ashes.

It's so eerie," Schuyler said. "Only yesterday I saw her in the White House . . . then she's dead."

"White House?"

"Yeh. She had been to see Barry Abramson. Something about wanting to hand deliver a

100

photograph to the president. Abramson — prick that he is — turned her down. Might have been her last request in life, too. I bet he feels bad now."

Palmer half turned. Something started to click in his head. Then he lost it. He pressed his face up against the cool window and began to cry.

FOURTEEN

He awoke in one of those panics of dislocation. Where was he? Too many hotel rooms, all the same. What city was this? Dallas. Yeh, it was Dallas. Now he remembered. He had flown here right after the funeral . . . the damn urn. And Christ, he wasn't alone in the bed.

"Hi."

She was blond, very young, very pretty, with blue eyes and curly hair. Palmer didn't recognize her.

"You're trying to remember, right?" she said. Palmer nodded. "Ellen. Waitress at the Onyx Club."

He felt her hand slide down his belly. It started to come back to him.

The funeral . . . Charlie stuffed into that urn . . . the late flight to Dallas. The snow had stopped or he wouldn't have gotten out. But what was he doing in Dallas?

Her hand found his groin and started to bring him alive.

Dallas . . . he had called Harvey Little right after the funeral. Little was surprised, thought he had heard the last of Alex Palmer. Palmer wanted a lead. Anything. Something to occupy his mind so he wouldn't have to think about Charlie and the urn. Little had a man in Dallas who knew something about the Kennedy assassination. The man was a Dallas cop. Little said he would try to arrange something. An hour later Palmer got a call from Little. The cop had agreed to meet Palmer.

"There's a Kennedy museum near the site of the assassination," Little had said. "He'll meet you there. Pay two dollars and go into the back room for the slide show. Watch it. He'll meet you after the lights go on. Wear a white handkerchief in your jacket pocket so he will recognize you." Little had hung up abruptly.

So Palmer had hoped an eight o'clock flight to pursue Harvey Little's "mole-ecular theory." It had been a long flight, there was a lot of drinking and then . . .

Palmer, suddenly aroused, leaned toward the blonde. She parted her legs and he slid in between them.

Thinking about moles was better than remembering that urn . . . Palmer had sat there at the funeral, staring at the thing. It did not make sense that a human being could love you and touch you and then fit into a little urn. There was nothing you could relate to. You stared and stared, trying to call up a shape, an image from lovemaking, but the urn blotted out everything. You had things to say, apologies to make, but no one to address them to. It was a silence you could almost resent, if resenting an urn was possible.

Palmer vaguely remembered landing in Dallas and

103

checking in at Reunion Center. He had stared at his reflection in the glass building as he stepped out of the cab. It looked unreal to him. He ducked quickly into the lobby and registered.

She was grasping him tight now, her legs clamped around his back, her groin pumping. Palmer was moving, thrusting harder and harder, hoping to escape.

"That was nice," the girl said when they were done. "Much better than last night."

"What did I do last night?"

The blonde's eyes twinkled. "It was what you didn't do last night."

"Oh." Palmer's thoughts drifted to the meeting Little had set up. It was for two o'clock. What time was it now? Palmer, who never wore a watch for fear of having time drag on him, dialed the operator.

It was one o'clock. Palmer quickly showered and sent the girl away in a cab. The museum was only a few blocks away. He crossed the railroad tracks, then turned left at Reunion Station. Palmer had a sense of déjà vu when he approached the site of the assassination. Cars wound down the curve past the grassy knoll, just the way they had done on that November day back in '63. Palmer had seen it so many times. It was eerie.

Palmer walked down a slope of grass and stepped into the street. It was approximately where Kennedy's limousine had been hit from above . . . or the side. Palmer's eyes drifted to the grassy knoll and the wooden fence. How easy it must have been. Dodging a car, Palmer ran across the street onto the grassy knoll, then made a right and headed toward the museum, which was directly across from the School Book Depository. There were two big rooms in the museum. The first was open free to the public, its walls covered with front page blowups from newspapers: KENNEDY ASSASSINATED . . . PRESIDENT DEAD . . . ASSASSIN KILLS PRESIDENT . . . KENNEDY SLAIN IN DALLAS . . . NATION MOURNS SLAIN PRESIDENT. . . .

Palmer walked beneath them, staring up, remembering the day years ago. A sign in front of a door leading to the second room announced: "A Film Documentary on the Assassination," beginning at one forty-five. Feeling numb, Palmer bought a ticket and went in, adjusting his eyes to the dim lights. To his right was a set of bleachers. Tourists with cameras strung around their necks were already seated, talking in hushed tones, as if something of the dead lingered in the room. Palmer took a seat in the second row and stared ahead at an incredible display. It was a plastic replica of Dallas, complete with buildings, streets, traffic lights, and green areas for grass. Near the bottom of the display, Palmer recognized the School Book Depository and the curve of the road which spilled past the grassy knoll. A little shiver went through him. Palmer nervously adjusted the white handkerchief, a signal for someone . . . Palmer looked around, trying to catch an eye, a glint of recognition. They all seemed to be tourists, many of them Mexicans. Little had said the contact would be made after the slide show. Palmer fidgeted in his seat, waiting for the lights to go out. Suspended above the plastic city was a white movie screen. Palmer thought about what a gruesome business the marketing of death was.

Suddenly the lights went out and Palmer tensed reflexively. He glanced over one shoulder, then the other, looking for what, he did not know. An attack in the dark? A knife slipped between his shoulder blades. . . .

The slide show began. A newsreel-type voice, imparting drama without emotion, introduced a series of slides, beginning with Kennedy's arrival by plane in Dallas. As the narration brought Kennedy to the outskirts of Dallas in an open limousine, a tiny bubble of light suddenly flashed on at the top of the plastic city. Palmer watched transfixed as a series of bulbs went on, one at a time, tracing Kennedy's route to the grassy knoll. Palmer found himself no longer looking at the slides. His eyes followed the path of the blinking lights. His gaze slid ahead down the map to the grassy knoll, then back to the blinking lights, four or five "blocks" away. Palmer felt himself urging the lights to stop their death march. The narrator's bloodless voice kept dragging Kennedy on. Palmer looked up at the screen. Slides showed Kennedy waving to crowds; hordes of them pressed up against barricades, eager for a look at the young President; Governor Connolly turned to say something to Kennedy; a policeman on horseback trotted past people who were taking pictures. . . .

There was something grotesque about it. Palmer felt like a witness to a tragedy he was powerless to stop. He was drawn again to the lights. They seemed to hypnotize him, the relentless beat of life and death. Palmer wondered if he smashed one of the lights would the death march stop. . . .

When the narration reached the shattering point in history, the lights stopped blinking and froze, the moment crudely accented by a gunshot piped in over the narrator. Palmer turned away. He could feel sweat dripping from his forehead. Slides depicted the capture of Oswald and the swearing in of Lyndon Johnson. Then the overhead lights went on. People slowly dragged themselves up from the bleachers, filing quietly out of the theatre. Palmer sat there waiting for the contact. Nobody made a move toward him. He waited until the last person had left and then, finding himself alone in the theatre, suddenly felt nervous and headed across the darkened room past the plastic Dallas. The door started to close suddenly. Palmer felt his breath catch in his chest.

"Wait!" Palmer shouted.

A black man in a dark suit appeared in the doorway.

"Sorry. Thought everybody had left," the man said, and swung the door wide to let Palmer pass.

Back in the front room again, standing beneath the headlines screaming of Kennedy's death, Palmer began to calm down. Silly thing, to have panicked like that. He looked around the room at the tourists, waiting for a sign of recognition. Palmer's eye was caught by a blowup of Oswald being gunned down by Jack Ruby. A few feet away, a headline from the *Dallas News* proclaimed: RUBY DIES OF CANCER. Palmer knew the whole shadow of death cast by the assassination, all the connections violently severed. He felt his heart racing again.

There was a phone booth outside the museum. Palmer dug out Harvey Little's number at the Salt Lake Hilton and charged the call. He got lucky. Little was in his room working on his novel.

"He didn't show?" Little's voice sounded tight.

"No. I waited, but nobody approached me."

"Did you wear the white handkerchief like I told you?"

"Yes."

"And he didn't show?"

Palmer could sense the tension at the other end of the line.

"What is it?" Palmer said.

"Lookit, Palmer. Get out of there. Fast. I don't like it."

"What's wrong?"

"The meeting was set up. I double-checked with the guy just two hours ago. He should have been there. Get out of there, Palmer."

Palmer started to ask a question, but the line went dead. Harvey Little had hung up, and he had been scared. Palmer stepped out of the phone booth and squinted in the sunlight. It was a cloudless, brilliantly sunny day. The same kind of day Kennedy had been killed on. Palmer walked quickly away from the museum, looking over his shoulder once as he left. In order to get back to the hotel, he would have to walk in front of the School Book Depository and across the grassy knoll. Palmer moved along at a brisk clip, turning his collar up. It was silly to think that anything could happen to him. It was a wide-open area in broad daylight . . . who would dare shoot him? The irony was not lost on Palmer. His legs felt slightly shaky as he ran down the slope of the grassy knoll. He tried to stop himself from looking back toward the wooden fence, telling himself it was all so silly. But he looked anyway. There were no rifles, no handguns pointed his way. Then he remembered the School Book Depository and glanced up at the window on the fifth floor, last one to the right.

Shuddering, Palmer started to run across the street, forgetting about traffic. A pick-up truck narrowly missed him, swerving sharply to the left and blasting its horn. The sound shook Palmer, and he bounded across the street and hurried up the hill on the opposite side toward the railroad tracks. He was soaked with sweat by the time he crossed the lobby of Reunion Center and pressed the elevator button. While he waited, he noticed the white handkerchief and yanked it out of his pocket, stuffing it in his trousers.

His room was on the twenty-third floor. All he wanted to do was pack his bag and get the hell out of Dallas. His shaking hand had trouble fitting the key in the lock; then it slid in and he opened the door. Palmer hesitated. At first he didn't know why, just that his mind screamed for him not to go in. Then, in the heightened state his senses were in, he recognized what troubled him about the dark room: the fresh odor of smoke. Palmer slammed the door and began running toward the elevator. He reached it and stabbed the down button, then spun around, bracing for an attack. Nothing came. The loud ring the arriving elevator made shook him. The doors parted and he rushed into the empty car, pounding the CLOSE button. The doors seemed to take an eternity to shut. . . .

"I haven't been in the room for over an hour. That's why I suspected somebody was in there," Palmer was explaining to the house detective, who was accompanying him back upstairs.

"Might have been a maid. They're not supposed to smoke, but who listens to rules these days," the detective said. He was a short man, neatly dressed in a grey, two-piece suit, pencil-thin mustache, narrow lips.

Palmer led him to the room, opened the door and then stepped back, letting the detective go in first. The room was a mess. Drawers hung open. Palmer's bag had been emptied, the contents strewn about. The detective unbuttoned his coat and walked cautiously into the bathroom, then emerged a couple of seconds later.

"Sure looks like you had company. Anything missing?"

"I don't think so," Palmer said. "Wasn't much to take. I can't imagine what they were looking for."

"Money. Jewels. The usual. This is one of the finest hotels in Dallas. A lot of wealthy people stay here. You'll want to file a report with the police, of course."

"Actually, as a matter of fact, I don't," Palmer said quickly. The detective eyed him carefully. He slid one finger across his mustache.

"Why not?"

"My name is Alex Palmer. Maybe you've heard of me."

The detective thought about it.

"Sounds familiar."

"I'm a writer. *Dirty Tricks. The Kent State Conspiracy.*"

Something in the way of recognition flashed in the house detective's eyes.

"That's why I wouldn't want this to be reported," Palmer said. "It would look like a publicity stunt. You can see what I mean."

The detective nodded, silently weighing his options. What the hell. Nothing seemed to have been stolen.

"Okay. We'll play it your way. But you'd better keep your door locked and bolted. Wouldn't want no big-time writer getting knocked off in our fine hotel, know what I mean?"

Palmer nodded, mouth dry. The little detective closed the door slowly and was gone. Palmer turned the safety bolt and slid the chain in place. He went over to the bed and sank down on it. Palmer remembered Harvey

Little's answer when he had asked him in Salt Lake why he didn't write what he knew: "Do you have any idea what happens when you mess with CIA?"

Digging out his bottle of Wild Turkey, Palmer poured a drink without ice and tossed it down to steady his nerves. He would not be frightened off. Not Alex Palmer. He was not like . . . his father. He would keep digging until something explosive surfaced and then he would write it. Every last fucking word. And to hell with them. Whoever "them" was. Palmer got out his little phone book and dialed the White House, asking for Schuyler.

"Alex, where are you?" the voice at the other end said.

"Dallas."

"Why?"

"I'm sightseeing. There's a lovely grassy knoll here you should see."

"Very funny. Are you all right?"

"Yes. More or less."

"I have some news for you. It's about that list of names you wanted me to dig up."

Palmer's grip tightened on the phone.

"The CIA Class of '57 was a big one, Alex. Some thirty names. I went through a lot of hassle getting this for you. If some of these people are Communist spies, our country is in big trouble."

Palmer lifted his drink and sucked some bourbon down.

"Alex, I've got one name on this list that's going to make you come in your pants, so make sure you're not wearing any expensive clothes."

"Cut the buildup, David, and tell me what you've got."

"Well, I hesitate to even tell you this, because I know what a paranoid muckraker you are. But I dare say even you wouldn't touch this one."

Schuyler paused, obviously enjoying himself. Palmer waited impatiently. In a pseudo-dramatic voice reminiscent of Joe McCarthy's, the president's counsel announced loudly over the phone: "And right here in my hand I have a list of thirty card-carrying Communists who have infiltrated the highest intelligence-gathering service of this great nation! They are out there, these agents of the Red Menace, spying on you every day, plotting the overthrow of your government."

"David, please."

"And right here at the top of my list of these card-carrying Communists is a name so big I shudder to reveal it. Yes, my fellow Americans, this agent of a foreign nation has risen so high in our government that the very foundation of this republic is in jeopardy. I submit to you the name of the highest-ranking Communist in America: President Joseph Demic."

FIFTEEN

David Schuyler heard his own heels clicking down the corridor of the White House and softened his step. The noise heightened his sense of where he was, and the last thing he wanted to do was to be awed by the place. He was trying to step out of the path of history, not into it. But how do you turn your back on all this? Schuyler struggled against being taken in by the majesty. Just another hall in a building. No big deal. He fingered the envelope in his hand, half wanting to tear it up and turn back before he reached General Worthington's office. A thousand young lawyers would give their right arms to be where he was today.

"Go right in, David, the general's expecting you," Worthington's secretary said.

Schuyler hesitated at the door to the presidential counselor's inner office, then took a deep breath and went in.

"Sit down, David, I'll be right with you," Worthington

said without looking up from a report he was studying. Watching the general, Schuyler again was struck by an awesome sense of time and place. James Worthington was one of the most respected men in America, and despite his heart attack was still an incredibly vital, imposing man. Six feet two, he had the type of broad shoulders meant to be squared off in a military jacket. His face was handsome and rugged, with blue eyes that disarmed you with their warmth.

Worthington looked up. "There's scotch and ice. Help yourself. It's been a while since we've had a chance to talk."

Something in Schuyler's face made the general pause. He noticed the envelope in the young lawyer's hands.

"Bad news?"

"Depends on how you look at it."

The general put aside his report and picked up his pipe with a slow, deliberate motion, watching as Schuyler mixed some Chivas and ice.

"Do I get to see the letter now or do you keep me hanging?" the general said.

"Sorry. I didn't mean to drag this thing out. It's just that it's difficult for me." Schuyler handed the envelope to Worthington.

Tucking his empty pipe to one side of his mouth, the general opened the envelope and began reading the letter. Schuyler watched nervously. When the general was done, he slid the letter back into the envelope, dropped it on his desk and leaned toward Schuyler.

"President Pierson's platform included a promise to trim government waste, son. This," the general said, picking up the envelope and dropping it in a nearby waste basket, "is a flagrant waste of White House stationaey."

Schuyler sighed.

"I'm serious about it, Jamie."

"You can't quit this army, David."

"This isn't the army, Jamie."

The general, his face suddenly weary, nodded. "Sometimes I wish the hell it was. God knows there is a lot wrong with the armed services, but it has its good points. Take a situation like this. A bright, but wet-behind-the-ears lieutenant like yourself comes into my tent and says he's had his fill of the front. Wants out. Know what I'd say to that young lieutenant, David?"

Schuyler shrugged, sinking further down into his chair. Out of the corner of his eye he noticed a stack of books on a table next to Worthington: Watergate.

"I'd say, 'Son, if I could hightail it out of here with you, I would. The war's dragging on me, too. But if we all turned and ran, that wouldn't end it. The battlefield would just shift closer to home. The enemy would march straight to that little town in New Hampshire or wherever it is you long to set up your comfortable little law practice. They wouldn't stop until they met resistance, so we might as well take a stand here and slug it out.' That's what I'd say, David."

General Worthington glanced at Schuyler, who looked like a glum schoolboy.

"I know what you're thinking. You're saying to yourself that the White House isn't no damn front. But you're wrong there, David. It is. Our nation is on the verge of a major crisis and the next week or two could very well decide the future of this country and the world. The battle will be fought here."

"Joe Demic doesn't need any lieutenants. Joe Demic is a damn one-man army," Schuyler blurted out.

"Aaaah. Now we get to the crux of the problem." Swinging out from behind his desk, Worthington went over and poured himself a drink. "The young lieutenant doesn't feel loved."

"Oh hell, it's not that, Jamie. It's just that all my life I've wanted to be part of something important, something vital. I've worked my ass off to get here, and suddenly I'm nothing more than an office boy. I mean, the damn guy hasn't so much as buzzed me in three days. I'm the president's counsel, Jamie. That should mean something."

Worthington smiled and put his drink down. "And I'm the highest ranking member of his staff," the general said. "Guess how many words he's spoken to me in that same time?"

Schuyler shrugged again.

"Almost none. Oh, there have been written memos, but no urgent summoning to the Oval Office. The man has isolated himself, David, for what reason I don't know. But the cold shoulder treatment isn't reserved for you. We all feel it. Maybe he's just digging in, preparing for the UN meeting and his summit with the Soviet president at Camp David. Whatever the reason, he's erected the Great Wall of China around himself, and nobody, but nobody can scale it."

Schuyler felt the warmth of the scotch and hoped it and soothing words from the general would break down his resistance. He didn't really want to resign.

"Jamie, I'm no quitter."

"I know you aren't, David."

"But hell, a person wants to feel needed."

"And you are."

"Fat chance. Demic probably doesn't even remember my first name."

"Not Demic, David. Me. I need you."

Schuyler's glass was empty. He held it up.

"Help yourself," the general said. Schuyler poured a stiff one. "David, you're the one person around this nut house that I trust. You're open and honest and refreshing. And you're not in awe of me. I like that. You aren't afraid to tell me I'm full of crap once in a while. It's important for me to have someone like you around. Especially with the problems that are coming up."

The general's words had the desired affect on Schuyler. He smiled.

"It'll be like I'm working more for you, than him, right? Schuyler said.

"Exactly. And David, this next week or so is going to make all the aggravation worthwhile. The world's tilting on end, and we're going to be at the center of the action. Even a man like Demic won't be able to get through this thing alone. We're going to have our fingers on the pulse of the world. History will break in front of our eyes. We'll be writing the chapters, David."

The general picked up a folder from his desk.

"The reports out of Russia are bad, David. The Soviets are in trouble. Their wheat crops are failing and their oil production is down to the point where they are now a dependency nation. Too many kopeks poured into weapons and not enough to put bread on Ivan's table. Hungry men are not easy to control, David. Rublov is skating on thin ice. Our intelligence says there are two factions struggling for power in the Politburo. The president and his handpicked deputy, Anatoly Brukhov, head up one of them. Brukhov is a hawk, and he's got Rublov's ear. It's no secret Rublov would like to pass on the reins to Brukhov.

"Then there are the moderates, led by Politburo chief Alexis Durichev. They favor increased ties with the West.

Durichev sees the advantages of working out a grain deal with us. The price we'd extract, of course, would be a reduction in the arms race, and Durichev would like nothing better. After all, the Soviets have been spending better then twenty per cent of their budget for over a decade on arms production. Durichev reasons that with a cutback, he could channel that money into areas which would build his public support — food, health care, a generally more Westernized standard of living.

"I'm convinced that at Burkhov's urging, Rublov is planning on invading Iraq, using the latest outbreak of fighting with Iran as a pretext for a 'peace' mission. What he really wants is control of the oil fields. It would solve Russian energy problems and provoke the kind of crisis that would be sure to divert attention from Ivan's woes at home."

"But we wouldn't stand for an invasion of Iraq. Surely Rublov knows that," Schuyler said, caught up.

"Maybe. Maybe not. That's what the Soviets want to find out. I get the distinct impression that Rublov wants to test Demic. After all, he's got nothing to lose. If things get too hot, he could always withdraw his 'peacemaking' troops."

Worthington stared down at the report.

"God, how much nicer it would be if Rublov would decide instead to invade Czechoslovakia," the general said.

"Czechoslovakia? Why?"

"Because our sources say the workers and students are tightly organized and ready to fight. If the Soviets invaded Czechoslovakia, they'd be in for a long, bloody fight. It would be their Vietnam, and the embarrassment would almost surely topple Rublov's regime and pave the way for the moderates."

"What does Demic hope to accomplish at Camp David?"

Worthington frowned.

"I wish the hell I knew. But then, there's that Great Wall." Worthington's face softened. "You see, we're really in the same boat."

Schuyler nodded. The stack of Watergate books again caught his eye.

"Why the sudden interest?" Schuyler said, pointing to the books.

"Can't really give you a good answer, David. Don't know myself."

Draining his glass, Schuyler got up and shook hands with Worthington.

"Thanks, Jamie. I was kind of hoping you'd talk me out of it."

Worthington walked Schuyler to the door. Something suddenly popped into Schuyler's head. Maybe it was the mountain of Watergate books that made him say it, or the scotch.

"Jamie, do you think it's possible that the president of the United States could be a Communist?"

Worthington did a double take. "What did you say?"

Schuyler laughed. "Never mind. It was nothing."

SIXTEEN

Getting the key to Charlene Lowenstein's apartment had been a snap. The landlady, an elderly German with a thick accent, remembered Palmer from the days when he was a pretty permanent fixture. She had always been overly friendly—Charlene had said it was guilt for what had been done to the Jews; Palmer had laughed at that. There were tears in the old lady's eyes when she gave Palmer the key. Perhaps she had been genuinely fond of Charlie after all.

Once inside, Palmer was almost sorry he had come. He felt like a vulture, picking over the remains of her life. His touch, as he pulled out drawers and lifted neat piles of blouses and sweaters, was absurdly gentle. He didn't want to disturb anything. But why? What difference would it make now? Charlene wouldn't be returning. Yet there was so much of her here: the ancient wool afghan spread on the couch . . . the porcelain collection of miniature animals which she kept in an empty tropical fish tank . . . the candle shaped like an oriental face, which Charlene had bought in Chinatown when the two of them were covering the financial crisis in New York. Palmer remembered how Charlene had lit the candle one night, then abruptly blew it out a half hour later, saying the melting face saddened her. Charlene Lowenstein had been a collector of things without value: old soda bottles, handheld mirrors with cracks, corks from fifths of Remy Martin, and finally, Alex Palmer. He had been a bundle of trouble and nobody in her right mind should have wanted any part of him. Nobody except Charlene Lowenstein.

Palmer got lucky and found the diary quickly. It was in the middle drawer of her writing desk, in a white plastic Buster Brown shoe bag. Palmer laid the diary on a coffee table in the living room and went into the kitchen. He laughed at what he saw in the refrigerator: an eight ounce jar of Hellman's mayonnaise, an unopened package of Hebrew National hotdogs, a jar of Guilden's mustard minus the cap, a bag from McDonald's, and a package of Kraft's American cheese, the slices individually wrapped. There was also a bottle of Taittinger's, and Palmer grabbed it by the neck, found a clean wine glass and took it into the living room, popping the cork and pouring. He took a sip, then walked over to the stereo. They had both liked the Beatles. Palmer picked up *Revolver, Sergeant Pepper's* and *Abbey Road* and put them on, remembering how Charlene had especially loved *Sergeant Pepper's* because she said it reminded her of the hippy she had never become.

They had both been at college when the drug craze

had first swept the nation's campuses — he at Yale, she at Radcliffe. Both resisted, each for different reasons. Palmer, arrogant and aloof, had been turned off by the artificial camaraderie of the dope smokers and pill poppers. He was a loner by nature and found something almost fascistic in the compulsive shared experience. He did not feel what the others felt when they lovingly sucked on their joints — that the world was beautiful and every man a brother. At twenty-one, Palmer had already seen more of the uglier side of the world than he had cared to remember, and the pot did nothing to mellow his perceptions. It had always angered him when they treated him as an outcast because he would not let his feelings go up in smoke.

Charlene's experience with drugs had been different. Palmer, listening now to "Norwegian Wood," remembered how Charlene had cried softly on his shoulder, recalling the painful years. She had wanted to feel beautiful like the others, be beautiful. But the drugs only made her paranoid, brought out all the ugly fears and self-doubts. The more she smoked, the more isolated from the others she felt. She was ugly. They were beautiful. She mustn't let them know. She would smile angelically, talk about beauty as she imagined it to be, and since her imagination was very good, she would fool everyone except herself.

Palmer's fingers closed in a tight fist. She had been warm and gentle. In public she acted tough, a caricature out of "The Front Page," but Palmer knew the person behind the byline.

Palmer tossed down more champagne. Somebody was going to pay for what had been done to Charlie, even if it cost him his life. Picking up the diary

Charlene's sister had written in Russia, Palmer thought about Schuyler's reaction to his suspicions about Demic. Schuyler had laughed when Palmer said he wasn't ruling out the possibility the president was a Communist. Palmer didn't bother to argue. How could he? The whole thing was so absurd, so impossible, and yet . . . Palmer hadn't told Schuyler about the photo of the Russian boy that Charlene had given the president just hours before she got the phone call that led to her death trip.

It was unthinkable that the president of the United States, a former deputy director of CIA, could be a foreign agent. And yet . . . Demic had joined the company three months after Joe McCarthy had died. The atmosphere, as the senator had been told on his death bed, was indeed ripe for infiltration. But that in itself did not mean that every red-blooded American who joined the government that year was a potential Communist, certainly not a man who rose to the top of the nation's intelligence-gathering community, retired before the scandals and then became a United States senator, a vice president and a president. Surely it wasn't possible. Palmer knew he was pursuing the slimmest thread, and yet the stakes were so high it was worthwhile. If his thesis proved out — and he lived to tell it — Alex Palmer would be the most celebrated investigative writer in the nation.

Palmer tried to recall all that Charlene had told him about her sister. Sarah had gone to Russia in 1953 with Henry and Claire Lowenstein. Henry had been Moscow correspondent for the *New York Times*. Sarah was seventeen, a Scarsdale High School senior on an incredible adventure. Charlene, an "accident," would be born a year later.

Palmer picked up the diary. On the inside page, Sarah Lowenstein had written: "My Russian Journey," and the date, Jan. 12, 1953. Palmer glanced at the first entry:

RUSSIA! Oh golly! We arrived in Moscow yesterday. There's a foot of snow and everything is so coolllllld . . . brrrrr . . . But it's all so exciting. I'm to enroll in a Russian school and I'm so nervous about that. I hope all the tutoring I've had in Russian pays off. I don't want to look like a dunce in front of the other kids, especially since I'm an American. The only bad thing so far is the apartment. It's so tiny, just three rooms. But Daddy says that's very big for Moscow and we were lucky to get it. Lucky????

Palmer flipped the pages until he found the last entry Sarah had made. It was dated June 23, 1953.

This was the most bizarre day of my life. Oh diary, I don't know where to begin. It was the kind of adventure that could never have happened to me in America. I don't even know how I had the courage to do what I did. But I was just so bored. Life in Russia is so drab. There's no gaiety or friendliness in public. People open up only in private, and then only if they know you. We foreigners (how strange to call myself a foreigner) are treated with respect but people seem to be afraid of us. Daddy said if we are seen going into a Russian's apartment, that person can be harrassed for it. Can you imagine it? In Scarsdale, if we had a Russian visitor, all my friends would rush over to see her.

And I'm so tired of all the lines. Lines for everything. You simply don't walk into a store and buy what you want, like at Lord and Taylor's. You must stand in line. Sometimes I get angry at all the fat Russian ladies, standing so passively with their bags, waiting and waiting and waiting. I don't know why I feel that way. Maybe it's because I stand there, too, like a dunce.

Anyway, I haven't even begun my adventure story. I'm thirsty. I have to run into the kitchen to get some milk. Be right back, diary . . .

I'm back. Where was I? Oh, I was telling you about how bored I was. We are staying in a village called Zukovka at the *dacha* of Vladimir Koslovsky. Daddy says Mr. Koslovsky is one of Russia's most prominent journalists and that it is a rare privilege for us to be allowed to stay with him. I guess working for the *New York Times* has its rewards, even over here. Zukovka is about twenty-five miles from Moscow, and it is where a lot of the important people have their *dachas* (*dachas* are like our summer homes in the Hamptons, only not nearly as big or nice).

It is very pretty here, even if there isn't much to do. Most of the *dachas* are on a big hill overlooking the beaches by the Moscow River. For the first week, I sunbathed and swam a lot, but that got pretty boring after a while. I've always been a nature lover—guess that's from my good old camp days—so today I decided to hike around in the woods near our *dacha*. I had been walking for almost an hour, and was coming out of the forest into a clearing when I saw him. He had a large, silver pail and was stooping to pick things off the ground, which he put into it. I didn't know whether to approach him or not, because Russians are funny about strangers, but then he saw me and waved, so I got real bold and walked over.

"Hello," I told him in Russian. "My name is Sarah Lowenstein."

Imagine my shock when he answered me in perfect English: "I'm Yuri. How do you do?"

"Are you an American?" I stammered, and then realized that he couldn't be, not with a name like Yuri.

"No. I'm not," he said, "but thank you for the compliment. I didn't know my accent was that good."

That was the strange thing. He didn't have any accent at all. In fact, as we talked more, I was amazed at how much American slang he knew. If I had met him at a party in Scarsdale and he had said his name was John Smith, I would never in a zillion years have suspected he was a Russian.

"How did you ever learn to speak such perfect English? Have you been in America?" I asked him. He smiled and said he hadn't. He's in a training program for future diplomats and learns English from tapes of American radio shows — *The Shadow*, Jack Benny, that sort of thing. He also reads a lot of American newspapers. Isn't that wild? I was really curious about his training, but he didn't seem to want to talk more about it, so I dropped the subject. I asked him what he was collecting in the pail and he showed me: mushrooms. It's apparently a very popular thing for Russians to do in the countryside. Yuri had been bored with his training and decided to take a break. I laughed when he said that because here I was, bored, too.

"Russians feel that mushrooms go very well with vodka," Yuri told me. "In fact, they say each mushroom has its own special vodka. For example, these milk mushrooms are supposed to go very well with refined brown vodka. Actually, I think it's all a lot of bunk. I think the only reason we Russians pick mushrooms is to have another excuse to get drunk on vodka."

We both had a big laugh about that. I had never heard a Russian speak so openly to a foreigner before. A Russian has to know you very well before he opens up, but his boy, well, he was more like an American. It was a very strange thing, but I guess it was from all that training. We gathered mushrooms together for a while and then we sat on a big rock to rest and it was then that he asked me if I'd like to go with him in his car to Moscow.

I didn't know what to say. On the one hand, of course, I really wanted to. But it was so brazen. I hardly knew him, and here he was asking me out on a sort of date. Mom and Dad would have told me I couldn't go, but they were supposed to stay on the beach all day with Mr. Koslovsky and Yuri promised we'd be back before sundown. I couldn't believe I heard myself say yes.

"First," he said, "we must get some vodka to drink on the way in." I told him I didn't drink, but he said, "I do," and laughed. Right there I should have changed my mind, but like I said, I was so bored and he was very nice . . . and cute, too. So we started down the hill toward where he said his car was parked. In order to get to the road, we had to cross through a pine grove and the ground was very hard to walk on and I almost tripped into what looked like a trench.

"It is a trench," he said, and proceeded to explain how trenches had been dug during World War II to defend Moscow against attack by the Germans, but the Germans had never come.

When we reached the road, I was surprised and quite impressed to see his car was a Zil. I mean, only very important people can afford to own Zils in Russia. They're like our Cadillacs. We drove about a quarter of a mile down the road and then he pulled over in front of a cement-block store complex. "You're not going to try and go in there, are you?" I said. "Of course," he replied. "Where else would I buy my vodka?"

I explained to Yuri how my dad had told me only the elite can shop there and that you needed a special card. No sooner had I finished telling him, then Yuri laughed and pulled such a card out of his wallet. Then he got out and walked toward the front door of one of the stores. Out of nowhere an armed policeman appeared and blocked his path. Yuri very calmly showed his card and was allowed to pass, just like that.

Yuri drove to Moscow very fast, steering with his left hand and drinking vodka with his right. I was more than a little frightened, but Yuri seemed so much in control, I found myself starting to relax. He offered me a sip, but I politely turned him down. In between drinking, Yuri laid out what he said would be our itinerary. First we were going to a *banya* — a Russian steam bath — then a soccer match, and if there was time, we would find a Communist Party meeting to attend. Yuri laughed when he said that, although I didn't see anything humorous in our going to a Party meeting. I just figured he was getting a little drunk.

"You're my sister, and you have forgotten your papers," Yuri told me. "If anyone speaks to you, you must smile and say nothing. You are deaf and dumb, and I am taking you into Moscow to show you a good time. We will have less problems that way, understand?"

I nodded my head, feeling a little deaf and dumb. Everything Yuri said seemed so extraordinary and crazy, but there was something about him which overpowered me. I have never met anyone so forceful. He was very much like some of the young corporation executives Daddy brought home for dinner in Scarsdale, except that Yuri was Russian and eighteen.

We arrived at the *banya* around noon. On the way to Moscow, Yuri had explained to me what to do once we were inside. There were separate baths for men and women, so I would be on my own. I paid the attendant with money Yuri had given me and was handed a rough sheet. For an additional ten kopeks, I bought a bundle of leafy birch twigs which Yuri had told me was for flailing myself in the steam room, an act which is supposed to cleanse you. A young woman with large brown eyes and a friendly face spoke to me, and I did my best to explain with my hands that I could not talk to her. She seemed very moved by my disability, and I felt kind of guilty about that. The woman took me under her wing, and using crude sign language, guided me through the *banya*. There was a changing room where we hung our clothes on hooks. I was very embarrassed to be naked in front of the Russian woman, fearing absurdly that somehow my body would give me away as an American. I undressed very quickly and wrapped the sheet around me the way the young woman did. The *banya* resembled a boiler room. There were open pipes and a pile of fire bricks in an oven in the center of the room.

As we walked in, a woman sitting on the highest balcony said something to me quickly in Russian about water. I was confused, and stood there. The woman on the top shelf was drenched in sweat. She clapped her hands, obviously indicating that I do something fast, but what it was I didn't know. I began to regret having come to Moscow with Yuri and wanted to be back with my parents. The young woman who had befriended me, however, came to my rescue, explaining to the other woman about my handicaps. Then the young woman took my hand and we left the room. There were two zinc tubs on a table near a water faucet, and with her hands, my friend motioned for me to fill one up and follow her back into the *banya*. I did, and then she dashed water onto the bricks, producing a burst of steam and a smile on the face of the woman on the highest of the seven stone steps. I repeated what she had done and then sat down next to my friend, feeling the sweat pour out of my body and wondering how Yuri was doing.

Some of the women would slap the birch twigs against themselves every so often, which seemed so silly, but I was afraid to be different, so I beat myself gently with the leaves. The torture, thank goodness, lasted only about six or seven minutes. I was led out of the steam by my friend, back to the changing room, where women sat around drinking beer and eating salami, black bread, and canned sardines. My friend gave the attendant money and she brought us both mugs of beer. Too nervous to refuse, I gulped the watery beer. It was sort of pleasant and I felt giddy in a short while. The young woman ordered another mug for each of us and some dried, bony salt fish, which you are supposed to chew. From my biology class I knew that the salt was good for you after excessive sweating. The beer was really making me feel nice and I paid for another round of drinks and fish. By the time I left, I was embarrassed at how drunk I was and when I met Yuri at his car, he made things worse by laughing at me.

The soccer match was not very exciting. There were almost a hundred thousand people in the stands, but nobody seemed to show much emotion. I don't know why I was surprised. Russians in the street are like that. But I thought at an athletic event it would somehow be different. It wasn't. Yuri had parked his car a couple blocks from the stadium, but said we would take the subway to the party meeting—"for the experience," is how he put it. When we filed out of the stadium, there were hundreds of soldiers outside, arranged in two neat lines through which we and the rest of the fans filed toward the subway. Yuri explained it was the Russian way of avoiding disorderly outbreaks, although I felt it was all pretty unnecessary, considering how subdued the crowd had been during the game. How wrong I was. The minute people passed the last of the soldiers, they seemed to lose all control, dashing in panic down the subway station steps for an approaching train. Yuri laughed like a madman, grabbing my arm and propelling me through the crowd so I wouldn't fall and be trampled. I had never seen anything like it, but Yuri assured me it happened all the time. "Russians," Yuri said, "go bonkers the minute they are out of reach of the authorities. That is why we are such big drunkards. Nobody could maintain such a morbid sense of control both in public and private."

I was feeling kind of dizzy and Yuri slipped his arm through mine for support as we stepped onto the train. My face got red when he did this, but I did not remove his arm . . .

Palmer, feeling suddenly weary, put the diary down. It was then that he first thought he heard a noise out in the hallway. Without knowing quite why, Palmer quickly walked over to the door and checked that it was locked. He slipped the safety chain in place, laughed a little at the stillness of his actions, and went back to the couch. The bottle of Taittinger's was almost empty. The tiny champagne bubbles seemed to have settled in his face below the surface of the skin, tingling pleasantly. Palmer picked up the diary again.

The meeting was held in a huge auditorium. There was a long table set up on stage with a half dozen chairs. The overhead lights were all very bright. I noticed that Yuri seemed to walk into the meeting with an exaggerated arrogance. We took seats near the front and waited while people arrived. Yuri's special card had been enough to get us both into the meeting, and the man at the door seemed impressed by Yuri. I found myself feeling proud to be with Yuri, although I couldn't really explain why. After we had been sitting five minutes, Yuri excused himself and went to the bathroom. I did not like being all alone. The party members seemed particularly morbid looking, even for Russians. I felt like I was at the funeral of someone I didn't know. When Yuri returned he seemed to be a little more drunk. He nearly tripped on somebody, and was noticeably swaying. "I finished the bottle," he said and laughed. I did not laugh. There was something all wrong about Yuri's behavior. It was not the place to be drunk, and he seemed to have done it on purpose.

When the meeting started, Yuri slouched down in his chair and folded his arms defiantly across his chest. He was the only one who wasn't sitting up straight and attentive in his chair. People glanced our way and I felt suddenly scared, but Yuri didn't seem bothered by the attention.

"Cows," Yuri said to me. "Cows?" I asked, confused. "Them," he said, sweeping his hand in a gesture meant to take in everyone. People near us turned to look. I reached out and pulled Yuri's arm down. The man who was speaking on stage seemed to skip a beat in his speech, then went on. I felt nervous and sick in my stomach. "Yuri, please be quiet," I whispered. He laughed. Somebody said, "Ssssh." Yuri went, "Mooo." Another person ssshed us. Yuri mooed louder. I felt my whole body begin to tremble. People were now staring openly at us. The speaker on stage stopped talking. Before I could do anything, Yuri cupped his hand over his mouth and let out a loud moo. I was now terrified, sweating worse than I had in the *banya*. A big man with a huge nose and thick arms stood up a few seats away and said something quickly to Yuri which I couldn't make out, but his harsh tone and the warning finger he pointed were clear in meaning. Yuri replied by mooing again at the man, and called him a cow. The man suddenly started climbing over people, his eyes red and bulging. Yuri popped up, smiling for some unbelievable reason, and stood waiting for the man. I moved away just as Yuri picked up a chair and slammed it into the face of the big man, who was toppled backwards onto the lap of a woman. When the man got up, there was blood streaming down his face and he had drawn a knife from somewhere. Yuri was no longer smiling. I cringed as the man lunged at Yuri. Yuri tried to kick him, but the man stepped aside and slashed at Yuri's leg with his knife. Yuri screamed and fell down. His pants were cut open at the right knee and I felt myself get sick when I saw the blood. The man raised the knife again but two other men grabbed him from behind and wrestled him to the ground. I started to cry and then felt arms pull me away. Yuri was screaming on the floor. His pants' leg was soaked with blood. I vomited and gagged on salt fish and beer. There were sirens and then a commotion at the back of the auditorium and the police came in followed by some men in white uniforms with a stretcher. They put Yuri on the stretcher and started up the center aisle. One of the policemen grabbed my arm and I was taken along. There was an ambulance out front. Yuri's stretcher was slid in and then I was put in beside him. There was a policeman in the back with us. The siren started and we pulled away. Suddenly I heard Yuri say, "Not the hospital. Take me to the Kremlin Clinic."

The policeman seemed to think that was very funny, but when Yuri reached into his pocket and pulled out his special card, he stopped laughing and quickly said something to the driver and then the car made a sudden right-hand turn. "Kremlin Clinic," Yuri repeated, and then passed out.

After Yuri had shown his card, the policeman seemed to treat me differently. I was someone special. When we stopped, and Yuri's stretcher was taken out of the back, I was very gently helped out onto the street. We were across the street from the Lenin Library, in front of a building that had no markings except for a hammer and sickle. There were a lot of Zils and black Volgas parked outside. Yuri was rushed into the building and I was brought along by the policeman. I was so scared I started to cry again. The policeman tried to console me, saying in Russian, "Do not worry. It will be all right." But I was worried. What were my parents going to think? I thought about trying to run, but where would I go? How would I get back to Mr. Koslovsky's *dacha*?

It was some sort of hospital, much cleaner and more impressive-looking than any other I had seen in in Moscow. I was asked to sit down in the lobby while Yuri was rushed away. In a few minutes, two men wearing black raincoats came over to talk to me. One of them spoke English and he asked me to tell him everything that he happened. He did not have the uniform of a policeman, but somehow I sensed he was someone with authority. Trembling, I explained how I had met Yuri and what had happened. When I was done, he glanced toward the other man, who had been writing everything down, and then told me I would be driven back to my parents. I almost cried when he told me that. Gosh, I was sorry I had ever done something so stupid. Just before we left, I asked the man who spoke English about Yuri, and he assured me he would be all right, that it was just a nasty cut on the knee.

When I got back to the *dacha*, it was dark and I was scared to face my parents. They were so relieved to see me, however, that they didn't even scold me. I told them everything that had happened and my father came over when I was done and put his arm around me and I could see tears in his eyes. I was doubly sorry then for what I had done.

The next day something very incredible happened. I got the phone number of the hospital from Mr. Koslovsky and called to see how Yuri was, but I was told there was no one by his name there. They said he had never even been there, and when I started to protest, they hung up on me.

Diary, I don't know what to think about all this. Yuri must be someone very important, so why don't they know what happened to him? I must find out, but I don't know how. I won't rest until I talk to Yuri. . . .

Palmer closed the diary slowly. That had been the last words Sarah Lowenstein had written. Two days later she had been found dead in the woods, strangled and raped by a man who was later caught and executed. Palmer remembered Charlene telling him that. It was not something you could forget.

On his way into the kitchen to throw away the empty bottle of Taittinger's, Palmer heard a click at the front door. He froze. Walking back into the living room, Palmer watched the door, barely breathing. The handle turned slowly. The door began to open, then stopped, secured by the chain. Palmer reacted fast. He grabbed the diary, raced toward the living room window and knocked over a lamp, which hit the floor with a loud crash. Pulling the window open, he stepped out onto the fire escape as an explosion rocked the apartment. Out of the corner of his eye, Palmer saw the apartment door swinging on one hinge and a man with a gun rush in. Palmer took the stairs three at a time, jumped to the ground and sprinted for his car as another gun blast came from the balcony. He opened his car, tossed the diary inside and after fumbling in panic with the keys, got the rented Mercury Cougar started and screeched away.

SEVENTEEN

It was sixteen degrees out, but Palmer kept the heater off as he drove. The chill kept him alert and that's what he wanted now above all else. His ears were still buzzing from the gunshots. Gunshots. Christ. What had he gotten himself into. Nobody had ever tried to kill him before when he researched a book, but then he had never messed with a president still in office . . . or the CIA . . . or whoever else was involved.

Palmer wasn't exactly sure where he was going, just that he had to drive. He found himself down by the Washington Monument. The monument looked like the barrel of a gun to him and he shivered and drove on by fast. He passed the Lincoln Memorial, the Capitol Building, the Treasury. Just aimlessly wandering, buying time. Time for what? To think things out. Palmer remembered his first visit to D.C. It was in junior high school. Thirty kids on a class trip: chaperones, singsong guide. *Look at all the nice marble statues, see what a great country this is.* Palmer spent the whole time trying to kiss some giggly blonde he had a crush on. Schuyler was also on the trip. Schuyler took notes on a thick pad and looked very serious.

Palmer's right leg began to shake from the cold. Couldn't be that he was scared. It was the bloody temperature. Palmer knew he should be scared, but somehow he wasn't. He was tense, unbelievably tense, but he was not scared. Palmer knew he would never be the type to grab an American flag and dodge bullets to plant it on top of some muddy hill in the heat of battle, but it would not be fear that would prevent him from doing so. Common sense, perhaps. Brushes with death seemed to heighten his senses. Maybe because his generation had grown up on TV, Palmer seemed to regard danger in a theatrical way: nice movie this is, guns, a getaway car, hero running from a vague threat through the night streets of D.C. Maybe I'm crazy, Palmer thought. He laughed out loud. Crazy, but not dead. It could be worse.

Palmer drove past the White House and felt an involuntary shudder. He pushed down hard on the gas pedal. There were tourists outside the iron fence, even at this hour. Perhaps they just wanted to spot HIM. The president . . . a glimpse of power. Palmer circled back toward the Lincoln Memorial . . . Lincoln freed the slaves so they could play basketball in the NBA. Palmer's mind was racing. Slow down, Palmer. Power was what had first attracted him to this city. If you wanted to see power on display, this was the place. Maybe the big corporations and the and the oil barons really ran things, them and the Mob, but you couldn't study them. Palmer had come here because presidents and senators and other elected power brokers operated more or less out front, and you could get a beat on them and take pot shots. There was power in cutting down someone else's power lines. That's what Palmer did when he wrote books. Now he had the highest possible voltage line in his grasp, and one false step and he'd get burned in a flash, like a moth zitzed in an electrocution device. Palmer felt suddenly exhilarated. He was homing in for the kill. This must be how big game hunters felt, Palmer thought. There was another dimension that bothered him, though—Charlene. Palmer knew the president had had her killed because of that snapshot. Just the thought made him flush with rage, and it was all wrong to feel that way. There was no place in a power struggle for emotion. No place in Alex Palmer's life for emotion. But there it was, big as life. He'd have to keep a lid on it.

Stick to the facts, Palmer said to himself. Journalism 101. Who, what, where, when, and why. What were the facts? Joseph Demic, president by virtue of John Pierson's death, was probably a Russian agent. Demic had been raised like a hothouse plant in the Soviet Union, trained as a perfect American, right down to the slang. After Joe McCarthy had died, Demic had somehow surfaced in government. But there were too many unexplainable facts. Joe Demic had been born and raised on a farm in California. There were a hundred people who would swear to that, and they had pictures to prove it. While Sarah Lowenstein was caught in a death trap with a wild Soviet youth in Moscow, Joe Demic was a star fullback for the Long River Blue Stars. It didn't make sense. It was a dead end and yet Palmer knew it had to add up, somehow.

Palmer tried to sort it out. It suddenly occurred to him that somebody might be tailing him. He glanced in his rear-view mirror. He made several turns. Nobody seemed to stick with him. Tailed. What paranoia. And yet, somebody had taken a couple of shots at him, there was no making that up. Palmer's thoughts drifted to Sarah's diary. Palmer remembered Sarah's description of Yuri, writhing in pain on the floor, knee slashed open, pants soaked with blood. Palmer's hands tightened suddenly on the steering wheel. The knife! A wound like that unless Sarah had exaggerated in her fear—would have left a nasty scar.

Palmer pulled over at the first phone booth he could find, dashed out of the car and dialed the White House. It was nine o'clock, but there was every reason to believe that with a summit meeting in the works, Schuyler would still be in his office. Palmer identified himself to the White House operator, then waited, glancing around at the Washington Monument and the Lincoln Memorial, trying to imagine how they would look collapsing under a wave of atomic heat. Not a pretty thought. Who's to say it couldn't happen now, even as he stood in the phone booth.

Schuyler's voice interrupted his thoughts. "Alex, where are you?"

"Doing a little sightseeing. Sorry to bother you. But I need to ask an important question."

"What is it?"

"Have you ever seen the president naked?"

"Have I what?"

"Seen Demic in the nude."

"Alex, are you getting kinky? I would think you have

enough problems."

"A scar, David. I'm interested in knowing whether the president has a scar on his right knee."

"Why?"

"Do I have to tell you now?"

"This line is secured, if that's what's worrying you. And before I go poking into the president's anatomy, I think I should know what this is all about."

Palmer explained quickly about the diary and the photo Charlie had given to the president. When he was done, there was nothing but silence at the other end of the line. Palmer heard his friend breathing.

"Alex, there was something on our AP wire twenty minutes ago about a shooting incident at Charlie's apartment. Was that you?"

"Yes."

"Are you okay?"

"Yes."

"The landlady said she hadn't seen or heard any-thing," Schuyler said.

"That was nice of her. Must be the German blood."

"Alex, I hope you realize this thing you're pursuing is incredible."

"Yes."

"Is there any chance of me talking you out of it?"

"None in the least."

"I didn't think so. Okay, what do you want me to do?"

"Find out about the scar. As soon as possible."

"And how do you propose I do that? I just can't burst into the Oval Office and say, 'Pardon me, Mr. Presi-dent, but would you mind terribly stripping down to your underpants, I need to look at your knees."

"What about a masseur? Does the president get rubdowns or anything like that?"

"Yes. Twice a week, as a matter of fact."

"Do you have any way of reaching the masseur?"

"I have his home phone number in my file. He does me once in a while. I can call him."

"Great. How soon?"

"First thing tomorrow morning."

"How about right now?"

There was a long sigh at the other end of the line.

"Alex, do I have to remind you that I'm a busy man? There is a crisis in the Middle East, and a summit meeting coming up."

"David, if Joseph Demic is a Russian agent, I would think the last thing you would want him to do is hold a cozy little summit with Rublov. The secrets Demic could tell him in one meeting could do awesome damage to our national security."

There was a long pause at the other end. The operator came on asking for change. Palmer dumped in a couple of quarters.

"Look, I'll call the masseur now. It may take a while to track him down. Do you know where Frazier's is in Baltimore?"

"Yeh, nice quiet basement restaurant with great crab cakes."

"Right. Meet you there at midnight."

The crab cakes were even better than Palmer had remembered, and he washed them down with a few icy cold mugs of beer. Schuyler was late. It was almost twelve-thirty. Schuyler was never late, and Palmer began to worry. Maybe he shouldn't have dragged him into this. Just because Palmer had a death wish, that didn't mean his friend shared his sentiments. But Schuyler was his contact inside the fortress of the White House. Atta boy, Palmer, use anybody you can, no matter what the risk. Still, if the president was a Russian agent, nobody in this country was going to be safe anyway.

Schuyler arrived at a quarter to one. Palmer's stomach tightened when he saw his friend's face. David Schuyler never rattled, but he was rattled now. Palmer lifted his beer quickly. The waiter arrived on Schuyler's heels.

"I'll take a double Johnny Black, easy on the ice. No, make it a triple, and give it to me in a brandy glass." Schuyler's lips were tight as he spoke.

"Triple Johnny Black. My my. I didn't know you hit the bottle like that," Palmer said, trying to lighten the air.

"Alex, there's a lot you don't know about me," Schuyler said coldly. Palmer tried to stare through his beer haze. This was a side of Schuyler he had never seen before.

"What did you find out?" Palmer said.

"I'll tell you in a minute. First I need my drink."

Need my drink. Christ, Palmer said to himself. Was this good old reliable Dave Schuyler. Seeing the fear in Schuyler's eyes, Palmer began to wonder again if he was in over his head. Schuyler tossed down a healthy mouthful of the scotch.

"Joseph Demic has a five inch scar running vertically down his right knee. The massseur said Demic told him it was from a spike wound in football."

Schuyler stared hard into Palmer's eyes. Palmer

145

would always remember the moment. The jukebox was playing Sinatra's "Chicago." Two old men at the bar were arguing. The one o'clock news was on TV and the bartender was standing up close to the set so he could hear over the jukebox. Palmer never would forget these things because the next words out of his friend's mouth would send a chill down his spine.

"My God, Alex. How could this have happened?"

Part 2

ONE

Moscow, 1935

Joseph Stalin twisted one end of his silver mustache and read the report prepared by Alexandyr Volodya, his deputy minister of security. Seated at a huge mahogony desk—a "gift" from one of the czars—Stalin seemed almost lost behind the massive desk. Out of the corner of one eye, he noticed Volodya fidgeting nervously. It is right he should be anxious, Stalin thought. The deputy's scheme was brilliant, an ambitious undertaking by an ambitious man. But so far, it had produced no results, and Stalin was not a patient man. If Volodya's scheme died stillborn, Stalin would chill the man's hot ambition with a tour of duty in Siberia. Stalin put the report down.

"Alexandyr, you have promised much but delivered

little."

"A thing like this takes time. Even the Soviet Union cannot control nature. At least not yet." Volodya forced what he hoped was a casual smile onto his face. Stalin recognized the misshapen grin for what it was. The smell of fear was in the room.

"By your own accounting, Alexandyr, there are a dozen sets of twins born every day in Russia."

"Yes. But you have seen the reports on the parents. They are unfit for the project."

"Yes. I will agree with you on that much. None has been satisfactory. A butcher, a shoemaker, a dissident writer, and his Jewish wife. Ugh. This project of yours, Alexandyr, is not floating very well. I would not like to see it sink. For your sake, of course."

Stalin smiled. Alexandyr Volodya tried to return it, but his dry lips seemed unable to move. In his expensive, British-cut tweed suit, Volodya could feel the sweat gathering at his armpits. He prayed nothing would show on his face. Above all else, Stalin admired a show of strength. He must not be seen to be waivering.

"It will work, Joseph. I know it will. It will just take time. We came close with that lawyer, didn't we?"

"Yes. But his wife was a peasant. He married beneath him. The best was the engineer and his wife, what was she?"

"A biologist, Joseph."

"Yes. Too bad she refused. He was willing. He understood his duty to Mother Russia. I should have sent only her to Siberia. But I was in a foul mood that day — too bad for the engineer. Why is it so important for the parents to consent? Why can't we just force them to comply. We have techniques."

"I have explained to you that the success of the project depends on the willingness of the parents. They are very important. To send an unhappy couple to America would jeopardize everything. It is too risky, and so much is at stake."

Stalin poured chilled vodka from a carafe into a short glass.

"Is there so much at stake, Alexandyr? How do we know that? Why is it so important to have one of our people planted among them? We are mighty. We are secure. Who could harm us? The German pigs, maybe. But surely not the Americans. There is a continent and an ocean between us."

Volodya thought carefully before answering. He was a visionary, but he must not reveal himself as such. Stalin detested "professional thinkers," as he called them. It was a label he must avoid if he was to rise in Stalin's Russia.

"Yes. Of course we are secure here. But some day we must move beyond our borders if we are to carry the people's liberation to the world. Is it so farfetched to think that some day Joseph Stalin might be marching down the streets of Washington?" Volodya paused to see if the flattery had registered. It had. "In order to carry out our mission of expansion, we will need people in these countries, people in high places able to relay information."

"We have many Americans faithful to us, don't we?"

"Yes. But traitors are never to be trusted. They turn in the wind too easily. A Russian-American, someone we could have absolute faith in, that indeed would be a valuable commodity."

Stalin quaffed the vodka, poured more and downed

it. He did not offer any to Volodya.

"This is a brilliant scheme, Alexandyr. But it smacks of too many ifs. I do not like things to be so far out of my control."

Stalin came out from behind the desk, standing near Volodya.

"I prefer to have things in front of me. Then, if I like what I see, I can pet it, like I do a dog." Stalin put his big hairy hand on Alexandyr Volodya's shoulder. "And if I am not pleased, I can smack it with the back of my hand." Smiling, Stalin gently cuffed his deputy minister on the cheek. "Two weeks, Alexandyr. No more. Bring me my little twins. You have raised my expectations. Don't disappoint me."

Volodya, the sweat running down his rib cage, turned and walked stiffly out of the room.

TWO

Rina Demichev opened her eyes tentatively. Instinctively, she reached down for the pain, but it was no longer there, just a dull soreness. Could it be over? Then she remembered. Yes. A baby had cried. There had been the endless hours of agony and then the wailing. Rina Demichev had not been sure whether the agonized cry had come from her or the newborn one. There had been so much pain for so long. She remembered praying to die. Again her hands strayed down to where the incredible aching had been. It was all a memory now. She was not dead. It was a miracle. How had she survived? Rina closed her eyes. It all returned to her. On her back, knees up, legs spread. Hour after hour, she had strained and pushed, her face red like beets, the muscles in her neck so tight she thought they might burst. No matter how hard she worked, the little one would not come, and then, after twenty-four hours she had given up and refused to work. That was when the full horror of it hit her. She had quit, but the pain did not stop. Somehow in her mind she had thought if she gave up, the thing would, too. But it didn't. It kept pushing, ripping her apart with the pain, and it was then that she realized for the first time that the baby was a thing separate from her, with a will all of its own, and that was the most frightening thing. Somebody else was in her body causing her pain. She had panicked, trying to jump off the bed, and it had taken four of them to hold her down. You will die, they said, if you keep this up, and that had only served to panic her even more. If only she could be rid of this thing, she would not die. Damn, hateful, disgusting thing. It was in her anger that she found the energy to push again, and shortly after that she had heard the slap and the wail and was free of it and then slipped away.

"Rina?"

She forced her eyes open again. The voice was her husband's.

"Joseph? Are you there?"

"Yes. Of course. I have been close by all the time. How do you feel?"

"Fine. Awful, actually. I wanted to die. It was a very terrible thing, Joseph. We must not have any more babies."

It was then that she first thought to ask. How stupid of her.

"The baby, Joseph. How is he? Or she. What is it?"

"Babies, Rina. It is babies."

Rina was confused.

"What?"

"Twins. You have given me a double pleasure. What a bountiful woman you are, Comrade Demichev."

"Two? You mean there were two? Oh God, no wonder."

Rina Demichev felt the tears slide down her cheeks. How guilty she felt. She had blamed the little one for all the pain when in reality there had been two. Probably they had been fighting for the privilege to greet the world first. Just like kids.

"Joseph . . . boys or girls?"

Rina felt her husband's hand on her arm.

"Two of the strongest, most virile Russian males I have ever seen. Born leaders. I can see it in their eyes."

Rina tried to sit up, but her arms would not support her.

"Healthy?"

"Very much so."

Rina closed her eyes tight and nodded, tears coming again.

"And what shall we call them? We were going to call the baby Yuri if he was a boy and Marina if she was a girl. But now we need another name. What shall it be?"

"Joseph. Joseph Demichev. I have always liked that name."

Rina laughed.

"Oh Joseph, you are such an egotist."

"And you are not, my lovely and brilliant wife? Future physicist."

"Oh, but Joseph, I will have to give all that up now. When there was one baby, I could manage. But two, Joseph? I will have to give up my studies."

"I will not hear of it."

They would have continued arguing playfully, had

they not heard the wailing. Two nurses entered the room, each carrying an infant. The babies were placed on the bed with Rina, one on each side. Rina frowned at them.

"So here are the culprits who have caused me so much pain."

She picked up the one to her right and hugged it to her chest.

"I will call you Yuri," she said.

From the minute Alexandyr Volodya had gotten the report from the hospital, he had known this was it. His heart had raced as he read the details gathered by the field agent. Joseph and Rina Demichev. They were perfect. Twin boys. Healthy, no apparent problems. *Stalin will be pleased. I can select my* dacha, Volodya thought. He picked up the report. Demichev was twenty-six, a brilliant young mathematician and professor at Moscow University. He was a party member, and his father Ivan had been a trusted aide of Lenin in the vanguard of the revolution. The wife was equally desirable. She was twenty-two, a graduate student in physics at Moscow University. She had graduated third in a class of over four hundred and was one of only eight women pursuing degrees in physics. Rina's father, Serge Magzen, had been a noted architect before being killed in an accident at a construction site. Her mother, Sonja, was a practicing physician . . . *a perfect pair. . . .*

Volodya put the report down. He slammed a fist triumphantly into his palm. *It would work now. He knew it would. It must.* They had laughed at him when he had proposed the project. Now they would see. Two boys, one raised an American, the other a Russian. Identical in every way.

Volodya called for his secretary.

"I want my car brought around immediately. And notify Sekev and Rostin that they are to meet me downstairs. Also call Stalin's office and leave a message. Tell him Alexandyr Volodya has some news he will find doubly pleasureful.

Joseph Demichev knew there was trouble the minute he saw the three men approach. Only men in authority walked like they did, confident, composed, eyes boring into him. What did they want of him at a time like this? Demichev instinctively glanced toward his wife's hospital room.

"Joseph Demichev?" one of the men said.

"Yes?"

"We would like a word with you."

Demichev tensed. What could they want with him? He thought of asking, but knew he would find out when they were ready to tell him. He fell in step.

THREE

"WHAT? YOU DARE ASK THIS OF ME?" Rina Demichev screamed. She reached down and drew her babies to her.

"I do not ask anything of you, my wife. I am only explaining what the people's state has proposed. We do not have to accept."

"I should say not." Rina Demichev sat up in her hospital bed. Still weak from labor, it took a great effort to raise herself.

"They want us to think it over for a week. I told them we would. It is our duty to do at least that."

"We do not need to think it over. You can tell them right now our answer is no. I have never heard of anything so absurd."

"The project has the blessing of Joseph Stalin," her husband said nervously, eyes averted.

"Is that supposed to mean something to me? Am I to give up one of my children so that Joseph Stalin can give birth to some devious project? Let Joseph Stalin give up one of his children. Let Joseph Stalin carry this grand idea of his around in his gut for nine months, let him vomit every morning upon rising, his belly swollen with something besides vodka and caviar. After Joseph Stalin has suffered the hell of labor, then let him come and say, 'Here, take one of my children, I have two.' To hell with Joseph Stalin!"

"RINA, PLEASE!"

"I will have none of it, Joseph. I have brought two boys into the world and I will watch them grow up tall and strong. Russian boys. Not Americans. My children. Not Joseph Stalin's."

Rina Demichev began to cry.

"Don't, Rina. You are weak. You musn't waste your strength. All we have to do is say no."

Clenching her pale fingers into a fist, Rina shook a warning at her husband.

"Do not be so naive, Joseph. It does not become you. You know as well as I do the consequences of defying our great leader."

"They cannot send us to Siberia simply because we refuse to give up one of our children. It is not human."

"Oh Joseph . . ." Rina turned her head away in disgust. With numbers, her husband was brilliant. But he could not add up the simple facts of life. Rina knew what would have to be done, and that was why she was so angry. Joseph, poor Joseph, he still believed in the Great Lie.

"Okay, Joseph," Rina said. "We will go home and

we will discuss it. Then we will decide."

Tears welling in her eyes, Rina looked from one baby to another. Oh God, she said, Which one will it be?

FOUR

Rina was startled when the doorbell rang. She had
been waiting for it all day, preparing herself, and yet
when she heard it, she was stunned. Perhaps she had
thought they would not come. Joseph had told her
they were to arive at noon. It was five minutes before
the hour. They were early. Her breathing came rapidly.

"You answer it," she said weakly to her husband.

"Of course." He avoided her eyes and left the bedroom.

Rina tried not to look at the two cradles. She had
not yet made her choice, and now it was time and she
had no idea which one to give up. Joseph or Yuri.
Rina had dressed in a white, lacy dress. She wanted
to look clean, although inside she felt soiled. Perhaps
the white, innocent look of the dress would make the

men feel guilty. That would at least be something. A small victory, but something.

She heard them downstairs and her stomach tightened. Maybe it was not too late, she could grab them and run. But where? Anywhere. If she had had the courage, she would have drowned them both. Better that than suffer this indignity. But the will to survive was greater than the shame. Somehow she would find a way through this horror. The child would be returned to her . . . somehow. She had to use cunning. Joseph had told her they would be going first to Poland, where they would be issued phony Polish passports in the names of Joseph and Rina Demic of Warsaw, then to a place called Long River, California, where there would be new papers, one of which was a forged birth certificate for a baby boy, born at a California hospital. They were to become farmers, inconspicuous souls of the earth. "There is an agent already there who will help us get started as farmers. He will teach us everything we will need to know," her husband had said. What a ridiculous thing. Joseph a farmer. He cannot even make his own eggs in the morning. She would do it, though. She would survive, because she had to get even. They would be made to pay for what they had done to her and her children. No matter how long it took, Rina Demichev would get even.

When Rina came downstairs, the three men were standing in the living room. They looked like clerks. Rina was startled by how ordinary they seemed. She had been prepared for devils. Picking out the shortest of the three, Rina fixed him with a cold stare, hoping he would turn away. He returned her look indifferently. It was she who cast her eyes down. Not yet, she told herself, I am not yet strong enough. She struggled against the trembling in her body. At all costs, she would maintain her dignity.

"You understand why we are here?" the tallest one said, addressing himself to Joseph.

"Yes," Joseph said softly. "It has been a very difficult thing for us, but we understand our duty to the state."

The tall one nodded, bored. The blood rushed to Rina's face. She hated Joseph for his weakness. He should have volunteered nothing of his feelings.

"My wife will make the choice. I, uh, felt it was better that way."

"Where are they?" the tall one said coldly.

"Upstairs," Joseph said, feeling a sudden weakness in his legs. "Do you want to go up now?"

"Yes."

Joseph nodded, numbed. "I'll . . . show you up." He turned to Rina, touching her arm. "Come, Rina."

Rina Demichev pulled away sharply from her husband's touch. Silently, teeth clenched, she brushed past the men and started up the stairs, holding tightly on to the wooden bannister. Her legs trembled as she climbed. When she reached the door to the nursery, she hesitated, heart beating furiously, then walked in. The babies were sleeping peacefully in their cradles. It was not real, none of this. Forcing herself, she looked down at the cradles . . . Joseph or Yuri . . . which one would it be? She had avoided the decision. Now it must be made. But how? How does one choose. Tears filling her eyes, she glanced from one to the other. Both babies were swaddled, only their chubby little faces showing. They were identical, but Rina could tell the difference. Joseph had warm eyes, brown the color of tilled earth. Yuri's eyes were also brown, but like bark on winter trees — there was something cold about them. Stiffly, Rina allowed her hand to settle on Yuri's cradle. She gripped the side of it hard, steadying herself. Her knees felt like they would buckle, but she managed to say it:

"Take this one."

FIVE

The pain in the knee is worse than the hangover, Yuri Demichev thought. He glanced down at the knee, throbbing under a thick wad of bandage and gauze. He tried to shift in bed to a position where the pain would be less intense, but nothing helped. Absently, he reached for a copy of *Tom Sawyer* on the table beside him, flipped through the pages, then put it back down. He felt as much like reading as he did running. Besides, he had read *Tom Sawyer* twice and could flash whole scenes by shutting his eyes, as he did now. He knew it was just a boy's story—and at eighteen he was no longer a boy—but there was something about the rascal Tom and his friend Huck which touched a chord in him. He could see them tracking the treasure, the picket fence with its new coat of white, and he wondered what it would be like going barefoot on hot summer days, being a kid when being a kid meant something. Yuri Demichev opened his eyes. He had never been a kid.

There was a knock on the door and then it opened. Yuri did not have to look up to know who it was. He closed his eyes and went back to Missouri.

"We'd like to talk with you," a voice said.

Yuri nodded, eyes closed. He heard two chairs scraping along the floor. They were pulling up close to the bed. This must be serious stuff. Yuri repressed a smile.

"Why do you have your eyes closed?" the voice which belonged to Boris said.

"I'm traveling. It makes it easier to see."

Yuri heard Boris sigh.

"I do not like talking to someone who has his eyes closed," Boris said.

"Then don't talk. It was not I who invited you in here."

"I think," said the voice which belonged to Anton, "that you are carrying your American training a bit too far, young man. Save your impertinence for—" Anton stopped himself short.

"For what, Anton?" Yuri said, opening his eyes. He sat up suddenly, wincing at the pain in his knee. "Save the impertinence for America and the Americans? Is that what you were going to say? Why don't you say it? Surely you don't think I haven't guessed what I've been programmed for?"

"In time, you will be told," Boris said flatly.

"In time? Why is it not time now? Why can't you tell me?"

"There are rules, set by others, timetables . . ."

166

Yuri closed his eyes. The white fence came back. There was silence in the room for a few moments. Boris and Anton. His Russian Abbott and Costello. Except that their act was not funny.

"It was wrong for you to have gone off to Moscow with the girl," Boris said, breaking the silence. "You might have jeopardized years of training . . ."

" . . . and blown your chance to get a *dacha,* right?" Yuri opened his eyes to stare contemptuously at the man called Boris. Boris Boris Boris. Always present. Always Boris. Like a father, but not. Boris with his ulcer. Boris with his dandruff. Boris with his spastic colon and loose bowels. the only thing that saved Boris was a brilliant mind, and Yuri knew not to push him too far.

Anton was far simpler than Boris. Anton was a modern Russian. He was what the manuals said you should be: neat, industrious, self-contained, and reliable. If you were conscious of what clothes he wore, it was only because you made an effort to look. Both men had had successful careers before being assigned full time to "Project Demichev," as Yuri liked to call himself. Boris had been a psychologist and author, Anton a professor of history at Moscow University, an expert on America. They worked as a team. Boris monitored Yuri's mental health, to insure that neurosis did not compromise his usefulness; Anton oversaw the Americanization process.

"Why did you do it?" Anton said.

"I was bored," Yuri said. "Bored with my training. Bored with both of you and all the silly tutors you send around. And frankly I am tired of all this secrecy. Why can't you just come out and say I'm to be sent to America on a mission? For the better part of thirteen years I have been inundated with American newspapers and books, and listened endlessly to American radio shows. I am probably more American than Russian. Why can't we end this charade?"

Boris, the psychologist, ignored the question.

"Here are today's newspapers." Boris picked up a pile from beside his feet and dumped them on Yuri's bed. Yuri did not need to look. He knew the list, like a menu grown too familiar: *New York Times, Washington Post, Los Angeles Times, Chicago Sun-Times, San Francisco Chronicle, Houston Post, Miami Herald* . . .

"What makes me so special, Boris? Why was I singled out for this extraordinary education? You led me to believe that on my eighteenth birthday I would be told. My birthday is just a month away. Why not tell me now?"

"It is part of your training to learn discipline," Boris said. "You will need great self-control on your assignment. Frankly, I'm not at all sure you have what it takes."

"Like hell I don't," Yuri said, arching his back, taking the bait.

"We'll see."

Yuri slumped back down in the bed, pouting.

"You were very lucky, you know," Boris said, glancing at a folder open on his lap. "The damage wasn't serious. All the cartilage and ligaments are intact. You will have a very nasty scar, though."

"Miss Bergman won't like that. She loves my knees," Yuri said, hoping to shock Boris and Anton. He knew they would not like it if they thought he was sleeping with his latest American tutor. He wasn't, of course, because Kathy Bergman was much too dedicated to the socialist cause. But let Boris and Anton worry about it. Yuri's thoughts suddenly turned to the other American girl, the one he had gone to Moscow with, Sarah Lowenstein.

"What happened to the girl I ran off with? You have not harmed her, have you? It was entirely my fault."

"She is no concern of yours," Boris said, flicking dandruff from his shoulders.

Yuri was suddenly worried. "Boris, you haven't got her in trouble, have you? Please, you must tell me."

"No, I haven't," Boris said, his eyes revealing nothing.

Yuri breathed a sigh of relief, then felt annoyed. His concern for Sarah was just another example of how feelings got you into trouble. He had seemed weak in front of Boris and Anton, and that was intolerable. He had to recoup.

"Actually," Yuri said, forcing a cocky smile onto his face, "she was quite a little whore. We had a good time together, if you know what I mean." Yuri winked. "I'd just hate to lose a piece like that."

Boris watched Yuri and was secretly proud. Yuri as John Wayne. Yuri the stud. Yes, the boy was an American. He had all the obnoxious qualities. The time had come. He was ready.

SIX

Boris reached into his pocket for the American antacid tablets — Tums — which he had bought for an exorbitant price on the black market. He popped three into his mouth. For lunch he had eaten a bowl of borsch and a slice of black bread smeared thick with butter, and it had given him a bad case of heartburn. Normally, the soup did not bother him, but he had added sour cream and chopped onions, and combined with the scare Yuri had thrown into him, his stomach was now raw and burning. It was Anton who spoke first, his mouth busy with his own lunch.

"Yuri is more than ready. I only hope we can keep him under wraps for a few more weeks."

Boris watched sourly as Anton worked on a lunch of herring and onions in a cream sauce, gefilte fish and horse radish, all washed down with chilled vodka.

Boris's mouth watered as Anton speared a chunk of herring.

"We have done all we could, Anton. The rest is up to our people in America. Yuri has been given the finest education available in Russia. He has been taught by the best Soviet scholars and given a wide sampling of American tutors. Were he to stay in Russia, Yuri would be one of the most brilliant students of his generation. We have seen to that. He was selected for his impeccable breeding, and his brains have not been wasted. Neither of us have had the benefits of such an extraordinary education. I dare say no Russian since the czarist princes has been so favored."

"Yes, he is almost like a prince, isn't he Boris?" Anton poured more vodka from a carafe.

"Very much so. His American education has also been exceptional. Not only could he pass any entrance examination from an American college with flying colors, but we could drop him onto any Main Street in the USA and he would fit in perfectly," Boris said.

"Fit too well. He has all the obnoxious qualities. At international seminars in Paris, I have met many American professors. They are just like him. Bold, cocky, overly opinionated, and abrasive. They will easily embrace him as one of their own."

"This latest tutor of his, Kathy Bergman, has been one of the best. Who recruited her?"

"Spasky in New York. Her parents fled Berlin just before Hitler came to power. They have strong Communist leanings. She was a natural with her background."

Thinking about the fate of this Bergman girl, Boris felt the acid drip again in his stomach. He popped two more Tums, painfully aware that this was his last roll and his black market contact was in Leningrad on business for two weeks.

"Is she sleeping with him?" Anton asked.

"Hardly. It is more of Yuri's American bravado. You know what happened to her. I don't think she has ever had a man, other than that one in New York."

"A pity," Anton said, winking. Boris shrugged. He obtained a woman once a month in Moscow and did so only because of his faith in Freud, who felt sexual abstinence had a negative effect of the mind.

"Joseph Demic will start at Harvard in three weeks," Boris said. "That is why we must act soon. Would you like to see the latest photograph?" Boris slid a picture out from an envelope.

"Remarkable," Anton said.

"Don't get cream sauce on it," Boris said sourly.

Anton stared at the snapshot. It was of a boy in his late teens, taken in front of a farm house. The boy was Yuri, only it was not.

"They are alike, right down to the pompadour. It is a very extraordinary thing."

"Yes. Alexandyr Volodya should be congratulated for his selection of the Demichev twins. A pity he is not around to see his project realized."

"Why did Stalin have him executed?"

Boris shrugged. "Perhaps Stalin's eggs were overcooked one morning. Or his toast was burnt. There is no telling what made Stalin do things. He was . . . a strange man." Boris stopped short of saying what he felt, that Stalin had been a mad man. Even after thirteen years of friendship with Anton, Boris did not risk such a statement. It was one of the maladies of Russian life that a person never fully trusted anyone.

"Yuri has grown up thinking his parents died in a car crash," Anton said. "What effect will this new explanation have on him?"

"It will disturb him for a while. A very short while, I believe. Yuri is an abnormally cold person. He will not long be troubled. He will be told his parents were traitors, that they fled the country illegally, leaving him behind because he was too sick to make the long trip. How could a boy love people who have done that to him? No, I do not think we need fear sentiment interferring with Yuri's mission."

Anton nodded, then let out a loud belch, rubbing his stomach. "Heartburn. How strange. I never get it." Anton reached for the Tums, but Boris quickly snatched them away.

"Sorry, this is my last roll."

"Pity." Anton rubbed his stomach again.

"Anton . . ." Boris seemed to struggle for a moment. ". . . Have you ever felt . . . guilty about our part in this . . . in what has been done to Yuri?

Anton shrugged. "The project was not our idea. Yuri had already been separated from his parents when we were assigned. What purpose would it have served to have turned down the assignment? They would have found others, and our careers would have been finished. What's to feel guilty about? Men who run the camps in Siberia, guilt is for them. We have been like parents to Yuri, good to him. We have educated him, taught him things that will make him a success. Why should we feel remorse?"

"We have helped take an infant and make him into a spy. That is what we have done," Boris said. "Let us not fool ourselves about his education or the tenderness of his upbringing. This boy was robbed of his parents, deprived of any semblance of a normal childhood. If we could have removed his brain and put in a plastic one designed by our state planners, we would have done so. You ask me what there is to feel guilty about? There is much, Anton, much."

"And that is all the more reason for us to insure that this mission is successful," Anton said. "If it is, will it not justify what we've done? Will not the good brought to the state and its millions of people not offset the harm done to one young citizen and his family?"

Anton watched as his longtime friend and associate struggled with it a moment. The acid in Anton's stomach dripped in a slow burn. He eyed Boris's Tums greedily.

SEVEN

The lesson had gone all wrong. She had wanted him to feel outrage. Instead, he had laughed. For all his American training, Kathy Bergman thought, he is still a Russian. He will never understand the evil of racial prejudice until he sees it firsthand in the United States. Still, it was appalling that he had howled with laughter through the entire taped episode of *The Amos 'n Andy Show*.

"This program," Kathy tried to tell him, "is an example of how American whites hold Negroes up to ridicule in order to keep them enslaved. As long as Negroes are portrayed like this, their right to equality will never be taken seriously. Capitalist toothpaste and tobacco companies pay for these shows in order to reinforce the insecure white population's belief that 'darkies' are stupid."

"Yes, but it is a funny show. I just love 'da Kingfish,' "

Yuri said, breaking into laughter again.

"I think, Yuri, you are missing the point. The show is about deprivation and prejudice."

"Amos and Andy don't seem deprived to me. Everybody on the show seems perfectly happy to me. All except Saphire, of course, and that's because the Kingfish is such a scoundrel."

"These are just appearances you are describing, Yuri. I expected more of you. For all his joviality, the Kingfish is really a pitiful example of what the white majority turns ghetto Negroes into. Through years of oppression, Kingfish has become a conniving, manipulating, devious hustler. Allowed to grow up in a normal environment, Kingfish might very well have turned out to be a decent, loving husband," Kathy said.

"A loving husband for Saphire? Ugh. That would be a fate worse than death. Worse than your American prejudice." Yuri laughed.

"I think we have discussed *The Amos 'n Andy Show* quite enough for today. We will move on to the newspapers."

"I didn't read them this morning."

"Why not?"

"Didn't feel like it."

"I see."

Kathy struggled with her anger. This would not do at all. If Yuri was not going to take his lessons seriously, why had she come all this way from America?

"Get the newspapers anyway, please. We will skim them together."

Yuri started to protest, then decided his behavior during *The Amos 'n Andy Show* had been enough rebellion for one day, and went to fetch the newspapers, still limping from the pain in his knee. While he was gone, Kathy

Bergman tried to compose herself, taking deep breaths and counting to ten, methods her father had used to control his legendary temper. It was from Hershel Bergman that Kathy had first learned to cope with a world full of injustice. She was proud of her father and mother, often reciting the story of their journey from Hitler's Germany to New York's Lower East Side. Hershel Bergman had been a fairly well-to-do lawyer in Berlin before the menace of Hitler had driven him and his wife, Helga, and twelve-year-old daughter, Kathryn, to New York. It took Hershel a year to meet all the requirements, and another year before he realized that no law firm in New York would take on a junior partner who was not only Jewish, but "acted it," as one honest lawyer had told him. "Be a little less Jewish, Hershel," the man had told him. "Work on Saturdays. Bring a ham sandwich to the office once in a while. It is all right for you to be a Jew, but don't flaunt it."

A man of deep principles and faith, Hershel had refused to take a low profile like so many other upwardly mobile New York Jews were doing. "I will not change my name, I will not cut my sideburns and I will not act like a gentile. Carry a ham sandwich to work? I would sooner invite Hitler over for the seder dinner." So Hershel had taken the last of his Berlin savings and bought a rundown townhouse on East Seventh Street, fixed it up and opened a practice in the basement while his family lived on the top three floors. Within a year, Hershel Bergman had a thriving, if not prosperous law practice. Impressed by his honesty and willingness to fight for a client, residents of the Jewish community began pounding on Hershel Bergman's basement door. They brought their problems — some legal, some not —

and spent long hours opening their hearts to the little baldheaded man with the Chaplin mustache and the sympathetic eyes. Unfortunately, few opened their wallets. In keeping with his principles, Hershel Bergman refused to see a client for nothing. That did not, however, mean he had to collect his fee. It was enough for Hershel to know that he had charged a client.

Helga, meanwhile, was also active in the community. No sooner did she learn that a neighbor had a problem, than she would set about to resolve it. Helga could cook, sew, doctor, and counsel like a professional, although she had had no formal training. As such, she became the next best thing: a "professional mother" to the community. The needy were never turned away from Helga Bergman's door, and often Hershel would play a little game in the basement when he heard commotion from above, trying to guess the number of people "my meshugenah wife has fed today" by the sound of the footsteps. It came as no surprise to him, therefore, when Helga suggested one day they convert the first floor into a sort of soup kitchen and confine their living quarters to the top two floors. Hershel did not complain, nor did he raise a stink when six months later Helga wanted to use the second floor to house homeless Jewish immigrants. In fact, Hershel used to joke at a local bar with his buddies that, "I am a successful American entrepreneur now. I have a law practice in my basement, a restaurant on the first floor, a hotel on the second and a penthouse on the top floor for my family."

It was only natural that Kathy Bergman grew up with a social conscience. She helped her mother in the kitchen, made beds and cleaned the second floor, and when she had a little free time after school, would go down to the basement and listen while her father explained American justice to Jewish shop owners. Although her teachers taught about the bounty of American life, Kathy saw a different reality at home, and came to feel that something was very wrong in her adopted country. Well before her sixteenth birthday, Kathy Bergman had already decided that she would dedicate her life to social change, and not even a horrifying incident with a drunk immigrant changed her mind.

It was during a hot Indian summer day, and, having finished cleaning the second floor, Kathy had gone upstairs to study. Her father was is in the basement with a client and her mother was out on an errand of mercy. Kathy heard a soft knocking on the door to the family apartment, which was never locked. "Come in," she said routinely, and then was startled to see one of their borders—a Jew from Warsaw whose family had died at Auschwitz—enter holding a knife. He was a big man—well over six feet—with huge hands and a straggly beard, and from the way he walked, Kathy could tell he was drunk. She tried to reason with him, and then failing that, closed her eyes stoically and prayed to God that he would at least not kill her. She could smell the man's drunken breath as he struggled to take off his pants. She opened her eyes for a moment and told him: "You don't have to do this, you don't have to do this," understanding that the immigrant was acting out of an intense hunger more than a will to do her harm. She started to repeat her words when she felt it pierce her between the legs. At first she thought he had shoved the big knife in there, but he still held that in one hand near her face. When she realized what it was, she was astounded—and appalled—that it could be so big and hard. She had seen

179

her father's penis in the bath once. It had been a tiny, harmless thing. But this . . . the man must be some kind of monster. The pain was horrifying; it seemed to be tearing her in half. The smell of the immigrant was so overpowering she feared she would puke and anger him more. Closing her eyes, she tried to retreat into her mind, and would have succeeded, had the man not given out a loud cry as if wounded, then collapsed on her. She felt something hot and sticky drip from between her legs as he withdrew, and feared the worst, that he had ripped her up and she was bleeding to death. When the man had staggered out of the apartment, Kathy had straightened her dress, put on her panties, and walked in a daze down to the basement. She would long remember Hershel Bergman's response. He sat there frozen for several moments, his angry eyes filled with tears. Kathy expected him to go after the man with a knife, an eye for an eye, a tooth for a tooth. But instead, Hershel Bergman picked up the phone on his cluttered desk, dialed the police and reported the incident in a shaky voice. Then he had gently taken his daughter upstairs and made her soak in the bathtub for two hours while he spoke to the policemen in the kitchen. When Kathy came out of the bathroom, they questioned her, too. The man was caught two hours later in a saloon on Broome Street, prosecuted and sent to jail for twenty years. Justice had been served. The justice of civilized men. It was a lesson Kathy Bergman never forgot.

Kathy also recalled how the incident did not change her parents' attitude toward the needy. Hershel's law practice was still open to the poor, and her mother kept up the soup kitchen and gave shelter to the homeless on the second floor. The only change was that Hershel had installed a strong lock upstairs on their apartment door. For Kathy, the incident did not end there, however. She became pregnant and stayed upstairs for the nine months, never once venturing outside. It was a time of intense learning and introspection. She devoured hundreds of books, learned to cook and sew, and even after the baby was delivered by a midwife in their home and given away, Kathy did not lose her ravenous appetite for knowledge. She returned to school and her grades reflected the change in her. Where once she had been an average student, now she was a brilliant one. She was graduated at the top of her class and was accepted at Barnard, where in addition to earning Phi Beta Kappa, she utilized her home "education" to start the Socialist League of Barnard. It was in her capacity as the group's president, that Kathy attracted a man named Ivan Spasky, who had a fascinating proposition for her.

That had been six months ago, and now, as she waited for Yuri to return with the newspapers, she wondered if she had made the right move. She had agreed to come to Russia for the opportunity to learn firsthand about a working Socialist system, but tucked away in Zukovka, tutoring this strange boy for an undisclosed reason, she had not really had the chance to learn anything. All she had been told was that her tutoring would be of great value to the Communist cause, and that afterwards, she would be allowed to tour the country and study the apparatus.

"Here are the newspapers." Yuri tossed them down onto a desk. "Can't we forget them today, Kathy? It's such nonsense."

"I don't consider studying the newspapers nonsense, Yuri. The papers reflect daily changes in American soci-

181

ety, and according to my instructions from Boris and Anton, you are to learn everything you can from them." Kathy stared at Yuri, who was pouting. She sighed. "Okay, Yuri. Then tell me what you want to learn today. I cannot just give you the day off."

"Dating."

Kathy was taken back.

"I want to learn dating," Yuri said.

"You mean boys and girls, going out and all that?"

"I believe that accurately describes what I'm talking about," Yuri said.

"But why?"

"Isn't it obvious? If I'm ever to go to America and blend in, I'll need to know how to ask a pretty girl out on a date."

"Well, I don't know . . ." Kathy blushed, and in truth she didn't know. She had never been on a date. Many boys had asked her out, but she had never said yes. Perhaps it was because of the incident . . . perhaps not. She did not like to think about it.

"I don't feel qualified to teach you American dating," Kathy said.

"Qualified? What qualifications do you need? You've been on a date, haven't you?"

"Of course," Kathy lied on impulse, her cheeks reddening.

"Well then, you're eminently qualified."

Caught off guard by her lie, Kathy allowed herself to be led over to a chair, where Yuri sat her down. Yuri then hurried out of the room. No sooner had he gone then he knocked on the door. Kathy waited for him to come in, feeling silly.

"You're supposed to say, 'Come in,' " Yuri said from

behind the door.

"In America we don't open doors until we know who it is," Kathy said, remembering that awful lesson.

"Well, you know it's me, so open it, baby."

Kathy winced at the crude Americanism, and opened the door.

"Why Yuri, how nice of you to come . . . " Kathy started to say, then broke up laughing. It was the first time Yuri had ever seen her laugh, and he was stunned at the change in her face. She was beautiful.

"You should laugh more often, it becomes you," Yuri said softly.

Kathy quickly regained her composure. "Oh Yuri, this is silly, I can't do this."

"But you must," Yuri said, grabbing both her hands. The quickness with which Kathy recoiled momentarily stunned Yuri.

"Please, don't touch me," Kathy said, turning away.

"I meant nothing by it," Yuri said. Kathy crossed the room and sat on a chair.

"Yes, I'm sure you didn't. But please, let us conduct this lesson more properly. Frankly, I would just as soon not continue, but if you insist . . . "

"Oh I do . . . " and Yuri had to stop himself from reaching out again. "Please. It is important to me to have this training." Yuri wanted to add " . . . from you," but thought better.

"If you insist," Kathy said.

"You make it sound like a death sentence," Yuri said, and then was sorry, reading the anger in the strange young woman's eyes. My God, Yuri thought, what has been done to her?

Kathy got up suddenly and walked over to where he

had dumped the newspapers. She picked one up absently — the *Miami Herald*. Miami . . . Kathy had been there once. It was during summer vacation after her sophomore year in high school. Her parents had sent her South by bus to help take care of a sick aunt who couldn't manage alone. Kathy had been thrilled by what she considered a great adventure, but after she had seen her first sunset and sunrise through the windows of a Greyhound, the magic wore off. It had been an exhausting experience getting there, and then the sick aunt had worn her out more. But now, so many thousands of miles away from home, Miami suddenly seemed nice in memory. Kathy realized that for the first time she was homesick. How ironic, to be in the heart of the world's greatest socialist utopia and be longing for New York, the capitalist capital of the universe. . . .

"Kathy . . ." It was Yuri, softly behind her. "I'm sorry if I've offended you. We can drop this whole silly thing . . ."

"Please, Yuri, it is not you who should be apologizing," Kathy said, turning. "It is I who should ask your forgiveness. I have overreacted terribly, and I'm embarrassed. I want very much to continue with this lesson. Truly I do."

Against his will, Yuri was moved, and he struggled with his emotions. This girl was not like the others. They had come to Russia for selfish reasons: to make money, travel, or invent a Communist identity where none existed. But Kathy was sincere, even if her perception of the movement was a bit naive. She seemed childlike in her political awareness, and yet she was womanly. He could not explain the disparity and it bothered him.

"So where are we going on this grand date, Yuri?" Kathy said.

"What? Oh. I don't care. I mean I do care, but it's up to you."

"How about the movies?"

"Fine."

"*Red River?*"

"For the hundredth time."

"Why not?"

They both laughed and Kathy went to a closet and took down a can of film. Yuri hauled out the movie projector and set it up facing a screen hung on one wall.

"Where shall we sit?" Kathy said, after Yuri had threaded the film, killed the lights, and tuned on the projector.

"On the couch."

"Both of us?" Kathy said.

"Of course. Even in Russia when a boy and girl go to see a movie heralding the wonders of Soviet steppe farming, they do not sit six seats apart. Surely you don't do so in America."

"No . . . " Kathy said hesitantly.

"Well, then . . . " Yuri patted the couch next to him. Kathy sat, a good foot away. She kept her knees pressed close together and folded her hands on her lap. "Are you sure you have never been to a Soviet film on steppe farming?" Yuri asked.

"Yes. Why?"

"Because you have the perfect form for viewing one."

Kathy looked down at herself and had to giggle.

"Ssssh," Yuri said, suddenly looking back in the darkened room.

"What's the matter?"

"The couple behind us is unhappy with our chatter."

"Oh." Kathy allowed herself a glance over her shoulder, and Yuri, catching her action, was pleased she was playing along. He stole a glimpse at her face in the light of the movie.

"Do you want to know how it comes out?" Kathy joked, both having watched the John Wayne film a hundred times. Ostensibly, Yuri studied the film often because he wanted to understand America's fascination with its Old West image. But Kathy suspected Yuri was obsessed with John Wayne. She noticed that after a viewing of *Red River*, Yuri was always just a bit more manly, walking with a swagger.

Kathy's thoughts were interrupted by the sudden pressure of Yuri's knee beside hers. She was both attracted and repelled by the touch. Before she could decide whether or not to move away, he slid his knee back, and Kathy was surprised at her disappointment.

"This Walter Brenner character, I don't think I like him too much," Yuri said.

"Brennan," Kathy corrected him. "Why?"

"It's wrong for a man to cook for other men. That is a woman's job."

"Not on the frontier. Men had to learn to cook because there were not enough women."

"Not enough women? That must have been a terrible deprivation."

Yuri moved his leg back and this time Kathy didn't bother to question her feelings. If anything, she seemed to press in closer to him, heart pounding. On impulse, she said, "This is my first date, you know."

Yuri turned to face her. "You're kidding?"

"No. I was very sheltered, I guess."

"But you're so pretty. Surely even capitalist boys recognized that."

"Oh boys did ask me, but I always said no."

"Why?"

Kathy turned away. She could not tell him. Her shame was too deep. "I just wasn't ready, that's all."

Yuri turned back to the screen, not really watching anymore. This was a strange thing to learn, even from a girl as difficult to understand as this. What could it mean? Kathy was twenty-two, how could she not have dated? Not have held hands. Not have . . . kissed?

"There were boys my age at family dinners on Passover and other holidays. I often talked with them," Kathy said quickly, suddenly feeling like a freak. She did not know why, but she didn't want Yuri to think badly of her.

"It is not the same thing," Yuri said, smiling.

"No, I guess not." Kathy blushed and looked at her lap.

Yuri shifted his body so that he was facing her. "Kathy," he said, "are you afraid of me?"

"Afraid? Yuri Demichev, why on earth should I be afraid of you?" Kathy lied.

"I don't know, I just felt you seemed a bit, well . . . standoffish. There is such an American word, isn't there?"

"Of course. But it hardly applies to me. I am not standoffish."

"Cold, then, perhaps?"

"That's not a very nice thing to say." Kathy's stomach fluttered at the renewed pressure of his knee against hers. The film had begun to skip badly, but neither seemed to notice. "I am just doing the proper thing. You

187

said you wanted to learn how American boys and girls behaved on a date."

"Yes, I do," Yuri said, sliding his hand close to hers on the couch. "And what is the proper thing for American boys and girls to do when they like each other a lot? Do they kiss?"

"Sometimes." Kathy began to tremble.

"Then kiss me."

Kathy's eyes locked on Yuri's. They were brown and handsome eyes, but there was something, something . . . almost cold. No, she was making excuses. Kiss him, oh God kiss him, a voice cried out inside, and then without realizing, she was saying it out loud, an anguished outburst: "Oh kiss him!" Yuri, surprised at the intensity of her words, was caught off guard. He hesitated a moment before bending to meet her lips. At the moment of contact, the door opened and bright light swept over them. Kathy drew back, stunned.

Boris and Anton stood in the doorway staring, then quietly they walked away.

EIGHT

Kathy was terribly embarrassed when she entered Boris's office. She closed the door softly behind her. Boris was alone.

"I'm so sorry, Boris. I know I failed you."

"Nonsense, nonsense. You have done an excellent job. This was just a silly little incident, bound to happen. Sit over here."

Boris motioned Kathy to a chair in front of his desk. Boris seemed very uncomfortable, and Kathy was sorry she had put him in this position. She would have to return to New York now, a failure.

"I've never done anything like this, Kathy began. "I know you probably don't believe me, but it's true."

"On the contrary, my dear. I do believe you. We know your background."

Kathy blushed. She did not like it that Boris knew

about the Pole. She felt suddenly unclean.

"Will I be going home now?" she asked.

Boris seemed to peer over her shoulder for a second before answering.

"Yes. But with a commendation for a job well done. You have been the best of Yuri's American tutors."

Kathy wanted to feel buoyed by Boris's words, but his apparent uneasiness undermined the feeling. Why had she done such a foolish thing.

"You know, Kathy, in this world some things may seem beyond understanding," Boris began. "We ask ourselves, why is it necessary to do this thing or that, but in the end, if we have faith, it all seems to come together, as in a puzzle."

Kathy did not know what he was talking about, but out of politeness nodded, and he continued.

"Sometimes I find myself asked to do unpleasant . . . very unpleasant things . . . for the cause." Boris was sweating, and he paused to mop his forehead with a handkerchief. Kathy wondered what she could say to ease his discomfort.

"Do you believe in God, Kathy?" Boris asked.

"Yes."

"I do, too. We're not supposed to, of course. Mother Russia is our God. But I believe. There must be something . . . someone forgiving. We are forced to do so many things that on the surface are ugly, but . . ." Boris shrugged, a pathetic, slightly embarrassed gesture.

Kathy noticed there was dandruff on the shoulders of his light brown plaid shirt. She felt sorry for him. "Boris . . ." she started to say, but never got the words out.

An arm slipped over her head and jerked her up in the

air by the throat. She expelled breath, then struggled desperately to suck more air back in her lungs. Her legs kicked wildly. A furious will to live sent her fingers tearing savagely into the heavily muscled, hairy arm that was squeezing the life out of her. Not this, not this, she cried to herself. She tore her fingers from the arm and reached frantically behind her, trying to grab, but could not latch onto anything. Her face felt like it would explode from the pressure, her eyes ballooning in the sockets. She looked at Boris. He had turned away. She tried to scream, but no sound came and then her bowels exploded in a wet gush and the urine slid down her leg. As she blacked out, all she could think about was the hairy arm. How sickening to have a man so close, she thought, and then died.

Boris, eyes averted and trembling, was horrified by the smell. Oh God, he said to himself, I hope this is all worth it.

NINE

Long River, California, 1953

Joseph Demic Jr. dipped his hand into the feed bucket, tossed some grain to the chickens, then set the pail down on the barn floor. That's the least of it, he said to himself, maybe forever. Tomorrow, it's off to Cambridge . . . Harvard. No more chickens, no more rising at the crack of dawn, no more milking the cows. A gentleman's life it will be for me. Hurry sun, make your damn run and be gone. The next dawn will find Joseph Demic Jr., son of Polish immigrants, on a train East, off to begin a new life. No, to begin life for the first time. I was not meant to be a farmer. Neither was my father, of course. Joseph tried to shake the image of the pathetic, bedridden man from his mind. He did not want to lower his spirits. It was not his fault the land had broken the man. With his delicate constitution, frail hands and body, Joseph Demic Sr. was never meant for the soil. His son could not understand why a man with such a good mind had wasted it, wasted body and soul for a stubborn, unyielding patch of earth. His father would never talk of life in Poland, or why he had come here and continued to farm when he was so obviously unsuited for it. Joseph was sure his father had been an educated man in Poland. There was no way he could have been just a farmer. Only in death would Joseph Demic Sr. make a union with the soil, and that would probably be soon. . . .

Walking over to where a chicken pecked at feed, the young man flexed his shoulders a couple of times, as if to shake his father's image off his back, and began to address the chickens:

"Hi. I'm Joe Demic. Nice to meet you. I understand we're to be roommates here at Harvard." Joseph extended a hand, which the chicken, after glancing up once to assess it was not a chunk of feed, ignored and went back to the grain.

Joseph shrugged. He had been warned by his counselor at Long River High to expect some snobbery from the Eastern prep school boys. "Don't worry about it, Joe," the counselor had said. "Once they find out what you can do in the classroom, they'll accept you. The one thing they admire most at Harvard is success."

Joseph had had more than his share of success. He had graduated at the top of his class, was student council president and captain of the football team. Brains and brawn. Harvard had liked the mixture. So had the girls. Joseph recalled some of the wild parties and realized he would miss high school. It was nice to be a somebody, even if it was in a small town. But the farming, that he wouldn't miss.

"Where did you say you had gone to prep school?" Joseph said to the chicken. "Andover? I had a chance to go East to Exeter, but I had a lot of chickadees back home and didn't want to leave the roost, if you know what I mean. . . ."

While Joseph was talking to the chickens, he did not see an ominous-looking black Chevrolet pull up at his house some seventy yards away. Two men got out and walked up to the front door. One knocked while the other picked with the edge of a matchbook cover at something lodged in his teeth. Place smells of shit and hay, the one digging at his teeth thought distastefully, and spit on the porch.

Rina Demic neither greeted the two men nor invited them in. She simply opened the door and walked back across the foyer into the living room. The men shrugged and followed her in. Rina sat on the couch, her eyes black and hard. She did not ask them to sit.

"The boy around?" the man who had knocked on the door said flatly. He was tall—at least six feet five—and chewed gum vigorously. Rina was struck at how similar these men were to the ones who had come for her Yuri eighteen years ago.

She shook her head.

"Good. It'll make it easier to talk."

The two men sat on cushioned chairs facing the couch. A voice from another room said: "Rina, is that them?"

"Yes."

"Bring me in," the voice said.

"Your husband?" the tall man said.

Rina Demic walked out of the room without answer-

194

ing. She went through the hallway and into a room at the rear of the house where Joseph Demic lay on a bed, pale and thin, up to his neck in quilt, despite the Indian summer heat. They had moved him downstairs to this little room because he needed constant attention and the frequent trips upstairs had been tiring Rina out.

"Does Joe know yet?" her husband said, struggling to push his frail body up in the bed. Rina helped him.

"No. I'm going to tell him today."

Joseph Demic nodded, tears coming to his eyes. Lately, in the final stages of the disease, he had taken to crying a lot, partly from the incredible pain, and partly from self-pity. Today's tears were of joy. A man of duty, Joseph Demic was finally getting his chance to fulfill his obligation to Mother Russia. Rina struggled not to show the disgust in her face.

"What if he won't go?" Joseph asked.

"He will," Rina said, her eyes averted. They will see to that, Rina thought wryly, but said nothing.

"This is a great moment for us, Rina," Joseph said, tears sliding down his stubbled cheeks. He reached out a thin, dry hand and took Rina's. His touch repelled her, but she submitted, even forcing a smile on her face, which assured him. In the old days, she thought, back in Russia, Joseph could see right through me when I lied. Now he sees nothing, only a dead memory he continues to invest life in: Joseph Demic, loyal Russian, faithful to the revolution his father helped start, fulfilling a mission the great Joseph Stalin sent him on eighteen years ago. It was all so absurd, but the man was dying and that meant something and so she kept silent. She would have her revenge, but it would not be at her husband's expense.

195

"Get my chair, Rina," her husband said. She rolled the wooden wheelchair over to the side of the bed.

"Are you sure you want to get up?"

"Woman, I've waited eighteen years for this. Do you think I'm about to let a little damn cancer stop me now?"

Rina winced at the word, never having used it in front of him. The word was full of terror for her, like Siberia was in Russia. She pulled the quilt back, careful not to show how repulsed she was by the smell of her husband. With one arm around his bony shoulders, she helped him slide off the bed onto the chair, which like the mattress, was pungent with the oily smell of death.

"Put a blanket over me. I don't want my comrades to see how much of my body I have surrendered to this capitalist soil."

With the cover tucked up around his neck, Joseph Demic was wheeled to the living room, where the two agents stood impatiently. The tall one had helped himself to some hard candies Rina kept in a crystal jar she had brought from Russia.

"I'm Joseph Demic," her husband said, stretching his pale face into a sickly grin.

"I'm Fydor Lenkov," the tall agent said, "and this is my comrade, Leonid Dronin. We've come to help you complete your mission, and to say on behalf of President Rublov, that the Soviet Union is proud of you."

Spoken in a dry, lifeless tone, Rina recognized Lenkov's words for what they were: an obligation committed to memory. She was relieved that Joseph had not realized that. His cheeks seemed almost to blush with pleasure. What a silly thing he has become, she thought. They must be made to pay for the destruction of her husband, too.

"As you know, we have come for the boy. Yuri is already in Boston, waiting to enroll in Jospeh's place at Harvard."

Yuri. Rina said the name to herself, surprised at the swell of emotion it touched in her. Yuri, the one with the cold brown eyes. Had she made the right decision? How could she ever know? In a situation like that, was there really any right decision? What did he look like, she wondered, and then laughed wryly to herself over the stupidity of the question. He would look exactly like Joseph, or else they would not be doing this incredible thing.

"What are we to tell our son?" Joseph asked.

"Only that Leonid and I are cousins on our way to Boston and have volunteered to give him a ride. That will be your final duty. From that point on, the mission is in our hands."

"What will you do with him?" It was the first words Rina had spoken to the men. She had not wanted to speak, but the need to know was too great.

"As a precaution, he will be drugged—a harmless sleeping potion—and we will drive him to Canada. There, a sea plane will be waiting. It will take us East, where a Russian fishing vessel is anchored in the Atlantic. From there we go home. Your son will then be told his part in the mission and rewarded for his service to the Soviet Union. If he wishes, he can enroll in our own prestigious Moscow University. He will be given the opportunity to pursue any career he chooses: doctor, lawyer, scientist . . ."

"Engineer?" Joseph said, eyes wide.

"Of course."

Yes, of course, Rina said to herself. A brilliant, young engineer to replace the brilliant, young engineer who was fed to the soil. What a wonderful sense of justice they have in the Soviet Union.

"He is a terrific student, my son, you know," Joseph said. Fydor nodded, disinterested.

When the men had gone, Rina turned to Joseph, his face beaming for the first time in years.

"Well, dear Joseph, this is the moment you have been waiting for. You must be very pleased."

"I am. I can die happy now."

"Do not speak like that, Joseph. The doctor said you have every chance to survive."

"Rina, stop. I have lost a lot since I came to this land—my health, my strength, my will—but not my senses. Death is already spreading inside of me, claiming little parts of me each day. I am holding on, but it is only a matter of time. All that is unimportant, however. There are things bigger than the individual, are there not?"

Rina did not answer.

"Will you not miss your son?" she said, finally.

"Of course. But my time with him was limited anyway. And now I will get to see my other boy before I die. He will come home to us on Thanksgiving vacation and, God willing, on Christmas, if I am still alive."

Rina wheeled him back to his room, brought him some chicken broth and sat by his bed until he had finished it and nodded off, expended by an emotional day. She tiptoed out to the kitchen, made a pot of coffee and sipped a cup at the table. Joseph Jr. would be done with his chores soon. John Brady, the hired hand, would come and relieve him, and then Rina would have to tell her son the whole, awful truth. It was something she was not looking forward to. Her thoughts wandered to her husband. Poor Joseph, how badly things had gone for him. Rina had worked hard, too—sunrise to sundown—but it had not broken her because she had welcomed the long hours. She saw it as penance for the act of cowardice she had committed. The harder she worked, the more she was cleansed. In Russia, she had been defenseless, but things would be different now. She would have her revenge.

Rina drained the last of her coffee and went over to the cellar door, closing it behind her as she went down the creaky stairs. Using a flashlight, she located some loose bricks behind a pile of coal in the bin, pried four of them loose and took out a small jewelry box. She replaced the bricks and retraced her steps to the kitchen. After peeking in on her husband, she opened the box at the kitchen table, staring for several moments at the object that lay within. Despite the passage of years, it was in excellent shape. Cleaning and oiling it frequently had seen to that. It had been eighteen years since she had bought it in town shortly after her arrival from Poland. She recalled how surprisingly easy it had been to purchase. No questions, no inquiring stares. Just fill out the form, slide the cash across the counter. It was as easy as buying canned beets. But of course, this was America.

Rina Demic picked up the gun, opened the chamber and began inserting bullets.

TEN

They were by the stream that bordered their farm when she told him. Tears were running down her cheeks when she had finished, and although Joseph stared long in silence at the stream, she thought his eyes were wet, too. Several minutes passed before either of them spoke.

"This . . . brother of mine. Does he look just like me?" Joseph said, staring at the ground. He picked up some black pebbles and tossed them in the water.

"Yes. At least I think so. I haven't seen him since . . ."

"Since you gave him away?" There was bitterness in his voice.

"Yes, since I gave him away." Rina touched her son's arm. "I do not blame you for thinking badly of me, Joseph. You can think no worse of me than I do. Not a day has gone by all these years when I didn't look in the mirror with disgust. I will not make excuses for what I have done. I cannot. What I can do is see to it that this madness is put to an end."

Rina took out the gun from a pocket in her cotton dress. Joseph gasped when he saw it.

"You are not thinking of killing these men, mother?"

"No. Not because I wouldn't like to, and certainly not because I am afraid. It is just that killing them will accomplish nothing. They would simply send others to do the job. No, I must make sure of the one thing that matters: that Joseph Demic Jr. survives."

"I would survive in Russia," Joseph said flatly.

"No. If they did not kill you before you got to Russia, a few years in their beloved Siberian camps would do the job."

"But why would they kill me? Surely they would want to reward you and father."

Rina shook her head. "Maybe I am being overly suspicious, but I don't think that with so much time and money invested in this project, they would risk letting you live."

Rina did not add her suspicions about what fate awaited her and her husband, and she quickly continued before her innocent young son could think of asking.

"This gun will help you to escape, Joseph. After the men take you away, show them the gun and make them pull over. After they get out of the car, drive away."

"But why should I go with them at all, mother? Why not run now?"

"Because of your father."

"My father?"

Rina Demic stared at her son, wondering if she could make him understand.

"Ever since he came to this country, your father has lived for just one thing: to fulfill his mission to Russia. Seeing you leave with the agents would allow him to die in peace. I don't know if you can understand that."

Joseph looked down, digging his fingers in the coarse, dry soil.

"Does my father give me up lightly?" Joseph said softly, afraid to look in his mother's eyes.

"No, Joseph. He loves you very dearly."

"But he loves Russia more?"

"It is not that simple. Your father is dying. His time with you is limited anyway. He reasons that it is better to fulfill what he sees as his great obligation, than to steal a few more moments with his son. It is not an unreasonable desire, considering his position. Surely even you must see that."

"I suppose. But what of Harvard? I've worked so hard. Am I to throw that all away for my father's fantasy?"

"Your father's fantasy, as you call it, has nothing to do with it. The Russians will not allow you to enroll in Harvard, no matter what. The other one, your brother, is already there, waiting for word that you have been taken away. They have committed themselves in that direction, and will not turn back because of a complication."

Joseph stood up angrily.

"Complication? Am I merely a complication? You talk like one of them," Joseph said bitterly. "But then, you are one of them, aren't you mother? Communists. My mother and father are both Communist agents."

Joseph walked over to the water, staring down at his reflection. In a matter of minutes, his whole world had been turned upside down. He dashed a stone into the water, shattering the surface. He felt a hand on his shoulder and recoiled.

"Joseph . . . " his mother began. "Your father will soon be dead. I am already dead. I died the moment they took your baby brother away. We are no longer of any consequence. But you, Joseph, you must survive. You must run and start a new life somewhere. Change your name. Live quietly. Do not attract attention. If you do as I say, they will never find you in this vast land."

Joseph turned around, tears in his eyes.

"But surely there must be something we can do, mother. This is America. We can go to the authorities, tell them everything."

"Yes. And you would buy time. A year, maybe two. But one day they would come for you. It would be made to look like an accident. Your car would go out of control, a truck might run you over, an electrical appliance could go haywire. The method would not be important. All that would matter is that they would have their revenge. Joseph, they have put eighteen years into this project. They will see it through at all costs."

"And Yuri . . . my brother . . . what will he do in my place at Harvard? Why is this being done?"

Rina stared deep into her son's eyes, the reality of the ordeal painfully clear.

"Yuri . . . my son . . . the one they stole from me. He will become a great spy."

ELEVEN

Once Joseph saw the route they had chosen, he knew exactly what they had planned for him. They had gotten an early start at five in the morning, and instead of heading East across Arizona and New Mexico, the "cousins" announced they would go up U.S. 1 and take the northern route to Boston. If you wanted to kill somebody and make him disappear, the stretch of U.S. 1 from Long River to San Francisco had hundreds of miles of convenient points to drop off a body. The highway snaked along cliffs overlooking the Pacific, and you could easily stop the car and toss someone down into the sea for the currents to sweep away. Joseph was sure he would never reach Boston.

They were about five miles north of Long River, and although the cousins tried to put Joseph at ease through light talk, he was not about to let his guard down. The set-up had been obvious from the beginning. Joseph sat in front with the driver, while the other agent was in back. In order to keep his eye on the agent behind him, Joseph positioned himself with his back to the door. The gun his mother had given him was in an inside pocket of his jacket. Every so often Joseph would scratch his stomach near the weapon, hoping that the movement would become familiar and not arouse suspicion when he finally went for the gun. The whole thing seemed so unreal. The only time Joseph had used a gun before was in hunting squirrels, and even then he had never felt comfortable. The first time he had killed a squirrel, he had stared down at the lifeless creature, its eyes open, blood trickling from its mouth, and was sickened by the sight of it. Joseph had wanted to throw away his gun, and he swore he would never use it again to kill one of God's creatures. But the urge had come over him three weeks later, and he went back into the woods that bordered the farm and shot another squirrel and this time when he walked up to it, it was only out of curiosity. Death, he discovered, fascinated him. He had knelt down and studied the squirrel, surprised at the urge he had to touch the dead thing, although too repelled to do so. The fourth time he had shot one, he gave in and poked the furry animal along the ribs, eventually picking it up to get a closer look. There were no answers to be found in dead squirrels, however, and Joseph had gradually lost interest in shooting them. But the fascination with death remained. He recognized that it had a lot to do with the state his father was in, although he would not permit himself to probe any further in that direction. There was nothing you could learn about death, he decided, short of dying. Killing didn't reveal anything.

Joseph's thoughts wandered to the early morning scene at the farm when the agents had come for him. His mother had kept her face averted. There had been tears in his father's eyes. The shrunken man beneath the quilt reminded Joseph of the dead squirrels, and he had wanted to pick up his father and study him: so this is what a dead man looks like. He did nothing, however, merely playing his part in the charade, and was surprised at how glad he was to flee the house.

Joseph suddenly shook himself out of it. It was chilling to think that something he did every day—daydream—now could be fatal. He scratched his stomach near the gun, forcing himself to think clearly. They were only ten miles north of Long River. Joseph knew that roughly two miles ahead there was a lookout area big enough for a car to park. It was here where he must make his move.

"What are you going to study at Harvard?" Fydor, the driver said.

"Liberal arts. I haven't really made my mind up yet what I want to specialize in." Joseph heard the words from a distance, as if they came from another person. He could feel the anger growing and was glad: It would be easier to do what he had to do if he was mad. He kept his eyes ahead, afraid to miss the lookout area. His stomach began to tighten as he rehearsed in his mind what he must do. Above all, he must not hesitate. If they thought he would not use the gun, it might encourage them to attack. He had no idea really if he could pull the trigger. He hoped he would not have to find out.

A hundred yards ahead, Joseph saw the lookout area. It was big enough for a car to pull over, and Joseph remembered Saturday afternoons after football games when he would take a girl there and stare down at the water exploding white and foamy on the big rocks below. Joseph reached to scratch himself again. Neither of the men gave him a second look. It was then that he pulled the gun and pointed it at the driver.

"Pull over," Joseph said, trying to keep the tremble from his voice.

"What is this?" the driver asked, startled.

"Never mind the questions. Just pull over."

Joseph stuck the gun up by the driver's face, keeping his eye on the agent in the back. The driver braked and steered onto the lookout area.

"Kill the engine," Joseph commanded, "and leave the key in the ignition."

Shrugging, the driver complied.

"You," Joseph said, pointing the gun at the agent in back, "I want you to get out first, put your hands over your head and stand over there by the edge of the cliff where I can see you. If you so much as lower your hands an inch, your partner is dead."

Joseph was surprised at how cool and authoritative his voice sounded. Inside, his stomach was drawn into a steel knot. The agent in back did as told.

"Now you."

"Can I ask what this is all about, son?"

Joseph felt suddenly furious.

"OUT!"

Silently, the agent obeyed, putting his hands over his head and joining his partner. Joseph slid into the

207

driver's seat, turned on the ignition and closed the door. He pointed the gun with his left hand through the window.

"If either of you move, I shoot."

Joseph felt blindly with his right hand for the gear shift. Grabbing it, he depressed the clutch and tried to shift into first. The gear wouldn't move. Joseph gave it two good jerks, but still it didn't budge. His eyes wandered to the stick for a fraction of a second, and it was then that it happened. On signal, the two agents dove for the ground in opposite directions, rolling as they hit. Momentarily stunned, Joseph did not react until he saw a glint of sunlight on something in the hand of the agent call Fydor. Joseph switched the gun to his right hand and fired. The agent dropped his gun, clutching his stomach. Joseph was shaken. My God . . . suddenly, the windshield exploded, glass shards ripping into the right side of his face. In shock at having shot a man, Joseph had forgotten about the other agent. Joseph rapidly fired twice through a hole in the windshield as a bullet whizzed past his right ear and burst through the back window. Both of Joseph's shots hit their target. The second agent lay motionless. Blood poured from a wound in his neck. A movement to the left of the car caught Joseph's eye and he turned fast to fire, but it was only the first agent rolling on the ground in pain. Joseph felt his head begin to spin, a wave of nausea overcoming him. The scene was too unreal. Two men on the ground, one dead, the other dying. The windshield was shattered, glass everywhere. Joseph felt pain on the right side of his face, and realized it was cut. He stared numbly in the rear-view mirror. Pieces of glass had bitten tiny holes in his cheek and blood was everywhere. He wiped his face with the sleeve of his jacket. The tension all broke suddenly, his body letting go in a series of convulsive spasms. He was seized with the overpowering urge to flee. It was the only thought in his head. Putting his gun down on the glass-strewn seat, Joseph tried with two hands to shove the stick into first. Come on you bastard, he said to himself. His sweaty hands slipped on the knob. It wouldn't give. Furiously, he worked at the gear, shoving, screaming at it, all the anger of the insane day coming out. It was only after he had succeeded in moving the stick into first with a noisy grind that the absurdity of the situation hit him. Where do I think I am going in a car with shattered front and back windows? What would I tell the police? Joseph started laughing, a crazy, uncontrollable laughter.

He sat there for several minutes, letting it out. When he was done, he tried to compose himself. He had to make some decisions, and make them fast. Joseph looked at the two agents. The one he had shot in the neck appeared to be dead. The other was still alive, though barely. It was only a matter of time before he would die. But did Joseph have the time? What if somebody found him before them?

Glancing in the rear-view mirror to make sure no cars were coming, Joseph got out and walked over to the wounded agent. A plan was starting to take shape in his numb mind, and he knew what he had to do first. The question was: Could he do it?

On the day he was supposed to be beginning a brilliant college career at Harvard, Joseph Demic found himself standing over a dying Russian agent and contemplating the unthinkable. He looks just like the

209

squirrel, Joseph said to himself. The agent twisted his head around slowly to stare up at Joseph, mouth open, teeth stained with blood. Just like the squirrel. Joseph's hand tightened on the gun. He moved his arm stiffly, a robot following command, until the gun was pointing directly at the man's head. The agent's eyes filled with terror. Poor squirrel. Pity the squirrel. Put it out of its misery.

Joseph Demic closed his eyes and fired.

TWELVE

Boris picked up the message and read it for the tenth time. When he got to the line that disturbed him, he felt his stomach churn, the meaning eluding him. Boris reached for his Tums. One thing was for sure, the California phase of the mission had not gone smoothly. The two agents were supposed to have disposed of the young man, then contacted him through London with the words: "Emily had twins, but one died at birth." Five days had passed, however, with no word. Worried, Boris had dispatched a San Francisco-based agent and a day later a message did come. Boris held it in his hands, shaking his head in dismay. It was not the message he had expected.

We regret to inform you that Uncle Harry, cousin Bob, and little Joe were killed in an auto accident. Their car went off a cliff on Highway 1 just north of Long River. Most of the wreckage was washed out to sea. No bodies were found.

Boris tried out a scenario in his mind that he hoped would put his doubts to rest: There had been a struggle, the kid had bumped up against the steering wheel, the car had skidded out of control over the cliff and smashed on the rocks below . . . the bodies were carried away by the tide. . . .

It was a plausible explanation, but not a certainty, and that disturbed Boris. In an operation this big, one that had taken so long to set up, could they afford to leave just one door open? And yet maybe he was overreacting. After all, what was the alternative scenario? Could a farm boy have overpowered two highly skilled Soviet agents? Most unlikely, Boris thought. And if indeed they had all gone over the cliff, how could anyone have survived such an accident? And why should Joseph alone of the three have lived? No, there was really no great cause for alarm. Everything would continue as planned. Yuri would be activated. He would get his degree from Harvard, then go to Washington to lead the infiltration. . . .

First, Boris must send two messages. He sat down at his typewriter and carefully punched them out, typing with two fingers. The agent from San Francisco was instructed to carry out the remainder of the mission at the farm. To Yuri, who was staying at the Parker House in Boston, Boris sent this message:

Congratulations on entering Harvard. We will be following your career closely.

Love,
Bob and Lora

THIRTEEN

Joseph Demic Jr. lay on the lumpy bed and stared at the grey ceiling, its paint peeling in several spots. He had been here two weeks, leaving the depressing little room only to go for meals at a diner on Sunset Boulevard. He had told himself it was better not to be seen, but the truth was he had no desire to go out. What could interest him, now that his life had been ruined? One afternoon he had gone to the Chinese Theatre to take in a movie, but had left halfway through, turned off by what he saw would be a happy ending. He did not believe in happy endings anymore.

Joseph was unsure why he had come here, except that maybe as a transient he would be less noticeable in a place like Hollywood. On the first day he had seen many others like him on the street and he had felt more at ease. They wandered, the lean ones, eyes alert, hunting for a buck, a girl, an opportunity. The irony of the situation was not lost on him. He reached for a pint of whiskey on the night table and gave out a bitter laugh: He was a man without dreams in Dream City.

From the moment Joseph Demic had loaded two bodies in a car and pushed them over a cliff, life as he had known it had ceased. For all practical purposes, Joseph Demic had gone over the cliff, too. Signing the register in the dumpy hotel, Joseph had hesitated, then scrawled in the name Daniel Johnson: Daniel for the lion's den he had escaped from, Johnson for the anonymity.

Daniel Johnson slid off the bed, went over to the bureau, and picked up the copy of the *Los Angeles Times* he had bought earlier. It was folded to the Help Wanted section. He took it back to the bed and lay down. His mother had given him a thousand dollars, half of which was already gone. Soon he would need a job. Perhaps I can dig ditches, or wait on tables, he thought bitterly. There was a very real part of him that wanted no part of it at all. A voice whispered for him to end it, but Daniel Johnson refused to listen. He had come close on his third night in the room. Drunk, having stared at the walls for hours, unable to sleep, he had gotten up in a daze, taken the gun out of his suitcase and brought it back to the bed, putting it down on the covers and staring at it, trying to summon the nerve. He went as far as placing the barrel in his mouth, but the burnt taste of the cold muzzle had shocked him, and he had thrown the gun across the room, later disposing of it in a garbage can on the boulevard.

He knew he had to live, if only because his mother wanted him to. An overpowering wave of depression swept over Daniel Johnson as he thought about his parents. He had never been away from home, and missed them both terribly. Better get used to it, he thought, you'll never see them again. Daniel Johnson felt his anger surge. He brought his fist down hard on the night table, knocking over the opened pint of whiskey. The liquor spilled on to the floor in a steady stream. Johnson watched it pour out. He had made up his mind to do a daring thing. Bounding out of bed, he scooped all the change off the bureau and went down to the lobby where there was a phone booth. Johnson dropped in some coins, dialed the number of his parents' farm and stared across the lobby at a clerk who was reading a newspaper with dark glasses. The operator came on.

"May I help you?" the voice said.

Daniel Johnson hesitated.

"I'm trying to call 876-2319 in Long River."

"I'm sorry, sir, that number has been disconnected."

Daniel Johnson's heart sunk. The booth seemed to spin around him.

"Disconnected? Why?" he managed to say.

"I wouldn't know, sir."

"How could I find out?"

"Well . . . I could connect you with an operator in Long River, and she might help you."

"Please. Would you do that?"

"Of course."

Daniel Johnson wiped at sweat forming on his forehead, took a deep breath and tried to keep the bad thoughts out of his head. If something has happened to them, then I'm all alone in the world.

"Yes, may I help you?"

It was the Long River operator.

"Yes. Operator, I'm trying to reach 876-2319. I've been told it's disconnected. Is there any way of finding out why?"

Daniel Johnson held his breath. The clerk across the lobby had taken off his dark glasses and was staring at him.

"Well, sir, I really don't have that sort of information."

"Listen," Daniel Johnson said desperately, "it's the Demic farm out on Carter Road. Surely you must know them."

"Oh, the Demics. Sure. My gosh, what a tragedy."

Daniel Johnson closed his eyes tight. He wanted to drop the phone and not listen, but kept his ear by the receiver.

"It happened about a week ago. The house burned down to the ground. Terrible thing. Both the husband and wife died. The son—Joseph I believe his name is—had to come home from Harvard for the funeral. They say he held up well. Are you a relative?"

Daniel Johnson's grip tightened like a vise on the phone, his body beginning to tremble.

"Sir . . . are you there?"

He let the phone drop. Long after he had left the booth, Daniel Johnson could still hear the operator's words: . . . the husband and wife died . . . the son had to come home from Harvard. . . .

Part 3

ONE

The director of the FBI took the call from the White House immediately.

"Do you have a file on a writer named Alex Palmer?" the voice from the White House said without a greeting.

The director bristled at the lack of pleasantries. They had never liked each other, and on the occasions when their careers had come in to conflict, the affairs had been hard fought and bitter.

"I think so. I'll have to check and get back to you."

The director hung up without another word, drawing some satisfaction. Not many men in the country would have had the balls to do that, he thought smugly.

There was a file on Palmer, and after reading it himself, the director phoned the White House and was told to send it over. Two hours later a second call came from the White House.

"This *Amerasia* thing, there's not much in the file. What can you tell me about it?"

The director, anticipating the question, had another file on his desk. He opened it.

"*Amerasia* was a left-wing magazine back in the Forties with strong Communist leanings. Evidence was discovered in 1945 that the magazine had in its possession some seventeen hundred highly classified documents stolen from the government during the height of the war."

"How was the evidence found?"

"An OSS security officer named Archbold Van Beuren was glancing at one of *Amerasia's* issues when he saw an almost verbatim reprint in the magazine of a secret and highly critical government report on British rule in Thailand, which he himself had written. He told his superiors, and a field mission was undertaken at the magazine's office on two twenty-five Fifth Avenue in New York. The date was March eleventh."

"What sort of field mission?"

"It was a break-in. The OSS sent one of its security officers, Frank Bielaski, to search the premises."

"Without a warrant?"

"Yes. That was their big mistake. Bielaski took a sampling of the documents he found at *Amerasia,* hopped a plane down to Washington and hand delivered them to Bill Donovan. Donovan ordered a twenty-four hour tail put on the magazine's editor, Philip Jaffe."

"And that's where Palmer's father comes in?"

"Yeh. The tail found that Jaffe met regularly with Lieut. Jack Palmer, who had been serving as liaison officer between the Office of Naval Intelligence and the

State Department. Palmer at one time had been a research assistant for Jaffe. The thought was that Palmer and another officer with Naval Intelligence, Lieut. Andrew Roth, were passing documents to *Amerasia*. After further investigation —"

"What further investigation?"

The director hesitated. "A search of the living quarters of three of the suspects."

"Illegal?"

"Yes."

"By whom? OSS?"

"No . . . FBI."

"I see. Go on."

"There was enough evidence found to arrest six people on June sixth, 1945 on a complaint charging conspiracy to violate the espionage laws. The case had been badly bungled, however. Almost all the evidence had been obtained on illegal break-ins, and there was no way it would stand up in court, so the thing was shoved under the carpet — a few token fines, no jail sentences. And that's the way it stood until Joe McCarthy picked up the ball seven years later."

"I can see how it would have appealed to him."

"He called it a whitewash," the director said. "Which, of course, it was. McCarthy forced the Senate Foreign Relations Committee to call key witnesses in the case, one of whom was Palmer's father. Jack Palmer had left the service and was a reporter for *Harper's*. McCarthy raked him over the coals pretty good. There were a lot of messy headlines and Palmer had to quit his job. He had been seeing a doctor for a nervous problem at the time, and the McCarthy affair must have put him over the edge. Two weeks after the committee finished grilling him, Jack Palmer killed himself.

"Was he guilty?" the voice from the White House said.

"That I don't know."

"Can you find out for me?"

"I can try."

"And Palmer's son . . . his file seems to have been put together shortly after his first best seller, but never updated. There are big gaps. I'd like to find out everything he's been doing since he left the *Post*. No fact would be considered too small, no detail too intimate."

The director of the FBI waited for more instructions, but the phone went dead.

TWO

War. General Worthington sensed it coming. He hoped to God he was wrong.

The presidential counselor's desk was littered with reports, none of them good. He was working his way through them, glasses perched on the tip of his nose, mind reeling from the potential for disaster on every page. The fighting between Iran and Iraq, of course, was the catalyst for the rest of the mess, and he began with that first.

From what CIA and military intelligence sources could gather, the Iraqis had the upper hand in the conflict, but were botching the job. It was no West Point operation. The Iraqi strategy was to use its air force to bomb and strafe stored oil and pipelines in an effort to deny supplies of aviation fuel, diesel oil, and gasoline to the Iranian forces. Ground forces, meanwhile, were putting the squeeze on Khurramshahr and Abadan — Iran's principal refinery city and its oil port. The tactical pattern, which Worthington recognized as militarily feasible, was to take the two cities plus Ahwaz and cut the pipelines that lead from Khurramshahr and Abadan to central and northern Iran. The ground operations were being handled clumsily, however, and if anything, the Iraqi efforts were intensifying Iran's will to resist. It was not going to be a swift and conclusive conflict by any damn stretch of the imagination.

The American naval presence in the area was what had the Soviets ticked off, and Worthington couldn't blame them. We'd react the same way if Soviet military ships were floating around Cuba. Two days after Moscow had detoured two freighters bound for Iraq, the Soviet president had used the situation to attack the American naval presence as (a quote from the *New York Times* was inclosed) " . . . a Sword of Damocles over the independent states of the Persian Gulf and Red Sea basin." Worthington laughed wryly at that one, and read on. Pentagon intelligence, meanwhile, was claiming just the opposite of Moscow, that Arab reaction to U.S. policy in the gulf was privately favorable.

Privately favorable. Worthington tossed aside the report in disgust. Privately? Why not publicly? Worthington knew the answer, of course. They wanted the help, but not the heat. The heat they saved for us. Bail us out and we'll be indebted. Indebted my ass. For how long? A month? Two? A year? Then the bastards would turn their backs on us. Will we never learn?

For the next two hours, Worthington read a rapidly growing file on next week's UN meeting and the scheduled summit afterwards at Camp David. What happens if the talks fail and the Persian Gulf crisis worsens? Worthington struck a match and touched it to his empty pipe bowl, picking up another folder as he puffed. Coming on the heels of the gulf mess, there was no doubt where the president's thoughts were leading when he had asked Worthington earlier in the day to begin implementing Presidential Directive Sixty-three. What a nice, clinical, antiseptic name, the general thought, opening the folder. Presidential Directive Sixty-three . . . odorless, colorless, as bleak and barren as the world would be if the directive ever went into effect.

Worthington had argued against the directive from the beginning, but Demic, armed with superior data and an iron will, had rammed it down the general's throat, which was about par for the course around here. The presidential counselor's office had gone from being a live wire in Pierson's administration to just a wire for transmitting Demic's orders.

"If you implement this plan," Worthington had argued, "it will be the single most important piece of intelligence we've got, and as such, could be our Achilles' heel. This one piece of intelligence in the Soviet's hands would be enough to threaten the future of the country."

"But why should we think the Soviets could ever get their hands on this?" the president had argued.

"They almost certainly won't but there's always that one chance in a million. We're putting too many eggs in one basket. Is it worth the risk?"

The president had thought it was, and after drawing up Directive Sixty-three, dumped it on General Worthington's lap. What the directive did was to outline procedures for moving all major political and military leaders out of Washington in the event of a nuclear attack. There were also directions for strengthening existing shelters and the creation of a network of command posts, but the key portion of it dealt with vacating the nation's leaders. And that was the part Worthington found fault with. Ever since the early Fifties, the government had prepared for the possibility of nuclear war by drawing up contingency plans for the protection and evacuation of the president and other personnel. The umbrella had always included no more than a dozen or so key people. Underground shelters had been built around Washington, stocked with food and other supplies. One of the bunkers, the Alternate Military Command Center, was set up at Mount Weather, fifty miles west of Washington. Another, built for the president in the Fifties was buried under Raven Rock, at Fort Richie, Maryland, sixty-five miles from Washington.

The highly accurate missiles of the 1980s, however, had made it extremely unlikely that the president's bunker could survive a direct hit, so new plans were drawn up calling for the chief executive and top military officers to run the war from an airborne command post, known by the code name "Kneecap." Shortly after Demic had taken over, a secret exercise was undertaken in which Demic was flown from the White House by helicopter to Andrews Air Force Base, where the air force maintains an airborne presidential command post, a modified 747 airliner equipped with advanced communications gear. The exercise, Demic said, had pointed out several weaknesses in the system which Directive Sixty-three was meant to correct.

And did, Worthington thought. But the president had not stopped there. After shoring up holes in his evacuation and command system, Demic had widened the umbrella to unheard of proportions. No less than forty of the most important military, political, and bureaucratic officials were included in the new evacuation system. Specific shelter locations were designated for each leader, with communications links to the presidential command post outlined. "We've spent years worrying about the vulnerability of our missile forces to a Soviet first strike," Demic had said, "but nobody thought about the vulnerability of our government. What good is it for us to survive an attack if we have no one left to command a counter strike and keep some semblance of a working government going?"

The point was well taken, but what bothered Worthington was that the location of every major official in the United States government was listed in the event of nuclear attack. That kind of intelligence in Moscow's hands would be lethal. Ground forces landed by submarine after a nuclear strike could easily mop up what was left of our government with that information.

Demic had refused to be swayed, and now, contingency plans having been drawn up, General Worthington was being asked to set the directive in motion. Putting down his pipe, the general leaned back in his swivel chair, his huge, battle-scarred hands rubbing at fatigue in his face. Evacuation . . . shelters . . . nuclear war . . . damn, Worthington thought. I came out of retirement to help write a chapter in history, not close the book on it.

THREE

Down the hall in the office of the president's counsel, the mood was equally gloomy, but for different reasons. David Schuyler had opened a fresh bottle of Johnny Red and fed a third of it into his personal think tank. Although precious few answers had come out of it, at least the world looked a little better. Damn Alex Palmer, Schuyler thought, washing down more Scotch.

In less than a week, Schuyler's private world at the top of the world had been turned upside down, and he had his good friend Palmer to blame for it. All Schuyler had wanted out of life was just to climb to a perch where he could breathe a little freer, the view unobstructed. Now that he had made it, along comes Palmer like a wave of smog.

Who ever heard of anything so preposterous: the president of the United States a Soviet agent. The mind boggled at the implications. And yet Palmer had built a pretty damn good case with circumstantial evidence. Was it just coincidence that Charlene Lowenstein was killed a few hours after she had showed the president a photo of a Russian teenager that looked like him? And what about Joe McCarthy's warning to Jim Bell on his deathbed? Had the senator really been visited by a Soviet agent who taunted him with information about a pending Communist infiltration . . . an infiltration which began the year Joseph Demic entered government? And finally, what about the scar? According to Sarah Lowenstein's diary, the Soviet boy had been knifed in the right knee, a wound that would have left a scar . . . the kind of scar the president's masseur said Demic had on his right knee . . . all circumstantial evidence, and all very frightening. . . .

Maybe that's what pissed Schuyler off more than anything. Here Palmer had dug up what potentially was the most terrifying political dirt ever, and he seemed cool and relaxed. What fairy-tale world did Palmer live in that he didn't understand the implications of messing with a president . . . a president who may also have ties to the KGB. If Joseph Demic had Charlene Lowenstein brutally killed for showing him a photograph, what would he do to Palmer for digging deeper? Or David Schuyler, for that matter?

Schuyler plunged into his Scotch. Am I becoming an alcoholic? Schuyler wondered. Me, who never used to drink? No. An alcoholic is someone who drinks heavily every day and I didn't drink yesterday, just the day before. Is there such thing as an every-other-day alcoholic? Schuyler shrugged and poured another.

Where was Palmer now? Probably in Long River.

He had taken an early flight to Los Angeles and was going to drive a rented car up to Demic's hometown. "If Demic, a star athlete, really did get a bad spike wound playing high school football, there would be a story in the local paper," Palmer had said. Palmer had also made Schuyler dig up and make a copy of the president's dental records. "Dental records don't lie," Palmer had said. "If I can find out who Demic's dentist was, and compare the records, we might have the kind of hard-ass evidence we need to bring the whole thing crashing down."

Schuyler had cringed when Palmer used the "we." Am I really a part of this? Me and Alex Palmer, alone against the world. Maybe I should tell General Worthington. Isn't it my duty to do so? And yet, it's all so crazy, how do I go about telling him? Better to wait and see what Palmer digs up in Long River. I can't go pleading a case against the president of the United States based on the evidence I have. No good prosecutor would. Atta boy, Schuyler, remember your training. When all is said and done, if the shit hits the fan and the White House turns into a battleground, I can always bail out and go back to being a private lawyer. David Schuyler will land on his feet, I guarantee you that . . . providing, of course, he lives that long.

Schuyler rushed for the Scotch, then pulled up short. Slow down. A respectable White House aide doesn't do it like that. Nice and easy, control the urge. White House aides take social drinks. Remember who you are: David Schuyler, counsel to the president of the United States, happily married man, father of two children, a pillar of stability. Schuyler's hand shook as he grasped the glass. "Oh Christ," he said out loud, and suddenly reached for the phone. Before dialing the familiar number, he closed his eyes and rehearsed the words: "Hello, this is Fred Mitchum. I've got to see you. . . ."

FOUR

"Jolly Harper is the guy you're looking for," the bartender was saying, right hand flying over the polished counter top with a rag. "Yeh, Jolly and the president were real tight."

Palmer slid his empty beer glass across the counter.

"Jolly probably knew the president better than anybody," the bartender said, pouring Coors from the tap. "Jolly played tight end, the president fullback. Hung around together. The president was the star, though. Jolly, he just pushed around bodies, once in a while caught a pass. Joe Demic, he could step some, didn't matter whether it was around you or through you. Tough sonofabitch."

Palmer smiled, wondering how much of what the bald old bartender said was true, how much fiction. He had been listening for over an hour now. Palmer tried to compare the Joseph Demic the bartender knew with the one in the White House. There didn't seem much similarity, but that wasn't surprising. A man who becomes president is no longer just a man. He's something of a king. Palmer had a theory about men who became kings in the White House, but he didn't think a bartender in the Half Moon Tavern in Long River wanted to hear it.

"I remember one time," the bartender was saying, "when these punks from Santa Barbara come into town, drifting I guess, and Joe Demic and Jolly were . . . "

Palmer nodded, not really listening anymore. After he had finished his beer, Palmer bought the bartender a drink and then went outside, squinting in the harsh late afternoon sun, feeling slightly tipsy. A tall, well-built boy wearing a high school letter sweater walked by, his arm draped around a pretty girl, the two of them laughing. Palmer tried to picture Joe Demic like that, strutting down Main Street, but it was impossible. The man in the White House could never have been a trouble-free kid, big man in a little town. No, Joe Demic must have been born at fifty, somber and burdened. And yet there were the pictures of the farm boy in *Life* . . . and the single shot, yellow with age, of a teenager named Yuri in the Soviet Union.

The bartender had given Palmer directions to Jolly Harper's used car lot, although it hadn't really been necessary. Palmer had spotted it on the way in to town. It was not the kind of place you could miss. Colorful plastic banners were strung over the lot, white light bulbs hung everywhere. There was a huge billboard on top of the office portraying what Palmer assumed was Jolly Harper laughing, the come-on being: WHY IS THIS MAN LAUGHING? COME SEE JOLLY AND FIND

OUT. Palmer parked his Mercedes out front. The brick walk leading up to the office had been painted gold. The used cars were all brilliantly polished. Above the office entrance a sign said:

> Jolly Harper
> Used Cars
> Real Estate
> Licensed Private Eye

"Are you really a private detective?" Palmer asked, after introducing himself to Jolly Harper.

"Shit yes. Licensed and everything," Jolly Harper said, shifting his considerable bulk on a leather swivel chair.

"What kind of cases do you have?" Palmer said.

Jolly Harper let out a bellow of laughter.

"None, actually. I've only had the shingle up a few weeks. Took one of them correspondence courses in my spare time. Got more spare time around here than spare tires." Jolly Harper's laughter filled the office. Palmer tried to imagine what the fat man had looked like playing tight end many years and many pounds ago. Palmer had no more success picturing the overweight toad behind the desk as a trim, youthful athlete, than he did the president.

"Why'd you become a detective?" Palmer asked.

"I'm a nut, I guess. I just like mysteries. Life's a mystery to me anyway," Harper said, his face suddenly boyish with embarrassment, some inner part exposed. "You know, I haven't had a case yet, but I'll tell you, people treat you differently when they know you're a private eye. Most folks, especially around here, got some secrets they want to hide. When they see me coming now they flash big smiles, trying hard to look like they don't have things to hide, but you know they do by the guilty look. I tell you, I'd love to dig into some of these people's lives. I bet you I could write a dandy detective book about them."

"Why don't you?"

"Can't write. Not like you, anyway. I read your books. Pretty good stuff. You're wasting your on time on real life stories, though. Why not try writing a novel like Dash Hammett or Ross MacDonald?"

"I don't think I could top real life, as you call it, for mystery and intrigue."

"Maybe. Maybe not."

Harper took out a pack of cigarettes, fumbled in his pocket for matches but came up empty. Palmer held out a gold cigarette lighter Charlene had given him for his birthday.

"Thanks," Harper said, puffing deep. "So what can I do for you? By the looks of the car you drove up in, Mr. Palmer, you aren't interested in buying one of my bombs. What's your poison?"

"I'm researching a book on the president, and I understand you played football with him."

"Digging a little dirt, huh?"

Palmer winced. Jesus, is that what everybody in America thinks about me? "Just digging," Palmer said carefully.

"I get you. You don't have to tell me the details. I'm in the trade, too."

"What I'm interested in knowing," Palmer began quickly, "is how long the president was sidelined with that spike injury he got during his senior year."

237

Harper looked puzzled.

"What spike injury? I don't remember him having one. For that matter, I don't recall Joe Demic ever having any type of injury. He was a rugged sonofabitch."

"Is it possible you might have forgotten?"

"Not possible at all. Jolly Harper has the best memory in Long River. Like an elephant, some people would say, none too kind."

"The president says he got a spike wound in the right knee which required stitches."

Jolly Harper's eyes seemed to narrow. Palmer thought he detected a smile.

"Oh, well if the president says that, then maybe I did forget," Harper said straight-faced. "Never knew Joe Demic to lie."

Palmer stared at the huge man, waiting for more. After several moments, Palmer said, "Demic came home for his parents' funeral. How did he take it?"

"Like a soldier. Joe wasn't the kind to show a whole lot of emotion."

"Did you talk to him much at the funeral?"

"No. Just told him I was sorry, that's all. He didn't seem to want any company, so I left him alone. He went right back to Harvard after the funeral. There wasn't any point in him sticking around, I guess. He didn't have any relatives left here. His folks were from Poland."

"Did you see him much after that?" Palmer asked, taking his gold lighter out again and a cigarette.

"Just once. In Cambridge. An uncle of mine in Boston had died and I went to the funeral with my dad. This was about a year after we had graduated from high school. I took the trolley over to Harvard and looked Joe up, kind of as a surprise."

"Was he glad to see you?"

"Yes and no. I mean at first it almost seemed like he didn't recognize me. I found him in the library. His roommates had told me he'd be there. Old Joe had his nose buried in some thick book when I snuck up behind him, put my hands over his eyes and did a, 'Guess who?' routine. When he couldn't guess, I removed my hands and he turned around, and for a moment he just stared at me, as if he'd never laid eyes on me before. So I said, 'Hey Joe, don't you recognize your old high school buddy Jolly? One year at Harvard and the guy doesn't remember his friends, gee.' Then Joe broke into a big grin and I realized he'd been putting me on."

"What did you talk about? High school days?"

"No. Joe didn't want to relive old times. He preferred to talk about what each of us were doing. It was a little awkward, I suppose, but that's the way it is when two guys go their separate ways."

"Did he sound at all strange?"

"Strange? How do you mean?"

"Did he sound different than he had in Long River?"

"Well, yeh, as a matter of fact he did, now that you mention it. Sort of had an accent."

Palmer felt his stomach muscles tighten.

"What kind of accent?"

"Oh hell, I wouldn't know. I mean it wasn't foreign. Not Russian or German. Sort of upper class, if you know what I mean. Harvard. Very British and all that. I just figured Joe was trying to keep up with the rest of them. Couldn't blame him really. After all, Joe Demic was only a farm boy from California, right?"

Palmer suppressed the urge to say no, to tell the fat

man whom he suspected the president really was.

"Is there a newspaper in this town?" Palmer asked. "A weekly, perhaps?"

"Sure is. *Long River Times*. Comes out every Thursday, more or less. Jim McDonnell is editor. He also writes all the stories, takes the pictures—when he can afford the film—and does the headlines. Jack-of-all-trades. If you're planning to interview him, though, you might have to wait a spell. Jim puts a sign on his door about now, saying he's out on assignment." Harper smiled. "The old boy's got him a girlfriend who works at the donut shop on Reed Street."

"I'll take my chances," Palmer said, getting up.

"Come on," Harper said, slipping his big arm around Palmer's shoulder. "I'll walk you outside."

On the brick path, Palmer thought of something and turned to Harper.

"I need to know the name of Demic's dentist when he lived here. Got any idea which one he went to?"

"Was only one then. Horace Melton. But he's retired now. Everybody either uses John Clark or Bob Coles. Coles bought out Doc Melton's practice, so maybe he's the man to see. His office is down on Kennedy Street, next to the bank. Can't miss it."

Palmer thanked him, got in his car and just before he drove away, watched as the fat man scurried back into his office. It'll be all over town in about five minutes, Palmer thought wryly.

FIVE

The *Long River Times* office was next to a barber shop with a striped pole in front. There was a chalkboard sign hung on the door which said: "Life's too hairy — gone fishing." Just as Jolly Harper had predicted there was also a sign on the newspaper's front door: "OUT ON ASSIGNMENT." Palmer got back in his Mercedes and drove to the dentist's office.

"Yes, may I help you?" a young nurse said. The office smelled from fresh paint. A workman with white-spotted overalls came down the corridor and disappeared into a room.

"I want to see Dr. Coles."

"Do you have an appointment?"

Palmer explained who he was, telling the girl he was doing a book on the president and needed to see his dental file.

"Are you the Alex Palmer who wrote the book on . . ."

". . . the presidents. Yes, that's me," Palmer said.

"Oh. . ." the girl said, blushing inexplicably. "I'll see if Dr. Coles can talk to you, sir." The girl hurried down the hall. Almost immediately she returned with the good doctor in tow. He was about Palmer's age, thin, with round shoulders, his face pale except for a nose red from popped veins. A drinker, Palmer thought, taking the smiling dentist's hand.

"Very nice to meet you, Mr. Palmer," the dentist said. Palmer detected the odor of whiskey and mouth wash. "It's not every day we get the nation's number one dirt-digging author visiting us here in little Long River. I'm just finishing up with a patient and then I can chat with you. Mary," the dentist said, putting an arm around the nurse's shoulder, "why don't you show Mr. Palmer to the back room. The painters are in my office, so we'll have to talk in one of my work rooms, if you don't mind."

Palmer followed the girl down the hall, passing a room on the left where a female patient, eyes closed, lay back on a reclining chair. Her plaid skirt was hitched up to her knees. Dead or under gas, Palmer thought. The dentist went into the room and closed the door. Palmer followed the young nurse.

"You can sit on the chair," the nurse said. "The doctor will be right with you." The girl left and Palmer got on the chair. He listened for the sound of drilling from the first office, but heard nothing. Naughty, naughty, Palmer thought. He glanced around the room. There were two medical certificates on the wall. Palmer couldn't read them from where he sat. Probably a correspondence school, the same one Jolly Harper wrote to.

Palmer jumped off the chair to look: UCLA Medical School. Palmer was surprised. What is a UCLA-trained dentist doing in a one-horse town like this? A scandal perhaps, a molested female patient in Los Angeles, hushed up in exchange for the dentist's agreement to get out of town . . . Palmer was tossing around a few shovels of dirt in his mind when the dentist walked in.

"Okay, now, Mr. Palmer. Where does it hurt?"

Palmer explained what he was doing in Long River.

"A book on the small-town roots of the president, huh?" the dentist said with barely disguised sarcasm. "Sounds like a departure for you, Mr. Palmer. One would have thought you'd be digging up some buried scandal in the president's past. But then, what do I know? I'm just a modest dentist scratching out a living in a little town."

The dentist turned his back on Palmer and picked up a bottle of Listerine. He poured some into a little paper cup, gargled and then spit out only a fraction of it in a nearby sink. Swallowed the rest, Palmer thought, detecting a whiskey mouthwash odor again. The dentist turned, eyes slightly glassy.

"I wasn't the president's dentist, of course. Old Horace Melton was. He was the only dentist in these parts for a long while, before the town grew. I bought his practice when he retired."

"I know. Jolly Harper told me."

"Oh, you've been to see the town's leading citizen already, have you?" The dentist's sarcastic tone made Palmer uncomfortable. "I'm sure then, that Jolly told you all about his exploits with the president. They were football heroes, you know."

"Yes, he did mention it."

"I'll bet. Hard to imagine, isn't it?" the dentist said, shaking his head. "That ton of blubber playing football, all the pretty little girls running after him. Sounds like something he'd make up, except that I checked it out with other people and they all say it's true. I wasn't born here, of course," the dentist added, as if disassociating himself from something unpleasant. Coles stared off for a moment, then shrugged and turned for the Listerine. "Damn bad taste in my mouth," he said, avoiding Palmer's eyes as he repeated his gargling charade.

"When you bought up Dr. Melton's practice," Palmer began quickly, "I presume you inherited all his files."

"Of course."

"Including Joseph Demic's?"

"Yes."

"Can I see it?"

"I wish you could," the dentist said. "I'd like to see it myself. Unfortunately, I no longer have that file in my possession."

Sensing that he had Palmer dangling, the dentist fell silent, his left hand wandering to the Listerine bottle. He started to uncap it, then apparently thought better and screwed it back on. Palmer hadn't taken his eyes off the dentist.

"You see, Mr. Palmer, the president's file, along with several others, was stolen from my office. I never really understood why, and the police have not been able to solve the crime. Since the office was broken into without my alarm being set off, it must have been a very good professional."

"Why steal files?"

"You tell me, Mr. Palmer. You're the famous investigative author."

"Was anything else taken beside files?"

"Not a thing."

"Strange," Palmer said.

"Yes, very strange indeed. It was right after John Pierson picked Demic was his running mate at the Republican convention. Maybe two days later. I was at home, getting ready to come to the office when my nurse called. She said the door to the office was open when she arrived, and that the file cabinet was broken into. After cross-checking the files with index cards I keep on patients, I figured out that twelve were taken, including the president's. It would seem, even to a layman detective like me, that the thief was only interested in the president's records. The others were taken in an obviously lame attempt to mask intentions. After all, what value could there be in having a record of Mary Gibbons's dental work, an eighty-five-year-old retired seamstress, right?"

Palmer nodded numbly, his mind trying desperately to come up with an explanation other than the obvious one: that the Russians were covering up the trail.

"After I found that nothing else had been taken, I dismissed the whole incident as the prank of a souvenir hunter . . . until now. First the president's file is stolen, then a year later a famous scandal writer shows up in my office. How very interesting, don't you think, Mr. Palmer?" The dentist smirked.

"Yes. Very." Palmer got up to leave. Then, on impulse, he reached for the dentist's Listerine. "You don't mind, do you doc? I've got a bad taste myself." Palmer started to unscrew the cap. The dentist reached quickly and grabbed the bottle, the smile gone.

"Sorry. I'd prefer that you didn't."

Smirking, Palmer walked out of the room and down the corridor, the dentist trailing quickly after him. Palmer stopped and glanced in the front operating room, where the female patient was just coming to from the gas. She had a pleasant, peaceful smile on her face. When she noticed Palmer staring, she blushed and pulled down her skirt. Palmer didn't bother to look at the dentist, who walked into the room and shut the door behind him.

SIX

"I must apologize for the condition of the room, Mr. Palmer, but the staff of the *Long River Times* has very little occasion to do any research. Actually, I am the staff of the *Long River Times*, lock, stock, and barrel, and I absolutely detest research. 'What's past is past,' they say. Another cliche I like that covers the situation quite nicely is, 'Let the dead lie.' Anyway, here you are. Feel free to use any material you'd like, and I'll be in my office if you need me."

His speech given, Jim McDonnell, silver-haired editor of the *Long River Times,* left Palmer alone in the tiny, stuffy room that housed bound volumes of every edition of the paper since its inception in 1921. There were no windows, just an old wooden desk, a metal folding chair, and a dim light overhead which barely allowed Palmer to read the dates on the huge cloth volumes, arranged in rows on shelves along three walls. Palmer sat at the desk, took out his gold lighter and lit up a cigarette. He then laid out the pen and pad he had borrowed from McDonnell, recalling the small town editor's cutting words: "You're a writer and you don't have pad or pen? Tssk Tssk." Smart ass.

Unable to read the volume dates in the dim room, Palmer opened the door, allowing light from the adjacent hallway to spill in. It was better, but not good. Glancing at the nearest shelf, Palmer shook his head in disgust. Many of the volumes were out of sequence. It was shaping up as one dandy job. Palmer rolled up his shirt sleeves, then began his search for 1952. Nineteen forty-eight, 1949, 1950, and 1951 were snuggled in succession, but the next volume was 1940, and the one after that was 1926. Figures, Palmer muttered. A couple of minutes later he located the volume, nestled between two war years, all three mixed up with the Roaring Twenties. Palmer lugged the heavy volume over to the desk and set it down with a plop, scattering dust.

At random, Palmer opened the big book in the middle, breaking off a piece of brittle page carelessly. The date was May twenty-third. The lead headline on page one was: ELEMENTARY SCHOOL TO VISIT STATE CAPITAL. There was a four-column picture of a scraggly bunch of kids in front of a school, flanked by a tall, grey-haired woman, unsmiling. How many of them are dead now? Lost in the war, strung out on alcohol, marking time in prisons? Palmer glanced at the faces, fascinated by frozen moments. He remembered coming upon an old photo of his mom and dad in one of his aunt's albums when he was eleven. His father had been dead six years and his mother institutionalized for three. The photo must have been taken shortly after the Palmers had been married. They were both smiling and looked very much in love. Alex Palmer could not recall his father ever smiling in real life, and the picture had made him cry and he had snapped the album shut and gone to his room, sitting alone for hours in the dark, crying softly. He had vowed never to look at the picture again, but a week later had gone back into his aunt's attic and dug out the album again and stared at the picture for several minutes and this time he didn't cry. Mastering the picture had made him proud in a strange way.

After studying the faces in the *Long River Times*, Palmer decided that none of the kids had grown up distinguished, certainly not like himself — number one dirt-digging author in America. Palmer carefully flipped the pages until he came to September. Football weather. Starting with the first week in September, Palmer looked up the sports section in the index and turned to find it. At first he was puzzled. Garden news was where the sports should have been. He rechecked the index. Page fourteen was supposed to be sports. But after page thirteen there was garden news. Palmer scratched his head. Then his eye caught the number on the top of the garden page and a chill shot up his back: page sixteen. A page was missing. Palmer could hear his own heavy breathing in the tiny room, which suddenly seemed claustrophobic. Bending his head down close, Palmer saw it. The job had been done neatly with a razor, the slice so close to the fold that only a close examination would reveal it.

Quickly, Palmer turned to the next week's edition. He looked up the sports pages. Gone. In a frenzy now,

Palmer turned from week to week, each time discovering the same thing. Every sports page for the fall months of 1952 had been cut out with a razor. Christ, Palmer muttered, sweat forming on his forehead.

He sensed it from the light changing before he actually saw it. The door to the little room suddenly swung shut. Already out of his chair, Palmer flung himself at the door, driving it open with a noisy bang. He jumped into the hallway, poised for attack. Jim McDonnell stood there holding a black cat in his arms. The editor's mouth was wide open, startled.

"Mr. Palmer, do you always exit rooms that way?"

Palmer let his body relax, his breathing still heavy. He felt very foolish.

"The door . . . I . . . thought, well, that is, I—"

"The cat has a nasty habit of making wee-wee in that room," McDonnell said. "I really don't know what his fascination with my research room is, but I try and keep the door closed."

"Yes, of course, I understand," Palmer said hastily, forcing a smile on his face. "I'm just a little jumpy."

"I can see that. Do you drink a lot of coffee, Mr. Palmer?"

Palmer stared at McDonnell, puzzled.

"Caffeine, Mr. Palmer," McDonnell said, and launched into a lecture. McDonnell was right. He was jumpy. The investigation had made him more paranoid than usual. Just before entering the newspaper office, for example, Palmer was sure a man in a blue Camaro across the street was watching him. The idea had made Palmer uneasy, but he had enough sense to dismiss it and get on with his work. Still, Palmer had made a mental note to keep an eye out for the Camaro when he came out. Palmer focused back on McDonnell, sensing he was winding up his lecture. Palmer wondered whether he should tell the man about the missing pages, then decided not to. It was bad enough that Jolly Harper and the dentist were probably spreading juicy tidbits around town. Palmer didn't need word of the missing pages leaking out.

"You're quite right about the caffeine," Palmer said when McDonnell had finished. "I think I'm going to give it up." Palmer nervously stroked the black cat, which arched its back. "Thank you for letting me use your research material. It was quite interesting. Your paper does a thorough job of reporting on the local sports scene."

Palmer thought he detected a sly smile on the editor's face. Does the sonofabitch know? Is he part of it? *It*. Jesus Christ, what is *it?* Palmer headed for the front door.

Outside, the temperature had dropped sharply. It was going to be a wonderful Southern California night and Palmer intended to spend it in Los Angeles, not Long River. He had learned all there was to learn in the town, which was to say nothing . . . and everything. Someone had gone to great efforts to erase all written records about the president. Palmer was convinced that if he dug further, he would discover more missing documents, and he didn't want to do that, at least not at the moment. It was risky to arouse too much suspicion among the locals. One thing was for sure, though: It was a good bet that young Joe Demic existed in memory only now. Every document connected with him had long since disappeared.

Palmer shuddered at the enormity of what he was uncovering. If it was true, and the president found out he was on his trail, it was not hard to speculate on what he would do to him. Palmer looked around for the blue Camaro, breathing a sigh of relief when he didn't spot it. That's when he saw the boy standing by his Mercedes. It was the one he had seen earlier with the letter sweater. Palmer walked over to him.

"Nice car you have here, mister."

"Thanks," Palmer said.

The boy ducked his head in the window and admired the interior.

"I've got my license, you know," the kid said. "Some day if I'm rich enough, I'm going to buy me a set of wheels like this."

"Who knows, you might grow up to be the president, right?" Palmer said. "Then you could afford any car you wanted."

"Like Mr. Demic."

God forbid, Palmer thought.

"Say, where's your girlfriend? I saw you walking with her," Palmer said.

"She had to go shopping with her mom. The stores are open tonight."

"You need a lift somewhere?"

"As a matter of fact I do. I just live a few miles out of town, and I'd appreciate a ride."

"Hop in."

The boy jumped in eagerly. Palmer looked around one more time for the blue Camaro before getting in. He fumbled in his pocket for the keys.

"Boy this car's worth its weight in gold," the kid said.

Gold. "Hell. I left my lighter in the research room." Palmer got out of the car, leaving his keys on the seat. "I'll only be a minute."

"Sure. Take your time."

When Palmer came back out of the newspaper office with his lighter, he saw that the boy had slid over on the driver's side and was pretending to be driving, turning the wheel back and forth. "Go ahead, start it up," Palmer said. "The keys are on the seat."

"Oh boy."

Palmer started down the steps, thinking about his first car, a twelve-year-old Chevy Impala he had bought in college. He paused a moment to remember the old junk, which he had repainted silver with a black racing stripe, and it was that hesitation which probably saved his life. A mighty explosion ripped through the Mercedes, the force of it hitting Palmer like a giant hammer. He was hurled off his feet and back onto the steps. His right shoulder hit the cement a second before his head did, cushioning the blow. He remember seeing a detached arm burning on the sidewalk and wondered whether it was his own before he passed out.

SEVEN

The story made the front page in the early edition of the *Los Angeles Times,* and later was given prominent play inside. Both UPI and AP put it out on their night wires within three hours of the incident, and since Palmer was a best-selling author, most major dailies across the country gave it a good ride. Translations of Palmer's first best seller had sold well in France, Germany, England, and Switzerland, so papers in those countries also picked it up from Reuters. On a day in which news was slow out of Iran and Iraq and no planes crashed, word of the attempted rub-out of a politically controversial author was hot stuff.

The edition of the *Los Angeles Times* which Daniel Johnson flipped through over breakfast carried a three-column headline which read:

AUTHOR PALMER ESCAPES
ASSASSINATION ATTEMPT

The story was not Johnson's cup of tea, and he was about to pass it over when his eye was caught by the dateline. He immediately put down his toast, got up from the table and took the paper and his lukewarm coffee into his study. Being used to his strange moods, his wife shrugged and continued to eat her soft-boiled eggs.

In the study, Daniel Johnson spread the paper out on his desk and carefully read the story. When he had finished it once, he read it again, and after playing over the ramifications in his mind, he scanned it a third time. Each instance, he came to the same conclusion. Daniel Johnson knew his life would never be the same.

Johnson got up and walked over to a shelf of books and pulled three out to expose a small wall safe. He worked the combination, swung the door open, and slid out a manila envelope which he took back to his desk. There was a typewritten page inside, which Johnson now read. The letter, dated March twenty-second, 1953, was addressed to Joseph Demic Jr. from the dean of admissions of Harvard University, and it told of his acceptance to the college. Tears suddenly filled Daniel Johnson's eyes. He put the document back in the envelope and placed it in the safe.

Once more he read the *Los Angeles Times* story, hoping to find a different meaning. But his conclusion was the same. Daniel Johnson had read both of Alex Palmer's books. If Palmer had shown up in Joseph Demic's home town, he sure as hell wasn't there to write a cover piece for *Ladies' Home Journal*. He had to be on the trail of some dirt, and there was only one scandal about Joe Demic worth attempting murder over, and that was the truth about the switch. How Palmer had discovered it, God only knows, but Johnson was sure the writer had done it. It was only a matter of time before the trail led to Daniel Johnson and then the Russians would finish the job they had botched so many years ago.

Johnson knew he had to do something. First he must learn how much Palmer was on to. It was possible that Palmer knew Joe Demic was a Russian agent, but not about the switch of twins. Johnson had to find out fast without tipping his hand.

The idea came in a flash. Johnson grabbed paper and pen. Slowly, trying to keep his hand from shaking, Johnson began to write: Dear Mr. Palmer . . . He stopped writing and crumpled the paper up. A telegram would be faster. He got up and headed for the door.

EIGHT

Palmer pretended he was asleep, but the nurse wouldn't buy it.

"Really, Mr. Palmer. If you expect to get well, you're going to have to start eating some food."

The nurse came over and stood by Palmer's bed.

"I've worked at hospitals where the food was a lot worse, Mr. Palmer. You should try to eat." Palmer didn't move. "Okay, Mr. Palmer. If you want to starve to death, it's your business."

Opening one eye slightly, Palmer saw the nurse pick up the untouched lunch tray and walk out. When she was gone, Palmer sat up in bed, wincing from pain in his shoulder and a dozen other places. It was easier to feign sleep than to tell the nurse why he hadn't eaten since he was carted in here the night before. He did not want her to know he was afraid of being poisoned. He had a tough enough time accepting it himself. He knew his normal level of paranoia had gotten out of control, but he didn't care. Maybe if he had been a little more paranoid last night, that boy would still be alive. Palmer felt sick recalling the awful explosion and the burning arm he had seen on the sidewalk. For a moment, he had thought the arm was his own, but later, regaining consciousness in the hospital, he had found all limbs intact.

Palmer recalled those first moments when he awoke in the hospital. Pain was everywhere. When he remembered the explosion, he immediately reached for his groin. It was all intact. Funny, he would have bet that a man regaining consciousness after an explosion would first check his arms and legs. The nurse, a Miss Tabley, had come in a few minutes later carrying a folder, which she spread open on the bed.

"No breaks, no internal bleeding, your right shoulder isn't dislocated, you have a dozen nasty bruises, but other than that, you seem to have come out of it in good shape. You're a lucky man, Mr. Palmer," the nurse had said.

Lucky man. Palmer laughed wryly. Sure he had survived the bomb, but so what. They'd get him next time. Now that they knew he was on to something, they'd make sure they didn't botch the job a second time. There was a death warrant out for him, and no place in America was safe. Certainly not this damned hospital. A single policeman had been stationed outside Palmer's private room. A lot of good that would do against the combined forces of the CIA, KGB, or who ever else was trying to get him. Food poisoning was just one of a dozen ways they could kill him. That's why he had refused to eat. Injections was another. Palmer had not permitted anyone to give him a needle, nor would he take painkillers.

Schuyler had flown in to see him in the morning. The White House counsel had looked grim and shaken. Palmer thought he detected the odor of whiskey. Paranoid about being bugged, Palmer had put the TV on loud and forced Schuyler to come up close and whisper. The whole atmosphere—with the armed guard at the door, Palmer bruised and bedridden, the TV blaring, and the two old friends whispering—seemed nightmarish.

"Who do you think did it?" Schuyler had asked, and Palmer had only laughed at the question. "Okay, supposing it was . . . him, how do we prove it?"

Palmer told Schuyler all he knew, and as he whispered the details, Schuyler's face grew pale. Mr. Unshakable seemed to be falling apart.

"We need definitive proof before Monday," Schuyler said. "That's when the president meets with Rublov at Camp David. I don't have to tell you what a disaster such a meeting would be from the standpoint of national security. No secret would be safe."

Palmer nodded. It was Thursday. That meant they had four days to topple a president. Four days. Christ.

"And if we don't find proof by Monday?" Palmer said.

"Then we're dead. This whole country is dead."

An hour later Schuyler left. Palmer had tried to sleep, but the combination of pain and thinking about the kid who had died in his place kept him awake until he heard the lunch cart being rolled down the corridor, and then he had closed his eyes and feigned sleep.

Palmer's thoughts were interrupted by the nurse again.

"Mr. Palmer, the sheriff is here to see you."

Palmer decided to open his eyes. The nurse gave him a frown, turned on her heels and walked out. The sheriff came in a moment later.

"Palmer, I'm Sheriff Keegan. I'd like to ask you some questions, if you think you're up to it."

"Okay. Sit down."

The sheriff had the look of a marine drill sargeant: compact of flesh, tight-lipped, short-haired, cold blue eyes, and an attitude of thinly disguised contempt for whatever it was that he thought the Alex Palmers of the world stood for. The sheriff leaned against the hard edge of the windowsill, and took out pad and pen.

"Any enemies, Palmer?"

"Have you read my book about the presidents, Sheriff Keegan?" Palmer said.

"Yes," the sheriff said, without expression.

"Well then I'm sure you know there are at least a half million God-fearing, righteous citizens, people like yourself, perhaps, who would love to see me hanged or decapitated. The bombing was probably the work of some nut."

"Nuts don't wire cars to explode, Palmer. Professionals do."

"So okay, some rich, right-wing nut hired a professional to do the job."

The sheriff wrote something down before continuing.

"What brings you to Long River, Palmer?"

"Business."

"Meaning?"

"I'm writing a book on the president."

"What sort of book?"

"A biography."

The sheriff displayed the same disbelieving look both Jolly Harper and the dentist had.

"And this . . . biography, it was the reason you were down at the newspaper office?" the sheriff asked.

"Yes. I was doing research, using back issues."

"I see. What particular sort of thing were you researching?"

"Sports. I was reading up on the president's exploits in football."

"The football-hero angle, huh?" the sheriff said, heavy with sarcasm. "And where did you meet the boy?"

"He was outside standing by my car, and asked me for a lift."

"You always pick up strangers?"

"No. Only when I'm in a friendly little town like Long River."

The sheriff nodded, his steel-blue eyes searching.

"You see anything suspicious, either going into the office, or going out?"

"As a matter of fact, I did. When I went in, I thought a man parked across the street in a blue Camaro was watching me."

"Did you get the license plate?"

"No. I didn't really think it was anything to get concerned about at the time."

"Getting blown up is something to be concerned about, Palmer. Having an innocent boy die in your place is something to be concerned about."

The sheriff's contempt for Palmer rose to the surface, jaw muscles twitching violently.

"You're right, sheriff. Next time I think I'm about to be blown up, I'll take notes."

Putting his pen and pad down on the windowsill with

a deliberate motion, the sheriff stared hard at Palmer.

"Lookit Palmer, if you think this whole thing is such a joke, why don't I just leave and take that officer at the door—a public employee who is being paid overtime by the taxpayers—with me."

"Is that a threat?"

For a moment, Palmer thought the man would charge him. The sheriff had a good lid on himself, however. He drilled Palmer with a fierce look, capped his pen, stuck it in his shirt pocket and said, "As soon as you're able, Mr. Palmer, leave my town. Don't linger." Then he walked out.

"What did you say to our beloved sheriff, Mr. Palmer?" the nurse said, entering the room. "He left in quite a huff. Almost knocked me over." A smile crossed her face for the first time.

"Nothing." Palmer shrugged. "I think he took the whole thing personally. You know, smart-ass writer comes to his town to get himself blown up on purpose, ruins his night. That sort of thing. I tried to be as helpful as possible."

"I'll bet."

"Is the guard still there?" Palmer asked out of curiosity.

"Yes. Why?"

"Oh nothing."

The nurse turned to leave, then stopped.

"Oh. I almost forgot. This telegram came for you." She took it out of her hip pocket. "Must be from one of your adoring fans."

"I have no fans, just beloved enemies, Miss Tabley."

Palmer opened the telegram and read it.

SORRY TO HEAR WHAT HAPPENED
TO YOU STOP LONG RIVER IS A STRANGE
TOWN STOP I LEFT IT 2 YEARS AGO BE-
CAUSE I COULDN'T FACE UP TO MY
BROTHER STOP BEST OF LUCK

ABEL KANE
26 SAN PULO DRIVE
SANTA MONICA

Nice to hear from you, Mr. Abel Kane, Palmer thought, shrugging. He crumpled the telegram and hurled it across the room into a wastebasket. Nuts. The world is filled with nuts. And I attract them. Why me?

Palmer knew, of course, but today he preferred to feel like a martyr: noble, crusading writer, victim of a vicious, senseless attack . . . etc. etc. ad nauseum. Palmer had agreed to meet with reporters at three o'clock. That left him another hour to kill. Not a blasted thing to do, either, except watch TV. He should have asked the nurse to buy some magazines. At least in hotels there were Bibles to read in desperate moments.

It didn't come in a flash. The thought process was much slower. The word Bible triggered a remembrance of Sunday School lessons. A dirty joke about Adam and Eve which a boyhood friend had told him followed next, and then something about the mythical Adam and Eve characters made him think of another Bible pair — Cain and Abel. And that's when he bolted up in bed.

"Jesus Christ!" he said out loud. "Cain and Abel. One good, the other evil. Twins. Abel Kane."

Palmer bounced out of bed, then nearly doubled over from the pain in his shoulder. "Shit." He moved more slowly across the room and retrieved the telegram from Abel Kane. Back on the bed, he smoothed it out and read it again. His heart pounded as the vague telegram became crystal clear. He stabbed the buzzer for the nurse.

"Mr. Palmer?"

"I need paper and pencil. I want to send a telegram."

"My, but you suddenly look much better, Mr. Palmer. The color seems to have returned to your face and—"

"Now, Miss Tabley. I need the paper now."

The nurse made a face but wheeled around and left, returning two minutes later with pad and pen.

"Please wait, Miss Tabley. I want to send this off immediately, if you don't mind."

"Well, it's not exactly part of my nursing duties, seeing that telegrams are sent, but for a distinguished author like you," the nurse said coldly, "I suppose I can make an exception."

"Thanks." Palmer didn't glance up to catch the nasty look. He wrote:

THANKS FOR THE GOOD WISHES STOP HOW'S YOUR BROTHER DOING
ALEX PALMER

When he had finished, he gave it to the nurse, his face flush with excitement. The nurse headed for the door.

"Before you go, Miss Tabley. Is it possible for me to get some food? I think I'm going to need my strength."

The nurse shrugged.

"I'll see what I can do."

NINE

A half-hour after the nurse had left, a teenaged girl came with a tray from the employee cafeteria. There was a bowl of greasy vegetable soup, a small salad with a milky glob of blue cheese dressing, a plate of soggy fried chicken surrounded by overcooked peas and corn niblets, a small carton of milk, and a strawberry jello with pieces of canned fruit. Palmer wolfed it all down. An hour after he had eaten and had finished talking with a half dozen reporters, the phone rang.

"Hello? Mr. Palmer? This is Nurse Tabley."

"Hi. Thanks for the food. It was yummy," Palmer lied.

"I just called to tell you that I stopped on my way home and sent your telegram. It was fifty-three cents more than you gave me. I laid out the money for you."

"Miss Tabley, you're a doll."

"Yes, I'm sure, Mr. Palmer. Goodbye."

Eight hours later the nurse on the night shift, a Mrs. Thornbuck, tiptoed into Alex Palmer's room while he was sleeping and left a telegram on his night table. It wasn't until the next morning that Palmer, having slept deeply with the aid of a pain-killing drug, discovered the telegram, which he ripped open immediately.

MY BROTHER IS DOING GREAT STOP HE IS PRESIDENT OF A BIG CORPORATION WHICH OPERATES IN THE RED

ABEL KANE

Palmer leaped out of bed, felt a sharp twinge in his left shoulder and wolfed down a painkiller. In minutes, he was dressed. His clothes were wrinkled and dirty and he looked like hell, but it was better than showing up in Los Angeles wearing a white hospital gown. He phoned for a cab, stuffed the vial of painkillers in his pocket and raced for the door, where he ran smack into Miss Tabley.

"MISTER PALMER! What on earth do you think you're doing?"

"Checking out."

"You can't do that. This is not a hotel. You have to be cleared by the doctor and—"

Palmer was winging down the hall before Miss Tabley could finish, the sheriff's guard standing next to her, puzzled.

"He can't do that," the nurse said indignantly to the policeman. "Stop him."

"The boss told me not to let anybody into his room. Didn't say nothing about letting the nut out."

TEN

He was an old man now and he spent most of his time reading by the fire. His *dacha* was small but comfortable and a boy came from the village each Tuesday with groceries and a bottle of cognac. It was pleasant to have a visitor, and Boris would make hot chocolate for Vladimir, who reminded him of Yuri. Vladimir seemed to enjoy the visits, too, and always stayed long enough to chop firewood for Boris, which he piled on the back porch so the old man would not have to tramp through the snow. Once, on a day when Boris had had too much cognac, he thought of telling Vladimir about Yuri, who had been like a son to him, but he had fallen asleep in his easy chair, and when he awoke, Vladimir was gone.

It was just as well, of course. Although he had been retired for twelve years, Boris was still bound by the Official Secrets Act, and Yuri Demichev's story was the single most important secret in the Soviet Union. No one could have guessed at the outset how high Yuri would rise in the United States government. Who but a fool would have suggested that a Soviet spy could become president of the United States? When Yuri had become second in command of the CIA, no less than Col. Alexsandyr Yanov, head of the KGB, had come personally to congratulate Boris. It had been the high point of Boris's life, and he was only saddened by the fact that Anton, his fellow worker in the project, had not lived to see the day. Anton, the healthy one, had died of leukemia, while Boris, Tums and all, had managed to live on to old age.

There were more pats on the back when Yuri was elected to the United States Senate, and again Boris's chest had swelled. But when John Pierson had chosen Yuri as his running mate, and they had swept into the White House, Boris was suddenly filled with apprehension. What if something happened to Pierson? That would make Yuri Demichev, a Soviet spy, president of the second most powerful nation in the world. Could the KGB dare allow Boris to remain alive with that secret? How easily Boris could imagine the discussion in KGB headquarters:

"Something must be done about Boris. He knows too much. It is a great risk."

"But Boris has been an honored comrade, a trusted one. He has never talked of the project before."

"Yes. But he is an old man now, and old men wag their tongues with age. He must be dealt with."

Boris had spent several anxiety-filled weeks waiting for the agents to come. It was an odd experience. At first he had been terrified by the thought of death, but as the weeks went on, he seemed to make a peace with himself, reviving his long suppressed feelings about Christ and the Church, and he was no longer afraid.

After the weeks had turned into months, and nothing had happened, Boris began to grasp an intriguing possibility: He may be more valuable to them alive than dead. The simple truth of it made him laugh out loud. He may be a security risk, but should something happen to Yuri, Boris was the one man still alive who could prove that the Soviet Union had planted the ultimate mole. In the event of Yuri's death, Boris would be marched out in public to tell his tale, the details so intimate it would be hard to doubt the truth of his words.

That is why on this day when the phone call came from the official at KGB headquarters, Boris's heart did not miss a beat, as it might have done months ago.

The official had asked Boris if he was strong enough to make a trip to headquarters and when Boris replied yes, he was told a Zil would be dispatched to pick him up. Boris had hung up slowly. Although he had nothing to fear, being summoned to KGB headquarters still made him uneasy. Perhaps something had happened to Yuri. But that would be impossible. Despite the strict censorship of news from the United States, even *Pravda* would not suppress word of the death of an American president. It must be something else. But what?

Boris dressed carefully for the trip. He did not want to look too prosperous, and at the same time he felt a person of his distinction should wear something a cut above the masses. He selected a conservative pair of wool slacks, but wore his best British boots and an American-made tweed overcoat. For his head, he chose an unstylish black fur hat made in Moscow, one he hadn't worn for years. When the knock came on his door, he found, much to his displeasure, that he was startled. He forced himself to appear calm, and tried to start light conversation with the two low-ranking KGB officials who picked him up. The almost rude way they brushed him off further served to make Boris anxious, however, so that by the time he was ushered into Colonel Yanov's office, a feeling of dread had crept in.

"Sit down, Boris," KGB Director Yanov said without a greeting. "This is Captain Lazishvili, head of our American division."

Boris nodded at the captain, a lean, athletic-looking man in his mid-forties with a black patch over his left eye and a shaved head. The man reminded Boris of the Israeli, Moishe Dayan. A dangerous look to cultivate, Boris thought.

"I'm sorry to have dragged you out of your comfortable *dacha* at this time of the year," Colonel Yanov said without emotion, "but a matter of extreme importance has come up."

"Is it about Yuri?" Boris blurted out too quickly.

The KGB director paused before answering, a slight smile at one corner of his mouth.

"Yes. It is about Yuri, as you call him. Joseph Demic."

"Has something happened to him?" Boris said, leaning forward, nervous fingers kneading his fur hat.

"I think this meeting will proceed better if you permit us to ask the questions, Boris," the colonel said.

"Of course, Colonel Yanov, of course."

Boris felt a spasm in his stomach. Acid began dripping. He reached in his pants for a roll of Tums.

"Still bothered by the stomach pains?" the colonel

asked.

"Yes. It's not so bad now that I've retired, but I still have problems from time to time."

"The Americans, they're good with these sort of remedies?" the colonel asked, nodding at the Tums. Boris wondered if he had errored displaying the American product in the KGB director's office.

"Yes. Not really so much better than our own products, but my stomach seems to have gotten used to these over the years."

"They give us the pains, then provide the best remedies, huh?" Colonel Yanov said. Boris was not sure whether the KGB director had made a joke, but when he saw the captain smile, he quickly joined in with a short, weak laugh. The colonel seemed to stare off for a moment. He was a handsome man in his late forties, with high cheek bones and a swarthy complexion. Like an American Indian, Boris thought, except for the deep blue eyes.

"The reason I've called you here," the colonel said, "is that a problem has come up in Joseph Demic's home town. Captain Lazishvili will explain it to you."

Boris swung around to face the captain, noticing a folder on his lap. Lazishvili began in a toneless, dry voice, imitative of the KGB director's, but much more high-pitched, almost feminine. The captain's eye was the exact shade of blue as the colonel's, and Boris wondered if the man wore a colored contact lense. He's eager to please, a weak emotional makeup, but probably very bright and ruthless. The psychologist in Boris went to work. It made him feel more comfortable to analyze, so he continued to study the man professionally as he listened.

". . . and our permanent man in place happens to be friends with this dentist, a Dr. Coles, and it was from him that he learned there was a writer in town asking questions about Joseph Demic."

"So?" Boris interrupted boldly, his confidence returning. "Is it not natural for American writers to track down their president's life history? We have covered all trails, we have nothing to fear from a biographer."

"Alex Palmer is not a biographer," Colonel Yanov said, a cold edge to his voice. He tossed a copy of Palmer's *Dirty Tricks* across the room. The loud smack it made landing at Boris's feet, shook the old man's confidence again. "Alex Palmer, as you can see, is a dirt-digger, Boris."

Boris glanced at the inside flap of the dust jacket, sweat forming on his forehead as he read silently: ". . . and author Palmer reveals in this extraordinary investigative study that dirty tricks in the White House did not begin with Richard Milhouse Nixon. Far from it. President Hoover . . ."

Boris got up on unsteady legs and put the book on Colonel Yanov's desk, then returned to his seat.

"Still," Boris said weakly, "what can he possibly hope to discover. Certainly he has no idea of the switch we made. He is probably looking for some scandal in the president's past, a cheerleader he knocked up, something like that."

"Why then," the colonel began, blue eyes boring into Boris, "is he interested in dental records?"

"Dental records?" Boris gulped.

"Yes. Palmer asked Dr. Coles for Joseph Demic's records. You are aware, of course, what that means?"

Boris nodded, stunned. The acid did a slow burn

down his stomach, but he dared not pull out the Tums again.

"Rest assured, of course, that Palmer's little inquiry proved fruitless," the KGB director said. "The records were removed long ago."

"Brilliant," Boris croaked, trying to flatter. "The agent is to be congratulated."

"Think so?" Colonel Yanov said. He picked up a piece of paper. "On this sheet are orders to liquidate the agent in Long River immediately."

"But why, colonel?"

"Because, acting on his own, the agent tried to kill Palmer. Not only didn't he succeed, but he ended up calling international attention to the incident. Every newspaper in the United States carried a story on it, as did papers in France, Germany, England, and Switzerland."

Boris licked his dry lips, his stomach on fire.

"What can I do to help?" Boris said.

"I want you to speculate on how this Palmer might have gotten on the trail of our operation."

"But colonel, there is no possible way. At least none that I can think of. Every precaution was taken," Boris said quickly.

"What about Yuri's tutors?"

"Each one was eliminated as his or her usefulness to us ended," Boris said, recalling the young, screaming faces that still interrupted his sleep from time to time. "Even the girl Yuri ran off with to Moscow. She, too, was . . . eliminated."

"Tell me again about the twin," the colonel said. "Tell me everything you recall about the switch in Long River."

The colonel leaned forward intently as Boris related the details of the car accident and the burning of the farm house. When Boris had finished, the colonel thought for a few moments before speaking.

"Is it not possible that this twin survived the crash?"

"I do not see how. And if he did, would he not already have surfaced?"

"Yes. It is unlikely he would have stood by so long and watched a Soviet agent, his brother, rise so high in government. Still, the fact that the twin's body was never recovered is a weakness in the scheme, don't you think?" The colonel looked at his captain.

"Well, I think perhaps it might have been at the beginning, but not now," Captain Lazishvili said.

"Why?"

"Because at the start, if the twin—presuming he survived the accident—had come forward and exposed Yuri, our whole project would have been wasted. But now, we have reaped much from Yuri's actions over the years. And even should he be exposed, think what havoc that would cause in America. The shock waves would be incredible, not to mention the loss of confidence among America's allies. We have only to look at the British experience with Philby to see how costly such an exposure would be, and the Philby incident was comparatively nothing next to this."

"A good point, captain. We seem to have the Americans by the balls."

Seeing a smile cross the colonel's face, Boris began to breathe easier.

"Still," the colonel said, "we'll have to keep our eye on this Palmer character."

"What method did the agent use to try and kill him?"

Boris asked.

"He attempted to blow him up. Instead, he killed an innocent boy. Palmer escaped with only some minor bruises." The colonel picked up Palmer's book, leaned back in his chair and studied the dust jacket with obvious distaste. "Too bad . . ."

"Too bad, colonel?" Boris said.

"Yes. Too bad he didn't kill Palmer."

Col. Alexsandr Yanov, Director of the KGB, dumped Palmer's book into the waste basket.

ELEVEN

"Another drink, general?"

Jamie Worthington lifted his empty glass and shrugged.

"Why not," the general growled. "Here."

David Schuyler took the glass over to his bar. The general was losing his patience, and who could blame him. Palmer had said he'd show up at noon — High Noon, as Palmer had dramatically called it — and it was now ten after one. It had taken quite a bit of pleading on Schuyler's part to tear the general away from the White House, and Palmer was really screwing things up.

"Where the hell is this Palmer character, anyway?" the general said.

"Flying in from California. I guess his plane was delayed." Schuyler handed a gin and tonic to the general, sat down on the couch, and nervously sipped his own Johnny Red and soda.

"Well, I don't understand why you can't tell me what this is all about. There's a major crisis in the Middle East, the nation may be on the brink of nuclear war, and you drag me out to your house to sip cocktails in the middle of the day, waiting for some nutty writer friend of yours."

"I don't know any more about it than you do," Schuyler lied. "All I know is that when Alex Palmer tells me he has to see us on a matter of extreme national importance, I have to respond. Palmer would not say something like that lightly."

Schuyler watched while the General sipped his drink, stewing. Schuyler had only partially lied. He knew a great deal about what Palmer was up to, but not why he had called this meeting. Palmer had phoned from Los Angeles to say he would be flying in today. He had requested the meeting with General Worthington, but refused to say anything further over the phone. Secrecy and paranoia were nothing new with Palmer, and normally Schuyler would have balked unless he got further information. But ever since someone had attempted to blow Palmer up, Schuyler had begun to come unraveled. None of the rules that had governed Schuyler's life now had any significance. Schuyler had taken pride in acting the public servant, and had always been careful to maintain the sort of life he considered worthy of a president's counsel. But what kind of president had he been serving? If Joseph Demic was a Russian agent, then hadn't Schuyler actually been serving the Soviet cause?

"Has the president outlined his plans for the summit?"

Schuyler asked, trying to drum up conversation.

"Yeh. More or less. You know Demic. Tells you only so much. Sort of like your friend, Palmer, huh?"

Schuyler nodded. "What's the itinerary?"

"After the UN meeting Monday, the president and Rublov will fly to Washington and then on to Camp David by helicopter."

"And then what?"

"And then they'll sit down in front of a Hammond globe, and the distinguished president of the Soviet Union will point a finger at one section of the world and say in English, 'Mine.' And the president of the United States will shake his head and say, '*Verboten*.' Then the distinguished Soviet president will point to the spot again and reiterate his demand, to which Demic will say *verboten* once more. At that point, Rublov will pick up the globe, smash it on the floor and storm out, leaving Demic with a dented world."

"That bad, huh?"

"That bad."

The general drew on his drink again.

"Why so pessimistic?" Schuyler asked.

"Because Rublov is in a bind at home. He desperately needs a show of force to stabilize his power, and he apparently has chosen Iraq as the battlefield. How much nicer it would be if he could be lured into Czechoslovakia, where dissidents are causing problems again."

"Seeing Czechoslovakia squashed would not sit well with the American public, either."

"But there is every indication Czechoslovakia would not get plowed under. The workers and students are very well organized. It would be a long and messy battle, a European Vietnam, if you will. That would certainly be enough to topple Rublov and pave the way for the Russian moderates."

"But —"

The doorbell rang. Schuyler bounced up and opened it.

Palmer hadn't shaved, his clothes looked wrinkled, but his eyes were bright and alert. Behind him was a man with a beard.

"Hello David," Palmer said.

"My God, Alex, it's about time. You've kept the general waiting over an hour. And who's this?" Schuyler pointed toward the bearded man, who wore dungarees and a leather jacket.

"This is Daniel Johnson," Palmer said.

"Well come in, come in. Don't stand out there."

Schuyler led them into the living room where the general, having drained the last of his gin and tonic, was sucking on the lime.

"General Worthington, this is Alex Palmer, and his, uh, friend Daniel Jackson."

"Johnson," Palmer said with a smile. "He drives a Budweiser beer truck in L.A."

Schuyler stared at Palmer. He had something up his sleeve, that was obvious. Why else the shit-eating grin? And who the hell was this Johnson character? A truck driver. Christ! The general's going to chew my ass real good if this is some kind of joke.

"Well, Mr. Palmer, I can't say it's a pleasure meeting you," the general said. "I've read your first book. I think the American presidency deserved a fairer shake. But I guess we all have to make a living. It's just that some of us do it in a more honorable fashion. And now, if you'll explain why you've interrupted my busy schedule."

279

"I'm sorry I had to drag you out here, general, but before I'm done, I'm sure you'll consider the trip quite worthwhile."

Schuyler glanced at Daniel Johnson, who was stroking his beard nervously. Damn if the man isn't familiar, Schuyler thought.

"On the flight here from Los Angeles," Palmer began, "I tried to think of the best way to explain to you what I've uncovered in my research for a new book. It's rather extraordinary, and frankly, a little unbelievable." Palmer paused to see what effect his opening words had. The general showed nothing. "I have discovered a scandal of astonishing proportions, one which will dwarf Watergate."

"Dwarf Watergate?" the general said, sitting forward suddenly. "What on earth could you have uncovered more of a national disgrace than that?"

Without answering, Palmer stood and walked over to the fireplace, staring at the unlit logs. The general glanced at Daniel Johnson. The truck driver also looked familiar to Worthington.

"General," Palmer said, turning around, "there's really only one way to explain all this to you. They say a picture is worth a thousand words, and in this case I think the cliche applies. I'd like you to follow me and my friend Daniel upstairs, and in a few minutes you'll understand why I called you here."

Palmer turned to Johnson. "Daniel? Are you ready?" Johnson nodded and got to his feet. "Gentlemen," Palmer said. "Would you follow me?"

Schuyler stood up. The general remained seated.

"General, I promise you this will be worth your while. Allow me my little theatrics."

General Worthington glared first at Palmer, then at the bearded, fidgety truck driver. Their eyes made contact. What the general saw was fear, the kind of terrified look he had seen on men at the front. Either they broke moments later, or else they performed great acts of heroism. The fact that the bearded man's fear had something to do with Palmer's discovery suddenly filled the general with dread. He stood up.

"All right, Palmer. I'm following. Lead the way."

Palmer motioned for Johnson to start upstairs. "Make a right at the top of the stairs. It's the first room down on the left," Palmer said.

"What's he going to do in my bedroom?" Schuyler asked.

"Bathroom," Palmer said. "He needs to use your bathroom."

"There's one downstairs."

"It's not properly equipped."

"Properly equipped? What the hell—"

"Patience, David, patience. You'll know soon enough."

Daniel Johnson crossed the master bedroom and stepped into the bathroom, closing the door behind him.

"Now, gentlemen, we wait," Palmer said.

"For what?" Schuyler said, annoyed.

"For my friend to get done."

Schuyler heard water running in the bathroom.

"What's he doing? Taking a bath?"

"No. Shaving."

"Palmer, have you lost your mind?" Schuyler said.

"Years ago."

Schuyler felt the general's restraining hand on his

shoulder.

"Be still, David. Let him play it out," the general said.

Palmer looked at Worthington. Has the general guessed already? Palmer could read nothing in his eyes.

"Well, if I have to play along with this, I'm going to be comfortable while I wait." Schuyler plopped down on his bed, kicked his shoes off, and stared at the ceiling. The general leaned against a dresser, watching Palmer.

"Do you believe in all the stuff you write?" the general asked Palmer.

"Did you believe in all the battles you fought?" Palmer shot back. The general smiled.

"No, I suppose not."

"Me neither. I know you'll find this hard to believe, but in a lot of instances I felt quite bad about some of the people I had to attack."

"Then why did you do it?"

"Simply because I thought it would be more unjust to stand in judgment over which public figures deserved to be spared and which didn't. You either shoot 'em all down, or you keep your pistol holstered."

The general nodded. The water was still running in the bathroom.

"A lot of your stuff is inaccurate," Worthington said.

"Probably. It can't be helped."

"You sound like an artillery captain explaining why some of his shells landed on civilian villages."

Palmer was about to reply when the water stopped running. Schuyler sat up in bed.

"You done, Daniel?" Palmer asked, close to the door. A muffled yes came from behind it.

Palmer stood back so they would have a good view. The doorknob turned and there was a moment's hesitation before it swung open. When Daniel Johnson stepped out cleanshaven, even Palmer gasped.

"Jeeessuss . . ." the general hissed. It was incredible.

"I think we'd better all go downstairs and have a drink," Palmer said shakily, unable to tear his eyes from the truck driver from Los Angeles. "Daniel Johnson has a very interesting story he'd like you to hear."

TWELVE

Johnson talked and they listened. It took an hour. When he was done, he heaved a sigh and seemed to shrink into the chair. A great weight had been lifted. The relief showed on his face in an almost imperceptible softening of muscle tissue. Palmer, like Schuyler and the general, had kept his eyes riveted on Johnson throughout his monologue, amazed at what he saw. Except for the slightly paler color of the cheeks, the man was Joseph Demic. Palmer could find nothing to break the spell. Even the voice was hauntingly the same — soft, yet carrying weight. Palmer would not have been surprised if the man had stood up and said: "I'm really the president. This is all a joke."

"And Alex says Charlene Lowenstein had a picture taken in Russia of this Yuri," Schuyler said.

"What happened to it?" the general asked.

Palmer explained how Charlene had shown the photograph to the president just hours before she was killed in the car crash.

"Coincidence," the general said weakly.

"You think so?" Palmer said, a cold edge to his voice.

"I don't know. My God I don't know anything anymore," the general said.

"Why didn't you speak up all these years?" Schuyler asked Johnson.

"Fear," Johnson said. "I was afraid they would kill me."

"What's to prevent them from doing it now?" the general said.

"Nothing."

"Then I don't understand."

"The difference," Johnson said slowly, patiently, "is that I no longer care. I am already partially dead. If a man spends years trying to kill certain things in himself—ambition, hopes, desire—he eventually succeeds. Like my father, I have lived a life I am unsuited for, and like him, I have paid a steep price for it. My son is somewhat embarrassed by me and my wife thinks it's a failing in her that I won't open up and reveal more of myself. How could I have told her what I am—a coward, a man who has put his own self preservation over the welfare of millions of people. It is only since I have come forward, that I feel somewhat like a man again. You know," Johnson said, drawing deep on his whiskey, "I was terrified at first when I heard what had happened to Alex in Long River. I feared that the path would finally lead to my door. And then, after a while, the thought that the charade was finally over filled me with an enormous sense of relief. I was damn glad it was over. I sat down in my study and cried. So many things came flooding back, so many memories. From that moment, there was only one path open to me. That is why I contacted Alex Palmer, that is why I am here today."

"You are a very brave man, to have done so," the general said softly.

"No. I am merely a man with very little left to lose. Twenty-five years ago I might have been a hero. Even ten years ago, when my brother left the CIA and first ran for public office, I might have been a hero. Now I am merely doing what is demanded of me. There is no room left to refuse. I have to act."

"And how will you act?" the general said. "What will you do? Or should I say, what will we do? Christ, so many things about Demic suddenly become clear. Now I know why he was so eager to meet with Rublov on Monday. Do you have any idea of the secrets he could hand over in a head-to-head confrontation? Missile sites. Defense capabilities. Why just the other day Demic ordered me to set in motion a new blueprint for evacuating this country's top officials in the event of nuclear war. I objected, naturally, that such plans would have a devastating effect if they fell into enemy hands, but Demic brushed me aside. I was angry at first, later puzzled. Now I understand perfectly. We must prevent Joseph Demic—or this Yuri—from meeting with Rublov, and we have only three days to do it. Any suggestions?"

"Daniel will have to go public," Schuyler said.

"And what would that accomplish?" Worthington said.

"It would prevent Demic from meeting with Rublov, wouldn't it?" Schuyler said.

"Oh sure. But at an awful price," the general said.

"What do you mean?"

"Do you have any idea how it would affect the American public if it was suddenly told that the man sitting in the White House, a former CIA official, was a Soviet spy? Do you think this country—any country—could survive such a shock? How could our government ask any citizen to have confidence in it after such a revelation? What official would be above suspicion? And what about our allies? Could there be any basis for trust anymore? No, David, having Daniel Johnson come forward with this story would be the worst thing we could do."

"Then what?"

The general looked at Palmer.

"Well, Mr. Palmer? I'm sure you must have some plan. The very fact that you're here and not sitting before your typewriter pounding out an exposé tells me as much. It must have been very hard for you to have passed over profit and notoriety for patriotic duty."

"Not as hard as you might think. And yes, I do have a plan, general. How well do you know former CIA Director Holmes?"

"Quite well."

"Well enough to ask a favor?"

"Of course. What favor?"

"I want you to ask him to kill the president of the United States."

THIRTEEN

It was Friday, October twenty-ninth. Palmer's eyes slid down the front page of the *Washington Post,* but he wasn't really reading. A voice announced an arriving plane from Chicago. Palmer glanced at his watch. There were still forty-five minutes before their scheduled departure to LaGuardia. Already the seats at gate twenty-two were jammed, which meant it would be a typical sprint to New York: elbow-to-elbow, barely time to wolf down a drink. Palmer looked across at Worthington. The general had insisted on taking a commercial plane in order to avoid questions. "You never know what government official is tied in to what reporter," the general had said. "If I go and requisition a plane, some hotshot news hound is bound to ask, 'What's the president's top aide hopping to New York for when the heat's on in Washington?' "

So they had booked a flight on Eastern and driven to the airport in Schuyler's car. The general, wearing dark glasses and a London Fog he'd borrowed from Schuyler, looked like a spy, but at least no one would suspect he was the president's number one man in the White House. Schuyler, rarely photographed, needed no disguise. Johnson, however, was a problem. It had taken the better part of an afternoon for Palmer to track down a stage director friend in Georgetown who had supplied him with a realistic-looking beard.

Palmer tried to read the *Post* again. Three top officials in Tehran had been assassinated in separate bombings. The Iranians were calling it the work of Iraqi terrorists and a fragile, two-day-old truce had exploded with the blasts. In Czechoslovakia, students had staged a sit-in at the main post office in Prague, protesting what they charged was government eavesdropping on their mail. Palmer folded the paper and dropped it on the table beside him. The real news, he thought, is being made by us.

Palmer closed his eyes, trying to doze. It was impossible. Too many things raced through his brain. He had worked hard all his life to control his destiny and now he had started something rolling that was too big and too fast for him. The prospect of racing to a conclusion he may not have control over scared the hell out of Alex Palmer. He was locked in, and for the first time in his life, he felt helpless.

He had not planned for it to proceed this way: killing a president. When he went hunting for Daniel Johnson in Los Angeles, he really didn't know what he expected to do once he found him. Probably he meant only to exploit the man, as he had done with so many others before—gather information and rush back to the typewriter. But the meeting with Johnson had done something to him. They had met at an agreed-upon spot on Santa Monica Boulevard and driven in Johnson's car to the beach, where they'd walked and talked for hours, making it to Malibu just as the sun set. Palmer had been impressed by the man's intelligence—stunned by it—and as the story unfolded he saw what a waste Daniel Johnson's life had been and thought of his own father—another waste. Palmer had turned his face away, looking at the white surf through watery eyes, thinking of his father. One day he had had a father, the next he was gone, a lifeless shape on the bathroom floor. Palmer remembered trying to rush past his mother's arms, but had gotten tangled in her big cotton skirt, struggling but not really wanting to get free. He had allowed himself to be led away that day, but part of him had stayed behind with the body on the floor, unalterably bound to it, a grotesque tethering that would shape the future of his life: Alex Palmer, the angry little boy. Alex Palmer, the dirt-slinging, ruthless author.

Palmer noticed that Daniel Johnson was staring at him. He smiled. Johnson returned the smile. There was no turning back.

FOURTEEN

"We had suspected for years that there was a high-rank-ing mole in the company, but were unable to get a fix on him. Demic even organized a top-to-bottom hunt him-self—or so I thought he was doing at the time. This is all so . . . extraordinary."

Wasted by cancer, Edward Holmes sat bundled up in a chair. He reached a shaky hand over to a nearby table for a glass of water, bending his head to meet it.

"Tell me, Mr. Johnson," the former CIA director said, setting the glass back down, "are you fully aware of what these men are asking you to do?"

Johnson nodded. His fingers tightened on the false beard he clutched in his hands.

"It is likely that you will never see your family again. Are you prepared to accept that?"

Again Johnson nodded.

Holmes went for the water. Palmer could not believe how much cancer had ravaged the once athletic man. Palmer remembered interviewing him for the *Post* years ago, but that man bore no resemblance to this burnt-out case, dying amidst the splendor of his Park Avenue penthouse.

"Will it work, Jamie?" Holmes asked.

"Possibly."

"That's not much assurance, considering what you're asking me to do."

"No it isn't, Edward, and I wish I could be more positive. But then I've never attempted something like this before."

"One thing in our favor," Palmer interjected, "is that Demic has no family. It would be a lot harder if we had to fool a wife or a son. And as far as I can tell, Demic has no really close friends. He's a perfect loner."

Holmes studied Daniel Johnson, who shifted nervously.

"It is a remarkable resemblance," Holmes said. "I must say it took my breath away when your friend here removed the beard. That was quite a performance you engineered, Mr. Palmer. First you march in here and tell me this absolutely unbelievable story, and then you pull the beard from this fellow and make it all so absolutely believable. The evidence you've gathered is amazing. There doesn't seem to be any room for doubt, does there?"

"No sir, there doesn't."

"How could the Soviets have pulled this off, right under our noses. This is ten — no a hundred times — worse than the Philby affair. I never figured the Russians capable of such a maneuver."

"Actually," Palmer said, "I don't think Stalin ever dreamed it would go this far. Mostly, it was luck. Setting up McCarthy for the fall was the first step. Then, when the American public had grown sick of Redbaiting, they pumped their subversives into the main line of government, the star being Demic. He was to be the perfect mole: a loyal Russian with an airtight cover; Harvard son of Polish immigrants; a farm boy from California. He was programmed to go as far as he could in the CIA. The fact that Demic turned out to be even more brilliant and successful than they had planned, was gravy. It is not too outlandish to think that had Pierson not conveniently dropped dead, the Soviets might have intervened some day to hasten him on his way."

"And why did you choose me?" Holmes said.

"I think you could answer that one yourself, sir," Palmer said softly.

The old man nodded. "Yes, I suppose I could. Demic would have to honor a request to meet here with me before he goes to the UN on Monday. I was the man most responsible for his rise in the company. Considering my condition, he wouldn't ask me to run over to his suite. And of course, an assassination is nothing new to a CIA director. Am I right?"

"Yes," Palmer said.

Holmes got up from his chair, the covers slipping from him. He wore cotton pajamas, which hung loosely.

"Do you know what I find most extraordinary about this whole affair? It is not that Demic could have gone so far, or that this man here is such an unbelievable look alike. What I find most stunning is the simplicity of your scheme which proposes to do away with an American president and replace him with a Los Angeles truck driver. It sounds so easy it's almost shocking. And do you know, I think it will work, that's the crazy part."

"Then you'll do it?" Palmer said.

"I don't know, son. I need time to think it over."

"We don't have much time, Edward," General Worthington interjected. "Today is Friday. Monday, Demic meets with Rublov."

"Will you give me until tomorrow morning?"

"Of course."

"And tell me, gentlemen," Holmes said, standing. "What will you do if I refuse to help?"

Nobody wanted to answer that.

FIFTEEN

Saturday came up beautiful. Blue skies and dazzling sun, the smell of burning leaves on cool breezes. It was a perfect autumn day. All across America, football stadiums were jammed with chilled fans. Alex Palmer, warmed by bourbon and the pumped-heat of his Washington Plaza suite, was watching the Notre Dame-Michigan State game on TV. Figures in helmets scrambled across the screen, colliding and separating. Palmer tried to focus, but his mind refused to take the lure. Hoping to perk up his interest, Palmer had phoned his Brooklyn bookie earlier in the day to lay the biggest bet of his life down on Notre Dame: five thousand bucks, giving three points. Palmer had hoped that by taking the plunge he'd get caught up in the game. But watching the scuttle of bodies, he knew that he could have laid twenty thousand down and it wouldn't have made a difference.

Palmer left the TV on and got up to pour another drink. He glanced into one of the suite's bedrooms, where Daniel Johnson lay sleeping, false beard sitting like a toupee on top of a clock by his bed. It is good that he is sleeping late, Palmer thought. Johnson had stayed up all night with General Worthington, going over government procedures and secrets. Worthington had also brought a copy of the speech Johnson would have to make before the UN, should the switch work. Switch. Even the word sounded absurd to Palmer. You don't go around switching presidents. It could never work. Palmer could think of a dozen reasons why it wouldn't, but he forced them from his mind. The gambit involved daring, and would only work if they moved boldly. Palmer didn't try to figure out the odds. Odds were for horse races and fights. It wasn't the same thing when a dirt-digging author and two White House aides tried to substitute a California truck driver for the president of the world's most powerful nation. There wasn't a bookie in Vegas who'd put a line on that one.

A new drink in hand, Palmer lay down on the bed, hoping the bourbon would make him drowsy. Unlike Johnson, Palmer had been unable to sleep. Maybe it was the general's words when he had left the suite: "I'll get the poison today. There's someone down at the Pentagon who owes me a big, big favor. He won't ask any questions. The poison's the newest rage—death is instantaneous, and the stuff is colorless, odorless, and gets destroyed by antibodies in the blood stream within an hour after it is taken, so it is undetectable by autopsy."

Poison. Christ. Ever since Edward Holmes had called that morning, there had been a knot in Palmer's stomach the size of a combination lock. "I've decided to throw the party. The guest of honor has been invited and he accepted," the former CIA chief said, then hung up.

Palmer took a big hit on his bourbon and went over it again. Two hours before the president showed up, Palmer, Schuyler, and Johnson would arrive at Holmes's apartment. Worthington would wait at the UN to help Johnson when he arrived. The poison would be put in the president's favorite scotch— Johnny Black. Holmes kept documents in a huge false compartment of a walk-in closet in his study, and it was there they would hide. Holmes would ask the president to meet with him in the study, which was well removed from the living room, where the agents would wait. Holmes would pour the president a drink, taking a Remy himself. If the president refused a drink, his tea or coffee would be spiked. The minute the president collapsed, Holmes would open the false compartment and Johnson would change clothes with Demic. Palmer and Schuyler would drag the body into the false compartment and hide again. After fifteen minutes, the president and Holmes would return to the living room. The switch made, it was all up to Johnson, who would have to think fast on his feet. It couldn't work, but then again, it might. What choice had they? If Demic was permitted to meet with Rublov, the lives of Palmer, Schuyler, and Johnson were worthless anyway, along with millions of other Americans. And if it worked, six months later a carefully chosen doctor would announce that President Demic had a severe heart problem and must resign. Vice President Thornburg, whom Worthington will have checked out beforehand to make sure he was not a part of Demic's cell, would then succeed him. The transition would be orderly, the Russians would have been frustrated. Would they blow the lid? Worthington didn't think so. Who would believe them? Besides, how would Rublov explain having lost such an invaluable mole? Questions would be raised. Rublov wouldn't be able to take credit for something Stalin had created; all he could take was heat for having blown the cover on Demic.

Palmer was thinking about the scheme when the phone rang. He leaped to grab it before it woke Johnson.

"Alex. I'm being followed."

It was Schuyler.

"How do you know?" Palmer asked, his heart suddenly racing.

"I know. I've made too many turns not to have lost him. He's been with me ever since I left my house. What should I do?"

Palmer tried to think fast. He'd been a fool to think they could sit tight safely, waiting for Monday to roll around.

"Where are you David?"

"At a phone booth a few blocks from the White House."

"Don't go to the White House. Come here."

"What good will that do? I still won't lose him."

"I don't want you to lose him. I want you to bring him here."

"Palmer, have you lost your mind? The creep's probably armed."

"So am I."

"What?"

"I've got a gun."

"Palmer—"

"David, just shut up and listen to me. I've got an idea . . . ."

SIXTEEN

The lobby of the Washington Plaza was crowded. Palmer sat on a sofa pretending to be reading the *Post*. The bulge inside his waistband dug into his gut. It was only a small caliber gun, but to Palmer it felt like a cannon. Where the hell was Schuyler?

Ten more minutes passed before Palmer spotted Schuyler entering the lobby. He was in a crowd, making it impossible to tell if he was followed. Palmer put the paper down on the couch and picked his way through a pack of incoming guests stacked up five deep at the front desk. He got to the elevators at the same time Schuyler did, their eyes catching for the briefest of moments, before the doors opened and they flowed inside. It was one of those rides where nobody spoke, the fit too tight, the air foul with garlic and onions. Palmer let his eyes play over the male faces, trying to pick out the one cut to be a killer. He was surprised at how many businessmen seemed to fit the role. Palmer kept his stomach sucked in, hoping to decrease the bulge from his cannon. Sweat was forming at the base of his neck and under his armpits. The elevator seemed to take an eternity.

When they reached the sixteenth floor, Palmer, who was closest to the door, stepped out, immediately realizing his mistake: He should have squeezed to the rear of the elevator when he got in. Now he was out before Schuyler and whoever was tailing him. Palmer stood frozen in the hallway a moment. On impulse he took out a cigarette and his gold lighter, dropping the lighter as Schuyler, two men, and a woman stepped out of the elevator. Palmer bent to retrieve the lighter. The ruse bought him time. The four people went their separate ways: one man and the woman heading to the right, Schuyler and another male walking toward Palmer's suite.

Palmer lit up and quickly fell in step behind the man tailing Schuyler. Palmer wondered whether he should unbutton his jacket to give him quick access to the gun. It was small comfort, but Palmer was relieved to see that the man was an inch or two smaller than he was and only moderately built. In a fist fight, Palmer thought, I could probably take him. The likelihood of the man being unarmed was slim, however, and Palmer slid his sweaty hand down the side of his pants, trying to dry his trigger finger.

Palmer's suite was at the end of the corridor, and as the trio approached it, Palmer tensed. Schuyler stopped at the door and knocked, glancing to his right at the approaching stranger. To Palmer's surprise, the man kept on walking past Schuyler, turning right and disappear-

301

ing around the corner. Wearing his false beard, Daniel Johnson opened the door and let Schuyler in. Palmer passed as the door shut. He was alone now, approaching the corner. His right hand slid close to the gun. He took a deep breath turning the corner, prepared to meet an avalanche of bullets. Instead, he saw the man standing fifteen feet ahead feeding coins into a soda machine.

Suddenly, Palmer had doubts that this was the man who had been tailing Schuyler. Unsure of what to do, Palmer kept walking until he had turned the next corner, then he hugged the wall and peeked back. The man was heading toward the suite again. Palmer moved quickly after him, stopping at the next corner to peek around it. This time there was no mistaking the man's intentions: He had his ear up to the door of Palmer's suite.

Palmer jumped out, gun raised. Startled, the man froze for a moment, then turned to run.

"Halt right there, police!" Palmer said, the idea popping into his head. To his surprise, the man did stop, raising his hands over his head. Palmer heard the chain slide back on the door to his suite, and Johnson opened it, a big vase raised menacingly in his hand.

"Get in," Palmer hissed. Johnson pulled the man inside and shut the door after Palmer.

"What is this?" the man said feebly.

"That's what we want to ask you. You've been following my friend here."

"I don't know what you're talking about," the man said, avoiding looking at Schuyler, who had a bourbon bottle clutched by the neck as a weapon.

"David, take that bottle out of your fist and use if for what it was intended. Make mine a strong one," Palmer said. He motioned with his gun toward the man. "You sit down and keep your arms folded across your chest where I can see them."

"Maybe I should frisk him," Johnson said.

"Don't bother, pal. Gun's under my right armpit. I forgot to put the safety latch on, so don't shoot yourself."

Palmer kept his gun trained on the man while Johnson dug out the revolver.

"What should I do with it?" Johnson said, holding the gun barrel with two fingers.

"Beats me," Palmer said.

"Empty the bullets out," the man said, his tone conveying boredom. "That way I can't shoot you, and you can't shoot me. It's a nice equation."

Palmer stared at the man: an unlikely assassin. He was in his late forties, hair thinning and lacquered stiff with something like Odell's Hair Tonic. He had weak eyes and a running nose. Somehow Palmer reasoned that a man with a running nose couldn't be a killer. Still, the man had tailed Schuyler, and somebody had tried to blow up Palmer in Long River, and Charlene Lowenstein was dead, and the man in the White House was a Communist spy. Appearances could obviously be deceiving.

"Who do you work for? CIA? KGB?" Palmer heard himself say, feeling somewhat foolish.

"Are you serious?"

"Dead serious." Palmer waved the gun. The man cringed.

"That thing shoots bullets, you know, pal," the man said.

Schuyler brought Palmer a bourbon on the rocks. He drank it fast.

"How many of us were you supposed to kill?" Palmer said.

"Kill? Are you off the wall?"

"Don't let him get you off guard, Alex," Schuyler said. "That's obviously what he wants."

"Right," the man said. "Then I'm going to leap out of the chair, knock the gun from your hand, fire from the hip and wipe out the lot of you. And do you know why? Because you're rude. You invite me into this swell pad of yours and then don't offer me a drink. Shame on you, Mr. Whatever-your-name-is."

"Palmer," Palmer said, having serious doubts again.

"The bastard knows your name, for Christ's sake," Schuyler said. "He was hired to kill you and me, remember."

"Not at seventy-five bucks a day and expenses, I wasn't," the man said. "At seventy-five bucks a day plus expenses I do a little tailing, make some notes, type up my report and hand it over to the client. The last time I fired my gun was eight years ago when I saw what looked like a big rat in my backyard and I shot it. Turned out to be my neighbor's black cat."

Palmer looked at Schuyler, perplexed. He lowered the gun.

"Keep it raised, Alex," Schuyler said quickly.

"David, I don't know anymore."

"Well I do."

Schuyler took the gun from Palmer and kept it pointed at the man.

"Name?" Schuyler demanded.

The man shrugged. "Jerry Diehl."

"Why were you following me, Mr. Diehl?"

"I'm a private detective and I was hired by someone to

304

report on your activities," Diehl said. "I wouldn't want to embarrass you in front of your buddies."

"Me? Why just me?"

Diehl shrugged again, a gesture heavy with weariness.

"Lookit, pal, I'm trying to be cool about this," Diehl said blandly.

"What the hell are you talking about?" Schuyler said.

"Why don't you just let me go and we'll save everybody a lot of problems. You don't even have to give me my piece back. I'll write down my address and you can mail it to me. Okay?"

Diehl got up.

"Sit down, God dammit!"

"Suit yourself." Diehl sat.

"Now again, I ask you why you were following me."

"I already told you. I'm supposed to report on your whereabouts."

"Why? Who are you working for, you creep."

The word creep made Diehl flinch, as if slapped. Maybe he had heard the name too many times before. He heaved a sigh and frowned. "Okay. It was your wife," he said flatly.

"Oh."

Schuyler lowered the gun, face pale. Diehl stood up again.

"Can I go now?" Diehl asked.

"Yes. Of course . . . I'm, uh, sorry about all this."

Red-faced, Schuyler retrieved Diehl's gun and gave it back to him. Diehl slipped it into his holster, straightened his shirt, and turned to leave. Puzzled, Palmer looked at his friend, but Schuyler wouldn't make eye contact.

"If it's any comfort to you," Diehl said, stopping at the door, "I won't be following you anymore. It ain't worth the hassle."

Palmer waited until Diehl had left, then said, "David, do you want to talk about it?"

"I guess so."

Schuyler tossed down a big gulp of bourbon.

"A woman?"

"Women."

"You?"

"Yup. Mr. Goody."

"But—"

"But how could I, right? I'm married to the girl of my dreams, a brilliant, beautiful woman, the mother of my children. Is that what you were going to say?"

"Something like that."

Johnson discreetly slipped away to his bedroom.

"Is Julie cold?"

"Not at all. Quite responsive, actually."

"Then?"

"Lookit, Alex, men cheat on their wives all the time. Why do you find it so hard to believe?"

"It's just that it's you. I mean, you're the last guy—"

"Maybe that's why I did it. Maybe I was tired of being 'the last guy.'"

Schuyler sank down into a chair.

"Alex, I'll say it once briefly and we'll let it go at that, okay? All my life I wanted to be Mr. Respectable. So I went to the right schools, married the right girl, and got the right job. And guess what? When I had all the right things, I found out they were all wrong for me. Want to hear something funny? If I had to do it all again, I'd be somebody like you—a maverick, a nonconformist. Bet

306

you'd never thought you'd hear that from me, huh? Bet I never thought I'd hear that from me, either. But the truth is, Alex, I'm suffocating. I'm addicted to all the little comforts and rewards that go along with being Mr. Goody in the nation's capital and I can't give it all up. So I do the next best thing: I make token rebellions. It started with an affair. Some cocktail waitress. I don't even remember her name. It was three years ago. Janet. Or Janice. Something with J. She was boring but I liked the idea of cheating. It made the sex better." Schuyler paused and looked at Palmer. "Am I shocking you?"

"A little, yes. But go on."

"After Janet or Janice, there was Carole or Cheryl, and then a couple of girls I met at a bar in George-town—literally two of them at the same time. The only problem with all these girls, though, was that occasionally they got attached, and then that ruined it. Attachments were just what I was trying to get away from. So somebody turned me on to hookers, and since then that's all I use. It's pretty nice, really, if you can handle the expense. All you do is dial the phone. No hassles, no silly little games. To you, it all probably seems stupid. But for me, locked into a straitjacket existence, my little indiscretions were almost a necessity. It's what kept me going."

Palmer waited for more, but Schuyler was finished.

"Let's get the hell out of here, David," Palmer finally said.

"Where?" Schuyler said weakly.

"I don't know. Anywhere. Let's go get rip-roaring drunk, the way we used to do on weekends at prep school. We'll go to a football game. We can catch the second half."

"Who's playing?"

"Oh Christ, David, I don't know. There must be a thousand football games today. This is Saturday, remember? An autumn Saturday in the good old U S of A, which, no thanks to Joseph Demic, is still alive and kicking. What do you say we drive out to the suburbs and find a high school game, sit in the stands and get smashed."

"Sounds okay. Maybe we can get some girls, too."

"Girls? Sure, we can get girls."

"What girls? Do you know some?"

Palmer stood up.

"Listen, fuckhead. This is supposed to be a spontaneous thing. I'm not the social director of Grossinger's. We'll go where ever the wind blows us. I thought you were down on the programmed existence."

"I am."

"Well, then move your ass, buddy. There's a whole world out there to conquer. And maybe, just maybe, if we get drunk enough, we might forget who we are and what we have to do two days from now. That'd be nice, wouldn't it?"

SEVENTEEN

Twenty minutes after Palmer and Schuyler had gone, Daniel Johnson got dressed and left the suite. He grabbed a cab in front of the Plaza, laid back and tried to relax, a monumental task. Ever since Alex Palmer had showed up in Los Angeles, Johnson's nerves had been shot. His every instinct told him to run like hell, but he knew that the time for running had passed. The general had spent a long night with him, ramming home a crash course on presidential duties and secrets. After Worthington had left, Johnson lay awake, wandering back over his life until sometime around dawn he came in his mind's eye to a farm scene. In it he saw a youth feeding chickens in a barn, and the boy was talking out loud about leaving for Harvard and how he was going to conquer the world. Daniel Johnson felt tears flowing, and when he could stand it no more he got up and splashed cold water from the bathroom sink on his face.

Looking out the window now as the cab weaved through traffic, Johnson wondered what his wife and son were thinking. Against Palmer's wishes, Johnson had left a note for them, saying only that he loved them very much but had to leave for reasons he could not explain. He had wanted to say he would return some day, but Palmer had insisted he leave that part out. "It wouldn't be fair to them," Palmer had said. "There is almost no chance you will ever be able to go back again, so let them begin the process of learning to live without you."

Learning to live without you . . . the words stung Johnson's mind. A wave of depression swept over him, followed by a surge of anger. Somebody must be made to pay for this. Johnson tried to focus the anger on his brother. He was at fault, and Johnson would take it out on him. In his heart, though, Johnson knew that Joseph Demic, like himself, was only a victim. What chance had the child named Yuri to resist the Soviet scheme? From the moment he was snatched away from Rina and Joseph Demic, Yuri had been programmed to be only one thing: a spy. The Soviet youth knew nothing of his parents. What feelings could they have stirred in him eighteen years later when he learned they were to be killed? He had no ties to these farmers in America. Yuri had been raised in an emotional incubator. It was entirely possible he had no conception of what it was to love. If Yuri had refused to carry out the assignment, they would have killed him. Why should he have sacrificed his own life for these strangers? No, Johnson knew that in Yuri's place, he might have done the same thing.

The president was not the enemy.

It was the Soviet Union which must be punished for crimes against his family. Daniel Johnson would help kill his brother because it was the only way to release the grip the Soviets had held on the Demics all these years. Then, when Daniel Johnson was president, he would cut off the grain sales, step up the costly arms race until the Soviet economy was pushed to the breaking point and . . . he had plans. Johnson was glad he had read so much about the Soviet Union all these years. It would come in handy when he set out to punish the Red bastards. . . .

Still, the thought of killing another person made Johnson shudder. He would like to have had a chance to speak with his brother before Holmes poisoned him, but that was not possible. And in any case, what would they say to each other? They really had very little in common, except blood. The president had never known his parents. Johnson had never been to Russia. For all it mattered, any of the tourists Johnson saw now outside the cab window could be his brother. Joseph Demic was a Russian spy, nothing more. And he would help kill him when Monday rolled around.

"Here you are, buddy," the cabby said, pulling over to the curb. "Three bucks."

Johnson fumbled in his wallet for three singles. He had no change, so he gave the man another dollar for a tip.

"Thanks. Looks like the tour is just about to begin. You taking it?"

"Yes," Johnson said. "I've never been here before."

"Well, have a good time. Nice place to visit, but I wouldn't want to live there."

"Me neither."

Daniel Johnson got out and stared at the impressive building. Then he hustled to join the other tourists lining up at the White House.

At six twenty-five, Barney Goldaper picked up his *Daily News* at the corner of West End and Eighty-seventh Street. Five minutes later he caught the downtown bus, switched at Fifty-seventh Street and got off at Park Avenue, walking the remaining five blocks north to the Lindsey. It was seven minutes to seven. He had cut it close. His wife was to blame. With his Shredded Wheat gone, his whole damn morning had been thrown out of whack. So disturbed had he been that he had forgotten to read the *News* for the first time in twenty years. Untouched, he tossed it in a waste can on Sixtieth Street.

Taking up his station on the red rug in the Lindsey's outer lobby, Goldaper, still seething, decided he would kill his wife. How would he kill her? With his bare hands, perhaps, but he didn't think he had the strength left at his age. Poison? Where would he get it? A knife would be messy, and he wouldn't want her to suffer, even if she had eaten his last biscuit of Shredded Wheat.

Lost in his fantasy of murder, Barney Goldaper did not notice the two men until they were a foot away from the door. Goldaper's practiced eye managed to assess them in the instant it took him to swing open the door: dark suits, no overcoats—despite thirty degree weather—penetrating eyes, confident manner. Cops.

"Good morning, gentlemen. May I help you?"

"Ed Holmes. He's expecting us," one of them said coldly.

"Whom shall I say is calling?"

"Joe Smith."

"Very good, sir."

After the men had gone up, Goldaper put them quickly out of his mind. He had learned that a meddlesome doorman was a source of annoyance. Of course

315

some of his tenants were famous people, and you couldn't help but notice when a senator or a singer like Ethel Merman went upstairs. Goldaper counted Edward Holmes among the special tenants, but in the five years that he had been living there, no one of any note had come to visit him, at least as far as Barney Goldaper could tell. No doubt some of Holmes's visitors had been CIA agents, but how could you tell? Did a CIA agent look any different than a plainclothes cop? Goldaper shrugged, turning his attention back to his wife and his plans to kill her.

At nine o'clock, a taxi pulled up in front of the Lindsey. Three men got out and walked up the red carpet. Goldaper immediately assessed one to be a lawyer, the second an artist. The third was bearded, and Goldaper couldn't get a beat on him.

"Good morning gentlemen. May I help you?"

"Yes. We're here to see Mr. Holmes," the artist type said.

"And whom shall I say is calling?"

"Uh, Mr. Smith. John Smith."

"Very good."

Must be some kind of government conference, Goldaper thought, buzzing Holmes's penthouse. When Holmes answered, Goldaper said, "Some other people to see you, sir. A Mr. John Smith and two gentlemen."

The three men passed into the lobby and Barney Goldaper watched them approach the elevators, then turned his back on them.

When the doors closed, Alex Palmer pressed the button for the twenty-eighth floor. Nobody said a word as the car ascended. Palmer glanced at Schuyler, then Johnson. Both were extremely tense. Who could blame them? In Palmer's pocket was a vial with enough poison to kill the president of the United States. A week ago, Alex Palmer was just an author with a fondness for killing reputations. Now he was taking the killing urge one step further. Palmer's thoughts wandered to the doorman. Why hadn't he told him his real name? What did it matter? If things went wrong when they got upstairs, they were all good as dead anyway.

Palmer was thinking about the doorman, about what it must be like to spend your life ushering people in and out of a lobby, when the car passed the twentieth floor. Suddenly, something the doorman had said came back to him and it was as if a live wire had been touched to his spine.

"CHRIST!"

Palmer stabbed for the buttons, hitting three floors at once.

"What are you doing, Alex?" Schuyler said.

The elevator came to a halt at the twenty-fifth floor.

"OUT! QUICK! GET OUT!"

Palmer dragged them out into the hallway. The elevator doors closed behind them.

"What the hell's the matter with you?"

"We're blown! The whole thing is blown!"

"What?" Schuyler said, shaken.

Palmer looked around, his mind racing.

"The doorman. Didn't you hear what he said?" Palmer said fast.

"The doorman?"

"When he called up to Holmes. He said, 'Some other people to see you.' "

"Yeah? So?"

"Christ, Schuyler, are you thick? Other people. Don't

317

you realize what that means?"

"Lookit, Alex . . . " Schuyler started to say, then suddenly caught the meaning and was unable to continue. "Oh my God!"

"Who spilled it?" Johnson said.

"Isn't it obvious?" Palmer said. "Holmes. The sonofabitch."

Schuyler, stunned, had to reach back for the wall to keep himself from staggering.

"What do we do now?" Johnson asked.

"Get the hell out of here, that's what."

Johnson reached to press the elevator button. Palmer grabbed his hand.

"No! They might have jumped in the empty elevator when it hit the twenty-eighth floor. We'll take the stairs."

"It's twenty-five floors."

Palmer started for the EXIT door without a word. Johnson and Schuyler raced to catch up.

On the twenty-eighth floor, the empty elevator having come and gone, the man called Joe Smith struggled to come up with an explanation. Where the hell were they? They'd called upstairs to say they were on their way, then suddenly they're gone. Could they have smelled a trap? But how?

Smith grabbed a walkie-talkie from his partner.

"Jack. They're on to us. They're running. Nail 'em at the front door."

Smith punched the elevator button.

Twenty floors below, dazed by the rapid descent, Palmer, Schuyler, and Johnson stopped to catch their breath.

"What happens if there's more of them downstairs?" Schuyler said.

"We're fucked."

"Gun . . . you've got the gun, right?"

"Yeh. Lot of good it will do against professionals," Palmer said.

Schuyler started to say something, but Palmer took off down the stairs again. It was a staggering task, racing down twenty-five flights. Nausea swept over Palmer, his head light. Too many packs of cigarettes, too much booze.

When they reached the bottom floor, legs like stone, Palmer stopped short of the door to the lobby.

"Let's catch our breath first. If we're going to have to fight, we'll need our strength."

"Palmer, I'm through. Can't go any further," Schuyler said, huffing badly. Johnson, a strange look in his eyes, hadn't said a word since they had started down the stairs.

"Right. You stay here, David. Let them cut you down like a dog on the stairs. Come on, Daniel."

Palmer made a move for the door. Schuyler grabbed him.

"Alex, don't go out there. They'll shoot us. I'm afraid."

"Shit, David, I'm scared, too. But we can't stay here. If we reach the street, we'll have a chance."

"Chance for what, Alex? If this thing has blown up in our faces, it's over. We're dead anyway. Where the hell can we hide?"

"I don't know. But it sure as hell isn't here."

Palmer started for the door again, but this time Johnson stopped him.

"This door," Johnson said. "It's marked one. But there is another flight of stairs. Where does it go?"

"Boiler room?"

"Did either of you notice whether there was an underground garage when we came in?" Johnson said.

"Christ, you're right. I think there was a garage," Palmer said. "Let's try it."

Palmer led the way down. The door at the bottom was marked only with a lower case g. Without hesitating, Palmer opened it.

"Garage. Beautiful," Palmer said. He studied the layout. There was about twenty cars and spaces for another three dozen or so. A ramp led down to what Palmer figured was another parking level. "Anybody know how to hot wire a car?"

Schuyler and Johnson shook their heads.

"Should have known without asking."

"Maybe somebody left keys in their car," Schuyler said. "I do all the time."

"It's worth a try."

"Alex, why don't you take out your gun for protection," Schuyler said.

"Can't."

"Why not?"

"Don't have it."

"But you said—"

"Told you that just to calm you down a little. Actually I left the fucking thing in my suitcase."

"Terrific."

"Forget about the gun," Johnson said. "Let's find a set of keys before they find us."

They had no luck on the first level. Running down the ramp to the second level, a car drove up towards them. They jumped in front of it, trying to flag it, but the driver gunned his engine and shot past them, nearly taking off Schuyler's leg.

"Bastard," Schuyler hissed.

"Can't blame him, David. This is New York."

On the second level they split up, racing from car to car. Palmer was about to check in the window of a Mercedes, when he heard a shout.

"ALEX! HERE!"

The keys were in the ignition of a white Cadillac Eldorado, but the door was locked.

"Step back," Palmer said. He took off his shoe and smashed it through the driver's window, reached in and opened the door. "Get in!"

Using a copy of the *New Yorker* that he found on the dashboard, Palmer brushed away the broken glass, sat down and started the engine.

"LOOK!"

Schuyler pointed toward the ramp. Two men were sprinting down it.

"You guys duck!" Schuyler and Johnson slid below the dashboard. Palmer floored the gas pedal. The big Caddy tore off in a screech. Thirty yards away, the two men on the ramp drew revolvers and went into a crouch. Slumping down as far as he dared, Palmer steered straight at them, the car moving forward in jerks as his foot vibrated in nervous spasms against the pedal.

"What's happening?" Schuyler yelled over the roar of the engine.

"They're going to shoot."

Schuyler groaned.

Palmer knew it was going to take luck. He waited until the last possible moment, then ducked completely below the dashboard, steering from memory. Two shots rang out, then two more, sounding like cannons. Startled by the explosions, glass showering down on his head, Schuyler glanced up, saw Palmer's head below the dashboard and screamed: "WHO'S DRIVING?"

"I am."

"JESUS!"

Judging the curve in his mind, Palmer wrenched the wheel hard to the right, swerving the car with a loud squeal. There was a sickening crunch, the Cadillac having whacked off a wall. Palmer hit the brakes, looked up, saw he was past the gunmen and floored the pedal again, more shots exploding behind him. Palmer saw daylight ahead, raced for it, then realized he might kill someone on the sidewalk and slowed down.

"MADE IT!" he shouted, then spotted two more men dashing toward him on the sidewalk. Palmer flew into the street, made a right and headed south on Park Avenue. In the rear-view mirror he saw the other two men jump into a car and pull out from the curb.

"They're following us!"

"Palmer . . . this car, look at it."

Schuyler's words sank in. The Cadillac's windshield was shattered. There was a big spiderweb hole in the rear window.

"First cop that sees us is going to nail us," Schuyler said.

"Is that bad?" Johnson said.

"God damn right. Who says we'd be safe in jail? And when they realize you've got a false beard on, and pull it off, what the hell are you going to tell them? That you're the president of the United States?" Palmer said.

"Then what do we do?" Johnson said.

"Abandon this fucking crate, is what."

Palmer waited until they were almost at Fiftieth Street, then steered to the curb and killed the engine.

"Hurry! Get out! Walk fast down Fiftieth Street. They won't be able to follow in their car, it's one way."

Moving as quickly as they could without arousing attention, they headed west on Fiftieth Street. Palmer looked back.

"They've abandoned their car, too."

"Why don't we grab a cab," Johnson said.

"Right."

They kept glancing behind them as they walked until an empty Checker came by. They hailed it and jumped in. The cab pulled away, and Palmer watched as the two men broke into a run, then stopped and jumped into the street, waving frantically for a taxi.

"Damn! They caught one, too."

"Now what?" Schuyler said. "Where the fuck do we go?"

Palmer's mind raced over a slew of possibilities.

"Driver," Palmer said, leaning toward the thick plastic partition. "Get us to Forty-second Street." Palmer took a crisp fifty, stuffed it in the driver's cup and said: "As fast as humanly possible."

The cabbie, a kid in his twenties with long, unkempt hair and rose-colored glasses, took the challenge without a word. He rammed his foot down on the gas pedal and the taxi shot forward with a noisy belch of exhaust, knocking Palmer back hard against Schuyler. In a matter of seconds, the cab was rumbling in high gear, banging through potholes with bone-jarring speed. Schuyler, hanging on tightly to an overhead grip, was about to say something to Palmer when the cab crunched through a monster pothole, and all three occupants of the back seat popped up like Jack-in-the-boxes, banging heads against the roof.

The cabbie mumbled something.

"What did the lunatic say?" Schuyler asked Palmer.

"I think he apologized," Palmer said, rubbing his head.

The words were barely out of his mouth when the driver swerved to avoid another pothole, pitching Palmer hard against Schuyler.

"The bastard's going to kill us, Palmer. Can't you slow him down?"

The cab flew across Lexington Avenue, just making the light. Palmer glanced back. The trailing cab was caught by the red light but plowed on through, horn blasting. Both cabs cleared Fifth Avenue, but halfway down the street there was a truck double-parked, blocking the road.

"Now what?" Schuyler said as the cab slowed down.

"Get ready to bail out," Palmer said, and reached for the door.

"STAY PUT!" the driver shouted.

Hitting the gas again, the driver leaped the curb onto the broad sidewalk, sending pedestrians scurrying with a blast of his horn. The cab sailed past the truck, then dropped off the curb back onto the street and raced toward Madison Avenue.

"No sweat," the driver mumbled.

His heart still racing, Palmer looked back in time to see the tailing cab repeat the maneuver, losing only a few yards in the chase. With the crosstown lights synchronized, they continued on a good roll past Madison. Approaching busy Sixth Avenue, however, the light went red thirty feet in front of them. Rather than shoot across four lanes of traffic, the cabbie braked hard. Almost instantly, three bums with dirty rags in their fists leaped off the curb. One had a bottle of Windex. He had his sprayer poised over the driver's side when the cabbie, seeing a break in uptown traffic, floored the gas pedal, knocking the Windex from the startled bum's hand. Palmer covered his eyes as they peeled across the avenue, cars bearing down on them fast, more horns blasting.

"No sweat."

This time the cab behind them was not so lucky. The three bums had jumped back into the middle of the street, shaking their fists at the fleeing taxi, and in so doing, blocked the path of the second cab.

"Beautiful!" Palmer said.

With a half dozen drivers hitting their horns, and the light having turned green, the bums finally moved, but the tailing cab had lost a full block in the chase.

"South on Seventh Avenue." Palmer quickly told them his plan. By the time the cab approached Forty-second Street, its lead was up to three blocks. Following Palmer's instructions, the driver made a hard right onto Forty-second Street, drove twenty feet and dashed for the curb. The three passengers jumped out and hurried toward the nearest movie theatre. Palmer plunked down a twenty at the ticket booth, motioning Schuyler and Johnson into the lobby. Palmer caught up to them and they rushed into the dark theatre.

"Let's catch our breath a moment," Palmer whispered.

There were only a half dozen people inside. It was a triple X-rated flick. Palmer glanced up once from his seat to see a jumble of naked limbs, then buried himself in thought. It had all caved in so fast. He fought against making any conclusions. It was more important to find a place to hide. Palmer tried to ignore the voice inside crying panic. With the two men beside him, Palmer had plotted to kill the president of the United States. A man with heavy connections to the CIA had blown the whistle on them, which meant that not only did the president know about the plot, but some portion of the spy agency was on to them, too. Demic's instructions would be to shoot to kill. In no way could he afford for them to be taken alive. Palmer suddenly remembered the vial of poison. He took it from his pocket, shuddering at the sight of it. Unscrewing the cap, he poured it on the floor, then dropped the vial.

Confident that they had shaken the tail, Palmer motioned for Johnson and Schuyler to follow him down the aisle toward a front exit. Light shot into the theatre as Palmer opened the door to the alley. Suddenly, something clanged and Palmer, startled, turned to see a young boy dash out from behind a garbage can and race up the alley. There was a middle-aged man in a three-piece suit sitting on the ground with his pants down, cock stiff.

"Come on," Palmer said, heading fast toward Seventh Avenue. They grabbed another cab and Palmer gave the driver the address of a bar near Sheridan Square. "I've got a bartender friend who owes me a favor. He's an artist and has a loft down in SoHo. Maybe we can stay there awhile."

Palmer had the cab wait while he popped into the Lion's Head Tavern and got the keys from his friend, then directed the driver to a warehouse on Spring Street. Glancing once to make sure they hadn't been followed, Palmer opened the door and let them into a musty-smelling hallway that led up a steep flight of stairs. The bartender's loft was on the second floor. It was about two thousand square feet, shaped like an L. The floor had been sanded, stained, and varnished. Decades of dirt had been scrubbed off a tall row of front windows. Hanging plants thrived in the sun. Wood walls had been torn away to expose brick, and several original art works were hanging. There was a platform bed, a captain's dresser, a beat-up couch with a red and gold afghan thrown over it, and a coffee table made from a slab of plexiglass and orange crates. The kitchen was at the far end and to the left of it there was a shower stall and toilet.

"Your friend leads the high life," Schuyler said.

"He's an artist." Palmer nodded toward several easels set up near the big windows.

After feeling for dust, Schuyler sat down on the coffee table.

"Is there anything to drink?" Schuyler asked. Palmer found a bottle of Cutty Sark in a cabinet beneath the kitchen sink, rinsed three glasses and handed them still wet to Schuyler and Johnson. He poured generously.

After waiting until they had started on a second drink, Palmer said, "We've got one thing going for us . . ."

"That's one more than I'd have thought," Schuyler said, annoyed that the glass trembled in his hand.

". . . and that's the fact that Demic probably won't want this handled in the open. I think the last thing he'd want is a sensational trial."

"Right," Schuyler said. "So he'll probably have his agents kill us. If that's what we've got going for us, then we're in big trouble."

"I won't deny that Demic is going to try and kill us,"

Palmer said. "But look at it this way. If he's going to do it—and keep it a secret—he can't afford to let more than a handful of people in on the thing. And that means instead of having to elude a hundred or more agents, we may be up against only six or seven. We've got a real good shot to get out of the country alive."

A depressing silence fell over them as Palmer's words sank in. Life as each of them had known it was over. Palmer and Schuyler would have to change their appearance, get work in common jobs. Johnson would have to assume yet another disguise.

"What about the general?" Johnson said.

"Demic probably had him nailed at the UN. Or maybe in his hotel room. A knife in the back, blame it on a mugger."

"Christ."

"Why did Holmes do it?"

"Obviously he never believed our story," Palmer said.

"But how could he doubt it? How, with the living proof in front of his eyes?" Schuyler nodded at Johnson, who had removed his false beard to scratch his chin.

"I don't know. I truly don't know."

"Lookit, Alex," Schuyler said, standing up. "I don't know about you, but I can't possibly go underground for the rest of my life. I wouldn't last. It's as simple as that."

"What do you mean?"

"I mean I'm not strong enough. I won't survive."

"You'd be surprised what you can do when forced to, David."

"I don't intend on finding out. I've got another idea, something you haven't suggested, so I will."

Palmer sipped at his scotch, anticipating his friend's

line of thought. "You'll take it to the press. March down to the *Times* office and tell your story. Right, David?"

"Right."

"And then what happens, David? We've already discussed the risk involved in exposing this thing. It could send the country into a panic."

"But Alex, if we don't stop Demic, what he'll tell Rublov this afternoon at Camp David would be more deadly than a panic."

Palmer nodded, silently weighing the proposition.

"And even if it doesn't work," Schuyler said, "surely it's better to take some action instead of running away hiding like criminals in South America for the rest of our lives."

"I have contacts at the *Times*," Palmer said, thinking out loud. "If Daniel told his story, and —"

Palmer heard it first. It was only a faint creak. Schuyler started to say something. Palmer cupped his hand over his mouth. The second creak they all heard.

"Them? How —"

Palmer's mind struggled desperately for an answer. Then, because he had once done some research on government eavesdropping, he suddenly felt in his shirt and pants' pockets. He found it sewn in the hem of his pants. It was only the size of a dime. Palmer turned out his cuff, exposing the bug. Schuyler gasped. Palmer searched frantically for a solution. The windows led to a fire escape. There might be more agents on the street, but if they could make it to the roof . . .

"Hurry!"

They raced across the loft, the heavy sound of their footsteps triggering a commotion in the hallway.

Palmer tugged at a window. "Stuck!" he said, then

noticed it was nailed shut. Security in a crazy town. "Stand back!"

He was about to hurl a wooden chair through the window when the door to the loft exploded open and four men rushed in.

"DROP IT!" one of them shouted. Palmer turned and flung the chair at the first gunman, then rushed him. Schuyler and Johnson followed on his heels. Palmer tackled the agent and they rolled on the ground. No match for his opponent, Palmer desperately sank his teeth into the stronger agent's wrist, biting hard into muscle. Warm blood filled his mouth. Screaming, the agent dropped the gun. It skidded over to where Johnson was wrestling with another gunman. Palmer scrambled on all fours for the gun but he was yanked from behind by the ankles and his chin banged hard onto the floor. Palmer tried to turn his head, but something that felt like a lead pipe thundered into the base of his neck and he collapsed, bolts of pain shooting into his head. His arms and legs felt paralyzed. Out of the corner of his eyes, Palmer watched helplessly as the man pulled a long hypodermic needle from his coat pocket and stabbed it into a bicep. Palmer opened his mouth to scream, but words never came.

NINETEEN

Boris was just dozing off in his easy chair when he heard the knocking at his back door. His mind was fuzzy from a long day spent reading Tolstoy and sipping cognac. Shaking himself awake, Boris tried to clear his thoughts. What day was it? Saturday? No Sunday. The boy who brought the groceries wasn't due until tomorrow. Or was it already Monday? Still hazy, Boris decided it must indeed be Monday and forced his body up from the chair, nearly knocking over a small table and a bottle of Remy. Now that would be a tragedy, Boris chuckled.

The knocking came again, louder. "All right, all right, I'm coming." He would have to scold the boy about that. There was no need to make such a racket. Boris suddenly realized he had not cleared away the lunch dishes. The boy had always remarked how clean and tidy he was, and Boris was annoyed with himself for having forgotten that it was delivery day. What an old man you've become, he thought.

The insistent knocking came again. Boris rushed to open it, his annoyance growing by the second. Angrily, he slid back the bolt and pulled open the door, a string of curse words ready to pour out. What he saw stopped him cold, however. A tall man in a black overcoat stood on the doorsteps. He wore glasses and in one gloved hand he had a gun. Boris said, "Oh . . ." and nodded as the gun went off.

TWENTY

In the study of the main house at Camp David, Gen. James Worthington sat on the couch watching the televised meeting at the UN. Rublov had just wound up a long address. The president was scheduled to take the podium in a few minutes. Worthington wondered who would come to the microphone—Joseph Demic or the truck driver from Los Angeles.

While he waited, the general sipped at his gin and tonic. For the first time in his life, Worthington felt like running from a tough situation. The feeling had started the moment he had given the poison to Palmer. He had taken the first step toward murdering the president of the United States, and the implications were terrifying. He had come to his senses quickly, however, and had begun carrying out a backup plan. On his own, he had decided that should the assassination fail, one final attempt must be made. That was why Worthington had flown to Camp David this morning. If the real Joseph Demic should walk in the front door later, the general would kill him.

Worthington had ruled out going public with his information, reasoning it would crush the nation. Better to kill him. The country had survived assassinations before, it would do so again. And Camp David was the only acceptable place to do it. There would have been no chance to do it at the UN. The metal detector system there would have prevented him from bringing a gun inside, and there was something unthinkable about doing the job outside on the street. Worthington had played that one through in his mind and had come to the conclusion that he would sooner see the country blown apart by hydrogen bombs and the Russians swarming over Washington than to become a sidewalk assassin. Some perverse sense of dignity prevented him from killing a president in public view. He could not bear the thought of millions of people watching him on TV, a recycled Sirhan Sirhan. Here at Camp David, he could fire the shots, then hand over the pistol to the Secret Service and surrender with dignity . . . or turn the gun on himself.

Worthington had gone over the situation a hundred times. If things fell apart at Holmes's penthouse, there was no reason to assume the president would know his top aide had been part of the attempt on his life. It was unlikely that any of the others would volunteer the information, at least not right away. And even if Demic did suspect Worthington, when the president got to the UN and found him missing, he would most likely assume he had fled somewhere. The last place he would suspect to find the general was at Camp David.

Worthington turned his attention back to the screen. The president was walking down the aisle. Worthington quickly left the couch and crouched close to the TV. From the long, tracking shot, Worthington could not tell if it was Demic or Daniel Johnson. The general switched frantically from NBC to CBS. Same camera shot. ABC was also shooting the president from a distance. As the president reached the podium, however, ABC went to a closeup. The general stared hard at the face. Was it Demic? Or Johnson? Worthington could not tell. But then, why should he? The key to the switch had been the fact that the two men were indistinguishable. Certainly somebody sitting in front of a TV screen couldn't tell.

Worthington went back to the couch, sipped his drink and waited for the president to begin his speech. Maybe from listening he would be able to tell something. The general closed his eyes and concentrated on the voice. At first it sounded like Demic. But then, something about the delivery made Worthington think it was the imposter. Moments later, Worthington changed his mind again. It was useless to try. He would have to wait, wait and pray.

Worthington wondered if God understood such prayers.

TWENTY-ONE

Air Force One took off at precisely two o'clock Eastern Standard Time. In the interest of security, the Soviet president flew separately in a backup plane, the second of three which took off from Marine Air Terminal near LaGuardia, en route to Washington. All air traffic had been halted in the New York area for the takeoff, and now, cruising safely at thirty-five thousand feet over the Atlantic, the president, flanked by his press secretary, sipped on a Johnny Walker Black on the rocks, sitting comfortably in a specially-equipped console chair.

"What was the reaction from your boys to my speech?" the president asked Barry Abramson.

"Good, Mr. President. Real good. They said it was tough. A 'no bullshit speech,' Tom Greer of AP called it," the press secretary said. He felt uncomfortable confined with Demic in the private compartment.

"Greer going to write it with that slant?"

"Apparently."

"What did the rest of the big honchos say?"

"The *New York Times,* the *Post,* the *L.A. Times,* and the *Miami Herald* all had favorable reactions, more or less."

"More or less?"

"Araton thought the speech was a little lean. Lean's one of his pet words. Means thin on content, fat on rhetoric. But I think he liked it on the whole."

"Why are the *New York Times* guys always the hardest to please?"

Abramson shrugged, anxious for the president to dismiss him. With Pierson, the press secretary had always felt comfortable. You could joke with Pierson, treat him like one of the guys. Demic was a cold fish. When he asked you a question, you sensed he was interested in what you had to say, but not you.

"Big pay, lots of prestige makes the *Times* boys think they're hot shit," Abramson said. "Probably are hot shit, in most cases, I guess."

"It's all a charade anyway," the president said.

"What is?"

"Speeches like that. The real business of politics is done over whiskey and smoke. Like with my head-to-head with Rublov later today. I probably won't even bring up half the bullshit I mentioned at the UN. And Rublov wouldn't expect me to. Hell, he plays the same game, doesn't he? Only difference, I guess, is he's got a little more freedom of movement. If he makes a slip publicly, he just says, 'Don't print that,' and that's that. Imagine me trying a number like that with the *Times* or the *Post?*"

The president laughed, swirling the ice in his drink.

Abramson, sweat forming on his forehead, forced a laugh. He glanced at his watch with an exaggerated gesture, hoping the president would take the hint and dismiss him.

"You know what I'd get a kick out of, Barry? For a year, I'd like to have all those hotshots assigned to Moscow. See how they'd like that."

"Some of them have already done that tour."

"Oh no, I don't mean as correspondents. I mean make the assholes work for Tass or *Pravda*. That'd change their outlooks a shade or two, wouldn't it?"

Abramson nodded, sweat sliding down his forehead. The White House staff had been griping that the new president was too distant. Now Abramson began to wonder if it wasn't better that way. Christ, it might frighten the hell out of them if they knew what went on in this guy's head.

"Don't get me wrong, Barry," the president said, as if reading his press secretary's mind. "I'm not against freedom of the press. Hell, they can print any damned thing they want about me—they always have. It's just that I wonder sometimes whose interests these guys are serving when they write some of the crap they do. Know what I mean?"

Abramson nodded again, not really understanding.

"You were a reporter for the *Baltimore Sun,* weren't you?"

"*Washington Post.* Twelve years."

"Why'd you give it up?"

"Money, I guess. Tired of the grind, too. Maybe I just wanted to be closer to the source."

"Ever regret leaving the profession?"

"Sometimes." Like now.

A white light began flashing on a panel along one arm of the president's chair. Demic picked up a phone from a table beside him.

"Yes?"

Abramson, seeing an opportunity, got up to leave. Demic motioned for him to stay.

"I'm glad to hear the British Premier was so pleased with my speech. Thanks for passing on the message," the president said and hung up the phone. He turned to Abramson. "More bullshit."

Checking his watch again, Abramson said, "I know you must be busy, Mr. President, so I'll hustle back to the main cabin and see how the hotshots are doing."

"Before you go, I wanted to ask you a question, Barry."

"Yes?"

"General Worthington. Have you seen or heard from him today?"

"Jamie? Gee, no. Was he supposed to be on board?"

"Yes. He was to leave with us from the UN, but he didn't show up there, either."

Alarm crept into the press secretary's voice.

"Do you think something has happened to him? Do you want me to alert the Secret Service?"

"No. Nothing like that, Barry. I'm sure we just got our signals crossed somewhere. I was only wondering if he had said something to you."

"No. I haven't spoken to the general all day. Come to think of it, I haven't seen him all weekend."

"I see. Well, I appreciate your taking the time to bullshit with me, Barry. Do me a favor, though. Don't mention Worthington's absence to the vultures."

"What do I tell them if they ask me where he is?"

"Say he's at the White House. Tell them somebody's got to run the shop while the president's away having vodka and caviar with the enemy. Tell them that. They'll like the line."

Long after Abramson had left, the president sat in his chair, sipping on a third scotch, rubbing lines of fatigue from his face. Worthington would have to be isolated, and fast. Things had come too far for one loose end to screw it up. Why hadn't the general shown up at the UN? The plan had been to either neutralize Worthington at Holmes's place, or in a car heading to the airport after the speech. Now, having shown up at neither place, Worthington was at large, and Demic didn't like it. How easy it would be if he could use all the agents under his command. But of course that was unthinkable.

Air Force One suddenly hit a pocket of turbulence, and the plane dipped sharply before the pilot got it under control. Demic, his seat belt off, was jolted out of his chair. He grasped the sides and kept himself from slamming headfirst onto the floor. He sat back squarely in the seat, fastening his belt immediately. How ironic, he thought, if after all the years of planning, his plane should crash now. What a shock that would be to the Soviet President. Demic's thoughts were interrupted by the blinking light on his console. The pilot was calling to apologize for the shakeup. As the president hung up, there was a knock on his door and two male flight attendants poked their heads in to inquire if he was all right, followed quickly by three Secret Service agents.

"I'm fine, just fine. Why don't you check on our reporter friends. We wouldn't want to lose any of them, would we?" The president winked conspiratorially and the stewards hustled away, flattered by the intimacy. To the agents, Demic said, "Check on Rublov. Call over and see if he's all right."

Turning his thoughts back to Worthington, Demic decided that it was likely that the general had backed out of the plot at the last moment. Perhaps he had fled somewhere. Of course there was always the possibility that the general was about to spill his guts to some reporter, but Demic doubted it. Wasn't Worthington's style. Somehow Demic sensed that a public disclosure — with all the implications for the general — would be too humiliating. Just what he would do, however, was still a puzzle, and that worried Demic. It had been a tension-filled day for the president, and just when he thought everything had gone smoothly, along comes this.

Demic tried to put Worthington out of his mind for a moment. There was nothing he could do about him. Within minutes of his landing at Andrews Air Force Base, Demic would have some kind of answer. If reporters didn't rush him with the word "spy" on their lips, he was probably in the clear. If Worthington was going to go public, he'd have done it already. Otherwise, it was safe to assume the general had sought another solution. Suicide? Possible. Demic shuddered. So many lives, so much intrigue. And all for this one meeting at Camp David.

And what shall I call the Soviet President when I sit down to talk with him? Shall I address him as "Comrade?" Demic let out a short laugh.

Comrade.

He wished to God it was over.

TWENTY-TWO

He had been at it for almost two hours now. There were six pages written, and still he was not done. Consumed by the task, General Worthington struggled to make his pen keep up with the furious pace of his thoughts. Nothing must be left out. The nation would only suffer more if doubts lingered.

Worthington was putting the document in an envelope when he heard the helicopter approach. Immediately, his breathing became shallow. He slipped the gun out of his coat pocket, surprised at how it repulsed him. After all these years in the military, Worthington was still not comfortable with guns. It was a feeling he had never imparted to anyone, certainly not his Pentagon friends. It wasn't that he was a pacifist. He believed warfare was a necessary evil. It was just that the instruments of death somehow turned him off. When you ordered men into battle, it was a decision reached with some agony and compassion, men dealing with men. There seemed something almost obscene about having to use mechanical means to do what was essentially a devastatingly intimate act: killing another human being. Hand-to-hand combat was something Worthington could relate to, bodies clashing on a battlefield.

There was no time to ponder such things. Worthington took the .22 caliber gun and placed it on top of a copy of the *Washington Post,* then folded the paper over it. Listening to his labored breathing, General Worthington waited for the helicopter to land. He heard the whirl of rotar blades close overhead and in a few moments the sound died abruptly. The president was down on the ground.

Legs feeling wooden, Worthington pushed himself off the chair and walked across the study. Closing the door gently behind him, Worthington stepped into the hallway and stood facing the front door, fifteen feet away. Worthington leaned back against the door of the study for support, lips dry, tongue thick and awkward. In his left hand he clutched the folded newspaper. His right hand was just inches away, ready to slip in between the fold. Voices in front of the house startled him, and he almost dropped the newspaper. Trembling, he waited. It would have to be done fast. The minute Demic saw him, he would react.

The sound of the front door opening startled Worthington. His hand slipped inside the newspaper. The first person through was a Secret Service agent, who gave the general only a perfunctory look and held the door open. The president followed him in, then stopped dead in his tracks, his eyes locking on

Worthington's. One glance told the president what was about to happen.

"Don't Jamie," the president said softly.

"Why?" Worthington's hand froze inside the newspaper.

"Let's talk about it."

Making a decision, the president walked swiftly toward the general, covering the distance in a matter of seconds. Stunned by the president's bold move, Worthington was unable to react. He stood paralyzed. Suddenly the president's firm hand was on his shoulder, and as if in a trance, he felt himself being led into the study. The general waited until the president closed the door behind them, then he dropped the newspaper at his feet and covered his face with both hands.

TWENTY-THREE

The sea was calm, and the man on the beach was able to make the stones skip a long way before they sank into the water. It was a cloudless day and the cold air, smelling of salt and seaweed, brought back memories of a winter vacation he had spent at Cape Cod while a student at Yale. He had not gone home for the holidays that year, choosing instead to steal away to a cottage by the sea paid for by a rich Radcliffe girl who had considered him a sort of waif and went in for mothering. In a way, she had been right. There had been no real home for him to go to. Just an aunt and some friends he had long since outgrown. It had been a peaceful two weeks: deserted beaches, days spent fishing, nights huddled under blankets by a fire. It had all been very romantic and silly and a very long time ago.

Alex Palmer picked up another stone and hurled it

underhanded. It clipped the crest of a small wave and disappeared. Bad sign, Palmer thought. Perhaps I will sink here without resurfacing.

Palmer turned his back on the sea, tugging the collar of his jacket up close to his neck. Cold as hell. A typical New England winter. If this was New England. Palmer had no way of knowing. All that he had been able to discover in the five days they had been here was that it was an island, roughly a mile square, with no other land mass within sight. Palmer had walked around it on the second day, when his head had cleared from the effects of the drug. The men who had brought them here had told them they were free to roam, and Palmer had immediately set out on foot, laughing at the agent's use of the word free.

It was a prison, and yet not a prison. They were allowed to move about, yet there was no place to go. The agents—there were four of them—had refused to answer any questions. Palmer had tried to pry some information, but all they would say was, "We are not at liberty to answer that." A stone wall. The one question Palmer had wanted an answer to most, he had never asked: Why are we alive?

As Palmer walked up to the house, he thought back to those first moments when he had regained consciousness. He was lying on a bed. What seemed like a thousand suns were exploding through a window framed with lace curtains. His head throbbed from the effects of the drug, but the warmth of the sun and the peaceful sound of waves breaking somewhere close by was so soothing that he lay for what seemed like hours, blocking out hundreds of questions burning at the back of his mind. When the sun left the window and the room grew chilly, Palmer thought about the others and got up to investigate.

It was an old Victorian house, clean and well cared for. Palmer had been the first to awoke. Johnson wake an hour later and Schuyler not for several hours more. Together, they had searched the house, and finding the agents gone, had dashed outside, hoping to discover a boat. Not only was there no boat, there was also no phones, no radios and no TVs. Isolation. Around dinner time that first night, they heard a motor boat, and staring cautiously out through the upstairs windows, watched as the four agents got out and walked up the beach, the boat turning and racing away.

The agents came with packages, and if they had any guns, they were well-concealed. There were steaks, potatoes, wine, and enough groceries to last for several weeks. It had been the strangest of meals. The tall, thin agent who had plunged the hypodermic needle into Palmer, cooked the dinner. They ate in silence at first, eyes averted from their captors. But gradually the situation became so absurd — three men held prisoner, sitting in silence eating porterhouse and sipping passable California cabernet — that Palmer felt obligated to speak. He asked questions, one rapidly following the other, all bringing the same useless answer: They were not at liberty to say anything. Palmer gave up and continued to eat in silence. That had been five days ago. Although he had read about men in captivity, he was surprised at how easily he conformed to the normal patterns. He found himself paying particular attention to the care of his body — washing, brushing the teeth, cleaning under his nails — and had already worked out a sort of crude daily schedule. Mornings he spent exploring the island, searching for a clue to where they were being held, keeping a sharp eye for ships which he might signal. It was a silly little routine — the island was as clean as a whistle, not even a stray beer bottle with a local brewery tag — but something compelled him to make the effort. At noon he met the others down in the dining room for lunch. Eating had become a dreary affair. The food was all right, but there was an almost unbearable weariness about the little group at the table, men who had been beaten and now waited for the final blow to fall. They had spoken long and passionately at first, trying to make sense of what had happened, wondering why they were alive and for how long they would stay that way. Gradually they had come to accept that they were being kept alive for interrogation, that Demic would probably want to know if there were others who knew his real identity. They were in for a hard time, and the only way to deal with it was to retreat somewhere, turn off, tune out, pretend it would all go away. So they spoke little at meals, as if fearing that human contact would break the comfortable little spell.

Palmer, who had long since grown out of the daily newspaper habit, was surprised at how much he craved to read one — even the worst rag. He could accept that he would never leave the island alive, but what he found hardest to swallow was that he would probably go to his grave never having been told the ending to their crazy story. What had become of Demic's meeting with Rublov? Had the president handed over the Middle East on a silver platter? Where was Worthington? And how long would it be before the Soviets, possessing all of America's important secrets, decide to make a first strike, to begin the end? Palmer, the weight of it bearing down, walked wearily up the beach to the two-story, white house for lunch.

A week passed when suddenly their whole routine was shattered by the simplest of events: the arrival of a newspaper. Palmer had been out on one of his morning walks. He was on his way back when he heard someone shouting his name. Palmer broke into a trot, fear dancing at the back of his neck. He saw Schuyler standing in the doorway of the house, calling to him. Johnson was next to him. Palmer was unable to read anything in Schuyler's voice. It could be fear, it could be something else. He increased his gait, lungs aching with the intake of cold air. There was something in Schuyler's hand, and as Palmer got closer to the porch, he could see it was a newspaper.

"Look Alex, look! Paper! The bloody *New York Times!*"

Palmer grabbed it, his breath coming in great bursts of steam. "How did you get? Where did it come from?"

"It was just lying on the dining room table when I came down for lunch. Just lying there, untouched."

"Do you think they left it deliberately for us?" Palmer said.

"It certainly seems that way."

"Maybe they were careless."

"They haven't been careless before. It seems unlikely."

"Yes. I agree," Palmer said, taking the newspaper like a precious jewel and walking into the warm house. He sat on a couch in the living room, spreading the paper on his lap. "What does it say? Have you read it?"

"No." Schuyler laughed. "I was too excited. I ran upstairs to show it to Daniel and then I went screaming for you. Pretty crazy way to act, yelling about a newspaper."

"Under the circumstances, my friend, I would have done the same thing."

With Schuyler and Johnson looking on, Palmer stared at the front page. Their eyes did not have to wander far. Screaming out at them, across eight columns was a rare *Times* banner:

SOVIET TROOPS MARCH INTO CZECHO-SLOVAKIA; KORINSKY PLACED UNDER HOUSE ARREST

"My God!"

"Czechoslovakia!"

Palmer turned to Schuyler, stunned.

"But isn't that exactly what Worthington was hoping for? Didn't he say the Czech labor movement and the students were extremely well organized, that if the Soviets made a move on Czechoslovakia it would be like a Vietnam for them?"

"Yes."

"Then why?"

For an hour they read the newspaper, poring over every word, trying to make sense of what they knew made no sense at all. The Soviets had wanted a toehold in Iraq. They needed the oil, wanted access to the sea. Why in God's name would they choose Czechoslovakia instead to make a show of force? Certainly Demic would not have offered any resistance to a move in the Middle East. Had Rublov made a colossal blunder?

Worthington had said that a long, drawn-out fight in Czechoslovakia would almost certainly push the Soviet economy to the point of collapse. And if that happened, Rublov himself was sure to go, replaced by a more moderate leader. Already an answer to this strange turn of events was forming in Palmer's head, but the idea was so implausible, so unbelievable, he refused to mention it to the others.

More newspapers followed after that. The agents left them daily on the dining room table, always untouched, always the *New York Times*. The situation developed exactly as Worthington had predicted. The Czechs dug in. Political analysts were saying the Russians had underestimated their neighbors. Daily, it was becoming a horror show for the Soviets. Demic, meanwhile, had drawn heavy criticism for his inaction. The president had seemingly bought the Soviet line that there had been extreme provocation, that the Korinsky regime had been corrupt, and a major portion of the Czech Communist Party had petitioned for help. It was all rot, and yet Demic was buying it.

One day Palmer found a quote from General Worthington, and then he knew that he had been right. He shared his idea with the others, and while they agreed it was possible, it was so incredible that they decided to reserve judgment.

"What other explanation for it can there be?" Palmer had said. "Why else is James Worthington not only alive, but still functioning at the White House?"

"Maybe it was Worthington—not Holmes—who blew the whistle on us," Johnson had said, and they had all agreed that that was an alternative possibility, but not likely.

On the third week of their captivity they had their answer. A snowstorm was brewing, and the little island was already covered with a thin layer of white. Palmer was in the kitchen making himself a snack, when he heard the whirl of a helicopter approaching. He dropped what he was doing and ran out onto the porch, trying to see through the snowfall. Schuyler and Johnson quickly joined him.

"Can you see it?" Johnson said.

"No. But it's somewhere south of the beach by the sound of it."

"Is it coming here?"

"Damned if I know."

Five minutes later they saw it. It was a military craft. It set down on the front lawn, the rotar blades sucking snow off the ground. The swirling snow prevented them from seeing who was stepping down from the helicopter. When they did, their breath was taken away, as if they had sustained blows to the chest.

"Gentlemen, gentlemen. Let's not stand out here on the damned porch. We've got work to do."

The president of the United States rushed past them into the house, three Secret Service agents trailing after him. Stunned, Palmer, Schuyler, and Johnson followed him in.

"Damned New England winters. Never did get used to them," the president said, walking over to the huge fireplace in the living room. The president removed his gloves and warmed his hands by the fire. He stood there a moment, thawing out, back to the others. Then he turned, hands on hips, and said, a rare smile crossing his face, "Well, sit down. Sit down. You'll have all your questions answered in due time." The president turned to one of the agents. "Fred. Get some scotch." Demic saw Palmer raise an eyebrow. "Oh don't worry, Mr. Palmer. The drink I'm going to give you is far less lethal than the one you had planned for me." Again the president smiled. Palmer blushed, against his will.

When the agent returned, he poured a short drink for the president and three stiff ones for the others. Palmer went for it immediately, cursing himself for the tremble in his hand. When he set it down on the coffee table, he noticed that the president was staring at Johnson.

"Rather unbelievable, isn't it," the president said. "Like looking at yourself. All these years I . . ."

". . . you thought I was dead. Or should I phrase it, hoped I was dead?" Johnson's cold eyes bore into the president.

"So much hate, brother for brother." The president sighed. "Well, can't say as I can blame you. Maybe you will feel different after I have had a chance to speak."

The president opened up a briefcase. "I brought along the latest edition of the *Post*. Here, take a look." Demic tossed it to Palmer, who unfolded in numbly and glanced at the front page. "As you can see, our Soviet friends are having the devil of a time with their little neighbors in Czechoslovakia. Seems the country has shut down. Strikes have closed every major industry. There have even been reports of hand-to-hand fighting in many villages. An altogether messy scene, wouldn't you say?"

Transfixed by the president's words, Palmer stared down at the *Post* front page.

"What is even more interesting, is the effect this is projected to have on the Soviet economy. There is an economic analysis by Walter Kohler on the op-ed page.

He gives some pretty intriguing figures. The Soviets gave between four and five billion dollars in subsidies to Czechoslovakia last year. That's a mighty big piece of change to invest in a little country. By our accounting, that's more than their burden in Cuba, which we had rated the Russians' most heavily dependent ally at a subsidy of three billion a year. The Czechs will have to turn to Comecon, the Soviet's economic grouping, and Comecon will have to find a way to keep the country going. The Kremlin will have little choice, because the Soviet Union now finds its economy so interwoven with those of its allies that it cannot afford to see any one of them fall into economic ruin. Shame. They should have thought of that before they plunged into Czechoslovakia headfirst."

Palmer his poise returning with each tug at the scotch, said, "You must have done a real snow job on Rublov, Mr. President."

Demic smiled. "Yes, as you have guessed, I did. I told Rublov that resistance groups were at an all-time low, according to our best intelligence. Went so far as to give him the names of twenty so-called key subversives in labor and at the universities. I told him if he rounded them up first, chances of resistance would be minimal. I also assured him that the United States would do little more than growl about it. Gave him a free hand."

". . . to hang himself," Palmer said.

"Yes."

His drink finished, Palmer looked toward the agent with the scotch, who came over and refilled his glass.

"When did you turn?" Palmer asked the president.

"Right from the beginning, actually. As soon as I was accepted in the company, I went to my immediate superior, who at the time was Holmes. Told him everything. He took me to Dulles, and I was asked to play double agent." The president turned to Johnson. His voice softened. "I would like to say that it was remorse for you and our parents that made me do so, but I won't lie to you, Joseph. There has been enough lying in our family. The Russians did not tell me that I had a family until just before I came to America. It would not be true to say I felt anything for you or our parents. How could I? I was raised as an orphan. What I did feel was outrage, although I kept it well hidden. Alone in my room in Zukovka, I wondered why they had done this to me. Who had willed it? But I showed nothing. I knew they would be watching me closely before sending me to America. The slightest bit of negative emotion and they would have killed me and aborted the mission. Whether I went through with my end of it or not, they would have killed you and our parents anyway. Your fate was sealed the moment they stole me from the crib. All that could be salvaged was my life." Demic paused to sip his drink. "The funny thing is, even if I hadn't been told the truth about my parents, I would have turned anyway. My training had seen to that. In the midst of Mother Russia, I had been raised as an American: spoiled, pampered, no lines to stand in, no government-issue clothes. I wore western jeans, listened to pop records, read the latest American best sellers. When it dawned on me that I was being trained to be sent to America, I was excited beyond words. And the more American I became, the less I could stomach Russia.

"When I turned, Holmes asked me to monitor a Communist cell he had discovered with the company. There were five of them. They were all native Americans who had gone over for various reasons — idealism, money, neurotic needs, whatever. The cell was one of several which infiltrated the government after Mc-Carthy's witch hunt. McCarthy unwittingly became the tool of Moscow. It was a perverse idea, really. They gave McCarthy a list of supposed card-carrying Communists — it was easy to dig up suspects because there was a leftwing strain on the fringes of government at the time. Because the list was largely phony, McCarthy never came up with much, and predictably, the American public grew sick of his Redbaiting. It was just what the Soviets had planned on. Shortly thereafter, we moved in."

"Jim Bell said McCarthy had a Communist visitor on his deathbed," Palmer said. "Was that you?"

"No. But it was someone Moscow sent. The Kremlin wanted to test the waters one last time. They knew if they told McCarthy the truth, he'd sound the alarm again, and they wanted to make sure that the issue was dead. It was. Nobody batted an eyelash."

"What did you have to give the Soviets?" Palmer said.

"In the way of secrets? Actually very little. And all of it selected, of course, by Holmes. I was able to convince Moscow that I would be more effective acting in a subversive manner, rather than in passing documents. It was Holmes's idea, really. Passing documents always involved a risk, and having invested so heavily in me, Moscow was easily swayed not to endanger my cover. Besides, they were reaping so many rewards domestically, why should they care?"

"Domestically?"

"Subversion. Screw-ups. Engineering events which weakened the fabric of American life. Bay of Pigs. The

Kennedy assassination. Increased involvement in Vietnam."

"You did all that?"

"Hell no. But I took credit for it. There was enough suspicion circulating in the press about CIA involvement in those matters that it was easy to convince Moscow that I had a hand in it all. When you think about it, there were any number of screw-ups in government that the CIA could be blamed for. Take Watergate, for example. Moscow thinks I was Deep Throat."

"And you weren't?"

"Shit no. But the Soviets didn't know that. Pat on the back was what I got for that one. And money. Lots of it. Maybe a hundred thousand in all. They were thrilled about the whole affair. And who could blame them? Every time they picked up an American paper, some journalist was calling for Nixon's head, writing that the very foundation of the country was being threatened by the coverup, that sort of crap. My God, the Politburo must have had a communal orgasm when Nixon, tears in his eyes, called it quits. And while the nation was making heroes out of Woodward and Bernstein, the Soviets thanked me for it all."

"If things were going so well, why did you leave the CIA?" Palmer said.

"Couldn't hack it anymore. The strain of leading two lives for so many years just got to me. Holmes was reluctant to lose me, but I had made up my mind and there was little he could do to dissuade me. I told Moscow that I might be a target of the congressional hearings Agee and Little had helped stir up. The Kremlin couldn't complain. They had reaped many benefits from me over the years — at least that was their perception. It was a two-way street, of course. I filtered much information from Moscow back to the company.

"After I had been away awhile, I got itchy to get back in the thick of things, and asked Holmes if I could run for the Senate. Politics had always intrigued me. Holmes got clearance for me, and I did well in the Senate. So well, in fact, that Holmes came to me one day with an outlandish suggestion. Despite any misgivings you might have about him, Ed Holmes is a man of extraordinary vision. He saw the possibility for a tremendous coup. It would take an incredible amount of luck, but we had nothing to lose. If I could work my way into the White House, we might set the Russians up for one punishing blow. It was a longshot, of course. More than a little pressure was exerted on Pierson to put me on the ticket. And as you see, we've cashed in rather nicely."

Palmer shifted nervously on the couch. Ever since he had entertained the possibility that Demic was a double agent, he had begun to hope that maybe Charlene wasn't dead after all. Afraid of having his hopes dashed, Palmer had put off asking the question. Now he heard himself say, "And Charlene Lowenstein? What about her?"

"Alive and well and residing in South America."

Palmer fought back his emotions. "How do I know you're telling me the truth?"

The president reached into his briefcase and pulled out a photograph.

"This was taken yesterday."

It was Charlene, in front of a house surrounded by jungle. In her hand, she held a copy of a newspaper. Demic took a magnifying glass out of the briefcase and held it out to Palmer.

"Use this to read the date on the newspaper masthead. It will show you that Miss Lowenstein was very much alive as of yesterday. Of course pictures can be doctored, so later I have arranged for you to communicate directly with Miss Lowenstein."

Palmer put the photo down, laying the magnifying glass on top of it. He felt like jumping up and kissing the president, but restrained himself. The president resumed talking.

"A corpse we snatched from a morgue was in her car when it burned, along with some of her identifying articles: wallet, jewelry, that sort of thing. A really easy job, actually. When we explained to her why we were kidnapping her, she said she understood the threat to national security, and promised not to write anything if we let her stay in the country. The temptation would have been too great, however, so we flew her to South America. Her mood was pretty dark until we softened the blow by giving her a rather sensational scoop, complete with documents, tapes, the whole bit. She's working on a book. It will be a best seller, without doubt. It will take her three years to finish, roughly the time I have left in office."

"Someone tried to kill me — twice. Or was I imagining that?" Palmer said.

"No, that was very real indeed. The shooting at Miss Lowenstein's apartment was my fault. I had sent a man around to get the diary, and when he came upon you, not knowing who you were, he fired. It was just a matter of you being in the wrong place at the wrong time. In Long River, it was the Russians. They apparently had a permanent man in place, and when you stirred up the dust, he tried to bury you. Botched the job. I've since

359

learned he's been eliminated."

"Why didn't you grab me earlier? Why didn't you take me when you snatched Charlene?"

"I didn't know, that's why. Your lady friend was very loyal. She said she had shown no one the photo. We really didn't know you were onto me until you started telling David here your suspicions. All the White House phones are tapped. I ordered it as soon as I took office. Not very nice, but very effective for security purposes. When I did find out, I was still reluctant to tamper with you. In Charlene's case, she was just a news woman on a beat. You were a well-known author, a controversial one. Your 'death' almost certainly would have brought some of your dirt-digging colleagues sniffing, and we didn't want that. So I let you play with it for awhile, hoping you'd reach a dead end. You didn't, so here we are.

"The funny thing is, while you had hoped to save your country by poisoning me, killing me would actually have done enormous harm to the nation. My meeting with Rublov was of utmost importance. After our little talk, Rublov couldn't wait to get back home and start the troops rolling into Czechoslovakia. And as you can see, it was the worst thing he could have done. We expect him to be removed any day now and replaced by a more moderate regime, one eager to pursue detente."

"But surely the Soviets must now realize that you are a double agent," Palmer said.

"Yes, of course. My double life is over."

"Aren't you afraid they will blow the lid on everything?"

"I don't think they'll try. Certainly Rublov won't want to admit he had been fooled all these years, that he had been tricked into blundering into Czechoslovakia. And proof is very flimsy. The last man living who had known me in Russia is dead." Demic paused, thinking about poor Boris. "It is a good bet the affair is closed. Well, almost closed."

"You mean us?"

"Yes. Or more specifically, you, Mr. Palmer."

"Why just me?"

"Well, Schuyler here is most unlikely to spill things. Nothing to gain, really. Ruin his career. There will be certain guarantees made to him which I'm sure will entice him to maintain his secrecy, for which he has already taken an oath. A congressional seat has been set up for him in Virginia. If he were to decide somewhere down the line to make a run at the Senate or the governor's seat, issues would be provided to insure that he would be thrust into the front-runner's position. Money would be no object."

"Why not just ship him out?"

"He's too visible. His absence already has made things difficult for us. And then there's the matter of General Worthington. I most certainly can't ship him out, as you say. So if I'm going to trust him, I might as well trust Schuyler."

"You have nothing to worry about with me, Mr. President," Schuyler said weakly, obviously not relishing the thought of three years spent on a South American banana plantation.

"I'm sure," Demic said, smiling. "As for my brother here, well, I think enough hardship has been imposed on him. I thought of two alternatives for him. I could send him to South America—with his family. But even that would be unfair. Instead, he will be allowed to go home. It stands to reason that a man who has kept a terrible secret buried for over thirty years, could keep a less painful one for three more."

"Thank you . . . Yuri," Johnson said softly, using his brother's Russian name.

"There is nothing to thank me for, Joseph. The United States government owes you a lifetime of favors. And we will begin to make restitution immediately. A job in the Russian Affairs Division of the State Department will be found for you in Washington. A house will be provided in Georgetown or anywhere else you choose. You will explain your recent absence to your family by saying you were instructed by the United States government to say nothing of your whereabouts while you performed a service to the nation, the reward being the State Department job. You have wasted a good mind for too long."

Unable to speak, tears in his eyes, Daniel Johnson simply nodded his head.

"And that leaves me," Palmer said. "I get the feeling you have not saved the best for last."

"You are correct in that assessment, Mr. Palmer. Quite frankly, you are not to be trusted."

"Meaning, South America?"

The president nodded.

"Will it do me any good to say I could keep your secret?"

No good at all. Your reputation speaks eminently for itself."

"Hopeless dirt-digger, right?"

"That's one way of putting it, yes."

"What if I refuse to go?"

The president shrugged. He walked back over to the

362

fire, warming his hands again. "Mr. Palmer, while your deeds as a writer leave me with nothing but repulsion, there is no denying your courage and good intentions when you set out to kill me. In fact, I was quite surprised — shocked really — that instead of going public with your knowledge and adding to your already notorious reputation, you actually sacrificed for the common good. Really quite unlike you. Mr. Palmer."

"I know."

"So, while you will be shipped out, you will not go unrewarded. Like Miss Lowenstein, you will also be fed a substantial dose of dirt, enough to keep your mind in the gutter for three years. At the end of my term, I will not run for reelection. As soon as an orderly transition to a new presidency is made, you and the others will be free to disclose everything you know. I would assume there is a helluva book in it for you, Mr. Palmer."

The president reached into his briefcase again.

"And then there is this, too," Demic said. He tossed a thick manila envelope on the coffee table in front of Palmer.

"What is it?" Palmer said, picking up the envelope.

"The contents of an FBI dossier on your father."

Palmer's pulse quickened.

"There is enough documentation in there to prove that your father had nothing to do with the *Amerasia* scandal. He was completely innocent, and apparently the United States government knew it. I thought you would like to have it."

Palmer stared at the envelope numbly, too stunned to speak. The president picked up his overcoat and briefcase, and with the three Secret Service agents in tow, headed for the door. He stopped in front of it and said,

"Palmer, when you write your book, if you can figure out how to tell the good guys from the bad guys, let me know."

He smiled and was gone.

THE SAIGON COMMANDOS SERIES
by Jonathan Cain

MORE EXCITING READING
IN THE ZEBRA/OMNI SERIES

TRIVIA MANIA
by Xavier Einstein

TRIVIA MANIA has arrived! With enough questions to answer every trivia buff's dreams, TRIVIA MANIA covers it all—from the delightfully obscure to the <u>seemingly obvious</u>. Tickle your fancy, and test your memory!